Interstate Providence

A Novel By

Samuel Miller

Printed in the United States of America

ISBN: 1942212046
ISBN-13: 978-1-942212-04-1

Hydra Publications
1310 Meadowridge Trail
Goshen, KY 40026

www.hydrapublications.com

Father

Chapter One
<u>Saturday</u>

What does it say about a man when his weekends become more hectic than his weekdays? Like most Saturday mornings, Hunter Damon wrote a list of 'things to do today' — boring chores and errands he couldn't find time to do during the week. Exiting the bank just before noon, he pulled out the list to check his progress. With one exception, the list that Saturday in early May didn't seem too different from any other.

~~Buy new watch battery~~
~~Pick up dry cleaning~~
~~Drop off letters/bills at post office~~
~~Traveler's checks~~
Lunch w/ mom
Meet up with guys @ Todd's
Get married--8 o'clock

"Nothing to do but get married," he sighed.

Scribbling 'get married' on his list proved too irresistible a novelty to pass up. Still, with the madness and minutiae leading up to the wedding, his final obligation was to show up on time. The irony amused him; hundreds of wedding details demanding immediate decisions over the previous six months had now culminated in hours of waiting.

Although the wedding's extensive planning, preparation, and pomp was for the benefit of the bride and her mother, Hunter often offered how he could lighten their burden. The women responded the same way, each time; "Show up and say 'I do,'" followed by a cool, callous glance suitable for a human sacrifice with quiet patronizing remarks about men. His responsibility had been reduced to idle waiting. As restless as the waiting made him, he knew the wheels were at least in motion.

Nobody would ever describe Hunter Damon as fastidious; however, an argument could be made that he only felt comfortable when he controlled at least part of the situation. Even with things beyond his control, he'd make token gestures to ease his mind – like, writing 'Get married' on his list.

By most standards, life was a fantasy for Hunter Damon. He paid a reasonable mortgage on a modest starter-home in an up and coming Minneapolis suburb. He had a year-old black Mustang convertible in the driveway for nice weather and a 15-year-old dependable Jeep for the harsh Minnesota winters in his small one car garage. A sample of items inside the house included contemporary furniture that didn't match, two framed pieces of original art, three plants, and a stereo hooked-up to a 37-inch television. These were a few of the material trappings any successful thirty-something bachelor might assume make up Mount Olympus of the American Dream. Or if not the summit, then close to the top.

Although owning a few creature comforts created an agreeable lifestyle, the even-keeled Hunter Damon never subscribed to the cynical notion of 'happiness equals possessions.' Of course, such a philosophy is easy to ignore after accumulating a few nice objects.

What he valued most was his fiancée, Hope Jones. Everything about her embodied loveliness. She was savvy, fashionable, sexy, and quite agile during intimate situations. Blessed with a dramatic, exotic comeliness, the 5'8" slender beauty's most striking asset was thick, luxurious scarlet hair cascading to the middle of her back. Her face epitomized symmetry, highlighted by voluptuous lips posed in a perpetual pout, a slender Romanesque nose and high cheekbones set below sparkling, deep green innocent doe-eyes. Just as impressive was her arresting hourglass figure that rivaled any modern equivalent to the Sirens' song. Hope was so striking that six years earlier she almost posed nude for a 'Girls of the Big Ten Conference' pictorial before backing out at the last minute because she was also decidedly demure. This was another trait Hunter admired in Hope. True, many times her unreasonable demands exposed a high-maintenance attitude, but Hunter understood paying a high premium for quality.

If Hope was as close to physical perfection as a woman could be, she had exceptional flaws, too. One of her stranger quirks was estimating the footsteps needed to walk from any point A to point B. If she'd underestimated, her last few steps would be awkward, longer than usual strides. If she reached her predetermined point B with steps 'left over', she would discreetly walk in-place to equal the number of steps she'd predicted. Hunter noticed this compulsion just a dozen or so times, but the notion crossed his mind that she'd perfected her spatial prognosticating after 27 years of walking and was, in reality, counting every footstep from every point A to point B.

Hope also had a paralyzing fear of sidewalk grates. She hated them and would drift several yards out of her way to avoid them. Also, when climbing stairs that had an open back, she preferred covering her eyes and risk tripping to seeing the space between each step. These quirks were annoying, but what worried Hunter was how he wasted more time and energy obsessing over her compulsions than they were worth; a reflection of his own control compulsions, perhaps.

Hunter's fiancée also came from wealth; not an essential attribute, but still appealing. Her father, Paul Jones, co-founded the Smarty-Jones advertising agency in Minneapolis 20 years earlier, and as fate would have it, he was Hunter's boss. In addition to perks like brainstorming sessions involving toys, he threw lavish parties for his employees.

Hunter met Hope at one such Christmas party. While he hovered over hor d'oeuvres, munching on cherry tomatoes, carrot sticks, and cucumbers, she sauntered over, tapped him on the shoulder, and introduced herself. Startled by her overwhelming beauty, Hunter spilled a bowl of sour cream and onion dip on his black shoes, filling his pant cuff in the process. His nervous bumbling came off as charming, in a spastic kind of way, and Hope found Hunter endearing. In their ensuing 'getting acquainted' conversation, Hunter used his faux pas to his advantage by dipping carrot sticks and potato chips into his pant cuff, teasing her that it was accepted party etiquette in many obscure parts of Australia. With each dip, he played it cool, never breaking eye contact or the rhythm of the conversation. Hope couldn't resist wondering what kind of man she had met.

Meeting Hope was the pinnacle in Hunter's life. Before that night, he struggled with a nervous, dispiriting desperation as if he'd been missing something. He suffered near constant frustration searching for something intangible, yet had no clue where to look or what to look for. More frightening was the idea that perhaps the mysterious piece eluded him because it simply didn't exist. Hope may not have been the long sought-after piece Hunter lacked, but she did help him concentrate on moving forward. She provided him with a sense of confidence, security, and affection he'd never known.

At the beginning of their courtship, he wondered what a woman like Hope saw in him. Added to that, worrying about the politics of dating the boss' daughter made for a few stressful months. After a fortuitous turn of events, Paul Jones offered Hunter a promotion, more money and an implied caveat of treating Hope well, or else. As more time passed, they fell deeper in love and then were engaged at the following year's Christmas party. Paul Jones, the business-minded materialist, treated their engagement like an obsolete arrangement from more barbaric times, where the son-in-law would take the reins of a business he didn't want, but would take for the economic security and club memberships.

The future looked bright for Hunter Damon. Not only did he get a destiny he never imagined, that day turned into one of the few perfect Spring days in Minneapolis; a fine day to get married. With several hours until the soiree, however, he had an agenda to keep. Next was lunch with his mother for a little 'my baby's getting married' talk.

The restaurant, Chez Chou-Chou, was (as regulars called it) 'tres frou-frou.' Conspicuously decorated with elegant minimalism, C3 presented an image overflowing with frilly pretension by flaunting its modesty. This image did wonders to sustain C3's popularity with the bohemians in Minneapolis because, despite an imaginative over-priced menu, the food was mediocre. The fancy presentation of his $12 Turkey

Sandwich Deluxe was not important. Instead, he spent lunch trying to get his mother to stop crying.

Lee Damon deserved those tears. A thin, graceful, soft-spoken woman in her seventies, the past several years, left her as fragile as the wisp of a smile she always projected. She'd had an ideal fairytale life until 18 years earlier, when the older of her two boys, Richard, left home after an ugly misunderstanding, vowing to cut-off contact forever. Richard's abrupt desertion created a tremendous void in her soul. Lee's smile persevered, even if it appeared a fraction less pronounced. Thirteen years later, tragedy struck again when her beloved husband Peter died of a heart attack, leaving Lee with a larger void and a smaller smile. For the past five years, Hunter remained close to his mother, if for no other reason than to preserve what little smile she had left.

After lunch, Hunter hurried to the home of his best man, Todd Morvich, for camaraderie with the groomsmen and a plan calling for beer, chips, and testosterone until 6 o'clock when the quintet would break to get ready. Hunter would dress at Todd's house, and the group would convene at the church. After 90 minutes of Lee Damon's concentrated emotional sensitivity, the coarse company of close buddies with vulgar needles and ribbings was what he needed. Listening to the three married groomsmen expound on married life, Hunter knew life would develop a different dynamic with a wife to answer to.

"It's amazing,' Alan Adaleman complained. "She can't pass a sale without buying something...anything. She's powerless. Then when these huge bills come in the mail she's like, 'but I saved money.'"

"My wife saves me a lot of money," Joe Cotton replied under his breath.

"Gail saved me 50% on three pairs of shoes she admitted she might never wear," Don Donerail lamented. "Makes you wonder if women get married to strike the gold mother lode," he continued, shaking his head in disbelief.

"Yeah Don, you're a big spender. Jane and I see you and Gail at yard sales and swaps at least once a month," Joe interjected. "Jane even made up a song. 'Don and Gail Donerail, can't pass by a garage sale,'" he sung.

"We don't go to *garage sales*," Don answered with mock dignity, his head high and shoulders back in a royal pose, "we go antiquing." He continued in his regular voice, "All I know, when we go to those swanky yard sales up in Wintergreen Hill, Gail gets in the mood."

"Amazing how much action you get by calling it *antiquing* instead of *scrounging*," Alan piped in.

"Hunter, you see the marital bliss you're getting yourself into? You've got time to run," Joe cautioned, pointing at his watch.

Clearly, many marriage maxims are universal. Listening to his friends' stories and anecdotes gave Hunter little pause. He knew marriage changes both spouses. Couples have been getting married for centuries. If it was so bad, why keep doing it? After awhile, he sat back, relaxed, and accepted that his day in the barrel had come. The guys joked and griped, but none of them would deny their marriage or wife.

Cracking open a fresh beer and feeling more at ease, Hunter thought about the woman he loved. The several weeks prior to that day, he'd grown more and more nervous — a little from the anticipation but mostly out of fear of this awesome commitment. His nervous crescendo had peaked, however, and Hunter looked forward to the changes. Soon, he would have love and stability.

Ironically, these were the last stable hours of his life for a while.

Chapter Two

Arriving at St. Christopher's Church just before 7:30, Hunter feared crucifixion for failing his one responsibility — showing up on time. He and Todd raced to the back parking lot reserved for members of the wedding as the guests were pulling into the front lot and mingling. Hunter skidded into the gravel parking space, and tossed his keys to Todd (who was responsible for getting the car home, since Hunter would be leaving in a limo). He then strolled to the rectory door, reflecting on his last steps as a single man.

Once inside, they met the other groomsmen while Father Patrick, the presiding priest, bolted around the corner in an ominous sprint.

"Where've you guys been? It's 7:30," Joe asked.

"Hey, we're a little late," the groom conceded. "It's not like there's going to be a wedding without me."

"Hope's father is looking for you, and he doesn't look happy," Joe answered.

"That's what his face always looks like," Hunter answered unconcerned.

Out of the blue, a squeaky, nervous, exaggerated bellow called Hunter's name. He'd heard this voice hundreds of times at the office preceding impending doom on the immediate horizon. In reality, it was the irrational voice of a pessimistic businessman with one eye on a perpetually falling sky. Rushing around the corner in a semi-dash came the father of the bride. Not far behind Paul Jones walked his dutiful one-time trophy wife Irene, a handsome woman who resembled a Grecian statue thirty years earlier, but had since substituted matronly grace, elegance and snobbery for faded beauty.

"Hunter, I've been calling you all day. You haven't answered," Paul said.

"I've been kind of busy preparing for a wedding Paul," he replied. "What's up? We need a campaign for Bank of

Minnesota by Monday?" Hunter joked hoping to lift wedding day tensions.

"Can we be alone?" Paul asked in front of the others.

"Guys, the guests are arriving," he told his groomsmen.

"Hunter," Paul paused as if organizing a rehearsed speech. Calling him 'Hunter' was a bad omen. For the past seven months, he'd been calling him 'son' when they were alone.

"Yeah?"

"Hunter, I'm serious, this would've saved some trouble if I got you earlier. As it is, this isn't easy to say, but...there's not going to be a wedding today," Paul blurted out, looking down.

"What?" Hunter recoiled confused.

"There's-not-going-to-be-a-wedding-today," Paul repeated, emphasizing each word.

Analyzing what Paul said, Hunter put the emphasis on 'today', meaning there would be a wedding, just not that day.

"Is somebody sick? Did something happen? Is everyone alright?" Hunter asked concerned.

"You might want to sit down for this," Paul sighed.

"What's wrong?" Hunter's worry escalated. That much build-up had to be a prelude to calamity.

"Listen to me. Hope's not here. She changed her mind last night. There's not going to be a wedding."

"Where's Hope?" he insisted. "Is she sick? Is she okay?"

"She's fine, she's fine, but listen to me. There's not going to be a wedding," Paul said for the fourth time.

"Why do you keep saying 'there's not going to be a wedding'?" he started to panic.

"Damn it boy, open your goddamn ears. She's gone. She doesn't want to get married. Not to you anyway...I mean, anymore."

"What? That's ridiculous. C'mon Paul, where's Hope?"

Paul pulled out two envelopes from inside his jacket. The first was elegant stationery, while the second was a standard office-style envelope. He handed him the first, not with a sense of sympathy, but rather an air of detachment out of loyalty to his daughter.

"Hope is gone. She left this note to give to you."

Hunter ripped open the envelope and started reading, but

two lines into it his face turned pallid. His eyes, which minutes earlier beamed with excitement, lost their shine, leaving him with an expression of confusion, desperation, denial, and dejection all at once — a look of utter desolation mirroring the shocking stare of Medusa as a fountainhead for disaster.

"No-no-no-no, this is not happening," Hunter panicked. "This can't be happening. Paul, I saw her 18 hours ago. What the hell could've happened in 18 hours? C'mon, where is she?" he persisted.

Surveying the damage, Paul glared at his wife with a 'this is your daughter's fault' look.

"You think I like this any more than you?" he continued, his voice getting squeakier. "There are four hundred people out there and I wasted twenty grand on the best damn wedding that's not going to happen."

Paul had grown close to Hunter, but fought the urge to feel sympathy for his would-be son-in-law. He'd known all day the wedding wasn't going to happen and took advantage of that time by getting into his 'business negotiations' mode. In Paul's mind, this was just another deal that fell apart at the literal last minute.

With his best stoic face, Paul handed the ex-groom the second envelope and continued in a gruff monotone. "And this is a severance package; a check for $10,000. We can negotiate the details later."

At this point, Hunter wasn't hearing things too well. Words took on a dull bludgeoning vibration as if he'd become trapped in a steel box collapsing in on him. He'd just heard the tail-end of 'doesn't want to get married. Not to you anyway...' when he got blind-sided with 'severance package.' Paul landed an excruciating 1-2 combination that left Hunter dizzy, dazed, and disconcerted.

"Severance package?" he asked baffled. "Severance package?"

"Hunter, I think under the circumstances..."

"You're firing me?" he asked dazed and incredulous.

"...it would just be too awkward," Paul finished.

"Awkward? Paul, awkward is your fiancée not showing up to your wedding."

14

"Yes," Paul agreed, placating his stunned ex-employee, "but I think it's clear our relationship has become strained."

Still not believing he was being stood-up at the altar, he'd just been told he was fired. He didn't care about losing his job, but Hope meant everything to him. He simply wanted to know why she didn't want to get married, in case there was a misunderstanding.

"Paul, where is she? If I can talk to her, everything will be fine."

Paul squirmed as he watched Hunter grasp at emotional straws. However, his answer was stern and final. "She's gone. She caught a plane this morning. She knew she couldn't face you, and she knew she couldn't go through with this. If it's any consolation, I just learned of it this morning."

As the coup de grace, Paul told him to do something tantamount to humiliation.

"Now, I think you better go out there and tell your guests that this wedding has been called off."

Hunter was crestfallen. As if being jilted and fired inside of sixty seconds wasn't bad enough, the responsibility of telling his guests he was stood up had fallen on his shoulders.

"Me?! How is that my job?" he protested.

"If you were man enough to marry my daughter, you're man enough to make the announcement," Paul answered with a tone that sounded rehearsed.

The irony of Paul's answer stung, but Hunter felt too wounded to fight it. As he peeked around the corner to scan the crowd, he could tell that rumors were circulating. Many guests had wide-eyed looks of disturbed intuition, others shifted in their seats, and still others glanced around for clues to confirm rumors being whispered. Since there were no bridesmaids anywhere, that must have tipped-off many guests.

Hunter took a few minutes to compose himself. He took deep breaths and rehearsed the quickest way to convey what had to be said. Starting to feel nauseous, he didn't want to be out there any longer than was needed, since vomiting on the altar would've made an already humiliating experience worse and wouldn't do much to endear him with God.

With his first steps out, the collective audible gasp from the crowd drowned out the organ. Trembling by the time he reached the spot where he was to have exchanged vows with Hope, he glanced around the crowd. Every eye focused on him as anxious guests waited to hear news they already knew. He glanced at the front row and saw his mother. They made eye contact, and she knew. Then, he told the rest of the guests.

"Uh, excuse me," he directed to the organist.

The organ stopped, and the last notes echoed inside the church. With almost 800 widened eyes focused on him, he felt very alone at the altar.

"Um, thank you all for coming," he continued, "I...uh, I'm sorry, but there's not going to be a wedding today."

The crowd gasped louder, and then added murmuring. Hunter paused, debating if he should expound, but chivalry prevented him from telling the crowd that the bride skipped town. He wasted no time getting back to the rectory and stood in a near catatonic gaze, needing a rational explanation to what just happened. Paul and Irene Jones extended their final awkward 'good-byes' without using the actual word 'sorry', and made a stealthy exit out a back exit, avoiding the backlash of an ugly scene.

The groomsmen rushed back, and the quintet stood there speechless; wanting to say things they couldn't put into words. With nothing to say, and wanting to be alone, Hunter told his friends to go home. A few guests tried to come back to console him, but as his sense of reality retreated for the sake of sanity, he disappeared into a small office for solitude. He plopped down on a leather couch, stunned, staring into space, trying to convince himself what had happened.

Hunter Damon was set to get married that day. He was anticipating an adventure that would change his life and give it new meaning. Although he didn't know it at the time, he was about to go on an adventure that would change his life in ways he never imagined.

Chapter Three

After 45 minutes, the strength returned to Hunter's legs, and he wobbled out of the rectory to the emptied church. His groomsmen offered to stay with him through the night, but if he was going to be alone, then he was going to be alone. Being jilted was a personal trauma he didn't want to share with a support group right away. Hurt, humiliated, and confused, he withdrew into privacy, preferring not to face anybody. With his head hung low and hands in pockets, he shuffled to the altar where he and Hope stood the evening before during their rehearsal. Scanning the church still decorated with beautiful, useless flowers, his eyes pulled focus to the front row seeing his mother still in her front pew seat of honor.

"I never liked that girl," her voice echoed with disdain.

Hunter managed to shake his shock.

"Mom, what are you still doing here?"

"My boy needs his mother," she said in the same protective tone she used twenty-five years earlier after his tonsillectomy. Lee had become devoted and loyal to her remaining family after her son Richard left.

"What do you mean, you never liked her? You loved her."

"No," Lee corrected him. "I loved that you loved her. There's a big difference."

"Mom, I still don't know what happened. She left this...note," he stammered, pulling the envelope halfway out of his tuxedo pocket. "I read it four times, but she didn't say anything about why she left," he added.

"Last night I cried because your father wasn't alive to see you get married. Now I'm glad he's not here to see this. This would've killed him."

"Good thing he's already dead, huh?"

Lee chuckled at her son's morbid joke. She knew he meant no disrespect.

"I guess you're not going back to work for that...asshole,"

she declared with authority.

"Mother!" Hunter replied shocked.

"It's true," she defended herself.

"Well, you're right," he conceded as he pulled out the envelope with the severance check. "He fired me. Said it would be too awkward."

"Oh Hunter," she moaned with sympathy. "You know what you should do? Go on a trip. You were going on your honeymoon anyway."

"I'm not going to an island resort alone," he reasoned.

"I'm just saying, spend some time with you. Get things together. You'll be okay."

He looked into his mother's eyes and recognized decades of experience and wisdom. He believed her. Even if he wasn't sure how everything would work out, he trusted his mother. Still, he was less than an hour removed from the most painful and humiliating event of his life. His eyes glazed over as he stared at nothing in particular.

"I think I'll just go for a drive. I don't feel like going home right now." The lost, desperate disturbance in Hunter's eyes worried Lee.

"If you need me, you know where to find me," she assured him, hugging her boy as tight as she ever had. Hunter snapped out of his gaze, compelled to say something to help his mother smile again.

"Strange. I figured I'd be holding a different woman with my last name," he recovered.

"Always with the jokes," she quipped as she turned to leave. Lee felt as much pain and anguish as her son, and on some levels she felt pain he'd never understand. Keeping her head high in her own elegant style, she reached the back of the church and pulled the door open when her son called out.

"Mom. Thanks. I'll be all right, okay? Promise."

Lee didn't speak, but put her hand to her mouth to suppress the enormous eruption of emotions she tried to hide, then left. Although the foundation of his personal empire had crashed around him like jagged rubble, Hunter felt safe in the sanctuary of God's house. He turned and stared at the sad, painful, lonely countenance of Jesus hanging on the cross He had to bear.

"So what do I do now?" he asked the crucifix. For half a moment, Hunter expected the sacred statue to transubstantiate and offer enlightenment like, "I already died for you, what more do you want? Figure it out yourself."

When he didn't get Divine advice, he scoffed at himself for expecting such a miracle.

As he paced down the aisle, the rhythmic clicks of the leather heels and soles of rented shoes hitting marble tiles accentuated the loneliness. The echoes amplified his alienation. Surveying the stained glass windows of martyred Saints caught forever in images of violent, grotesque tortures, he reached into a diminished well for a last gasp attempt at optimism. "At least I'm not one of those guys," he rationalized.

Dusk had fallen by the time Hunter exited the church. The sound of his footsteps, though still laborious, had changed as the leather heels and soles crunched the gravel on the parking lot. He wondered if Todd had the foresight to leave the keys in the car. Since he and Hope were supposed to leave in a limousine, Todd had agreed to drive his car back to his house. Being stranded at the church would have added cruelty to a tragic ending to his day, but fortunately, peering in the car, he saw the keys on the front seat with a handwritten note.

Sorry buddy. Give me a call when you feel like it. - Todd

Slumping in the seat for a few minutes, Hunter personified irony. Dressed in a tuxedo, he exemplified a handsome symbol of confidence and potential; an upper crust gentleman with unlimited promise for achievement. A man on the go, a man on the move, a man going places – but he sat paralyzed and unmotivated in his car for 20 minutes. Even after psyching himself into starting the car's ignition, he didn't know where to go. He only knew that he didn't want to go home as if it had been just another end to just another Saturday night.

He decided to drive around for a while.

After driving on near empty streets for an hour, Hunter realized he'd been driving in a daze. The shock combined with his familiarity of the neighborhoods made driving an automatic response to lights and signs he'd experienced every day. If this nighttime drive was going to be cathartic, he needed the perfect combination of thinking and driving. He needed roads with no stoplights where he could push down the accelerator and eliminate pent-up aggression.

Coming to a cross street leading to the highway, he jerked the wheel hard right in a flash of inspiration. Although staying cautious on the few residential blocks heading to the highway, his restlessness increased like a rambunctious racehorse on its way to the starting gate.

Hitting the highway on-ramp with the fury of nothing to lose, Hunter floored the pedal with an angry appreciation for speed. He accelerated up the ramp and dusted past a car already traveling at a good pace in the merging lane. The impulse to worry about police entered his mind, but the anxiety of a hundred dollar speeding ticket paled in comparison to his angst. He just didn't give a damn.

Then from nowhere, Hunter felt the uncontrollable urge to howl like a maniacal madman. Unable to repress his confusion any longer, he bellowed until on the verge of tears, but laughing so hard he couldn't cry. How would he deal with the pain of rejection from the woman he loved or the humiliation he endured in front of hundreds of people? With his thoughts solidly in denial, a small rational voice whispered through the whooshing breeze into his mind.

Hope had been so preoccupied and excited with planning their wedding, the idea it might not happen seemed an incomprehensible scenario, like witnessing the face of God — something not even imagined as remotely plausible. Now faced with a precedent, he knew better than to assume what was or wasn't possible. He had no other choice than to continue his uncontrollable chortling. It was a pressure cooker response, and he didn't know which was more therapeutic; his maniacal cackling or his reckless speeding down the highway. Between confused chuckles, Hunter thought about his father and wondered.

"Where are you Dad? I sure could've used you today."

At 80 mph, his driving had little direction and reason until he decided to up the ante upon reaching an on-ramp to a connecting Interstate. His laughter soon tapered off into slow giggles that eventually evolved into long guttural moans that foreshadowed his submissiveness to the obvious course of action.

"What the hell," he said aloud. "I'm getting out of town."

Chapter Four

For the first hour on the highway, Hunter perfected a blend of soul searching and self-pitying – a strategy any man tossed in the same situation of being jilted and fired might conjure. While being fired dumped extra salt in the gaping wound, his finances were the least of his concerns. To prepare for his new life, he'd started saving money to acclimate himself to marriage. Now that he was unemployed, his sizable nest egg had become an emergency fund that could last at least a few months. If he added the severance check to that stockpile, he knew he wouldn't starve any time soon. But the mere idea of taking the severance check bothered him, as if it was a buyout. The rejection of being fired hung heavy in his heart, but not nearly as profound as losing Hope.

Before meeting Hope, Hunter had languished in the tedious motions that had become familiar. It wasn't that he was failing, but a jagged emptiness chipped away at what had become a brittle existence. He knew deep inside that his success over the past year and a half was due to Hope. That self-admission became a key that unlatched many doors of memories about her.

Their year and a half courtship had been ideal. They'd enjoyed a couple long romantic vacations and several short, equally romantic weekend getaways. Thinking of their trip to the Bahamas 13 months earlier, Hunter remembered an evening stroll on the pink beach where he snapped a mental picture of a specific moment. The setting sun shimmered off rippling clear blue water while curling waves crashed to the shore and scampered up the sand as if to greet them. It was at that precise moment when he realized he was the happiest he'd been in his life. He was calm, he was loved and most importantly, he loved.

Then his mind jumped to a Saturday morning at a bed and breakfast in Northern Minnesota. As they bonded in the glow of post-intimacy, their playful conversation turned to planning a life together. Hunter remembered verbatim the things said and promised in those few hours together in bed. Between tender caresses and unbridled lovemaking, they planned years of decisions in their fantasy future, settling tough choices like how to discipline children and details like color schemes for kitchen tiles. Hunter had more precious memories of Hope than he could count. Fleeting moments of seemingly small, otherwise insignificant events that confirmed in his soul how much he loved her. Those times she wasn't even aware of, when something she did something that stirred an intense reaction of adoration inside him.

They occasionally fought, but each fight brought them closer because they were fighting for the same reasons. While they were on the same side, they sometimes had different ideas of the best way to take their journey. The emotional outbursts, though rife with anger and frustration, were evidence of their commitment. Nobody likes the negative repercussions and baggage of fighting, but the drama of their disputes supplied the necessary Yin to their lives' blissful Yang.

Indeed, things were said, and things were promised. The bottom line was he loved Hope and couldn't accept she just...left. Questioning if the intensive and exclusive emotions he'd invested over the past 18 months had meant anything was an explosive mistake. Now what could he do? His love had been unwavering.

He had so much love to give Hope, but now she didn't want it? Was there something wrong with his love? For months he'd known he couldn't live without her. Now he was forced to do exactly that.

His dangerous downward spiral of self-doubt narrowed. Its chaotic curves dove deeper, steeper and faster until ending abruptly, dumping him into a darkened abyss where crazed inner-demons lay in wait to crush everything good within him. Any other time, sheer terror would be the primary predator mercilessly ripping his mind to shreds. This time, however, the extreme melancholy took over.

The dejected musings surged with little prompting, but like everything else, even the shock of the day's events yielded to fatigue. After three hours, he'd reached Eau Claire, Wisconsin, a small city an hour or so from the Minnesota border.

Any other night he would've second-guessed squandering money on a hotel room so close to Minneapolis, but that Saturday night was different. Who cares? What the hell are a few bucks in the grand scheme? Besides, if he didn't find a bed to crash onto, he would find a tree to crash into. So what the hell? Who cares? This 'new attitude' Hunter realized how different his world had become. Things had changed. He was alone now. As alone as he'd ever been. He began embracing his 'what the hell' attitude. 'What the hell? The world can turn on a dime at any given moment.' Or, 'what the hell? The life you planned got shattered to pieces because of someone else's decisions.'

Trying to fight losing control of his life, he took a quick inventory of what was left. He had plenty of money to last a good while. He had time. He had a car and an open road heading to a near infinite number of destinations. Most important, he had freedom from obligations binding him to anybody or anything. It's funny how ultimate and sudden freedom can make a man feel more like a slave than ever before.

Hunter embraced at least one silver lining in feeling exhausted; there's not a tragedy powerful enough for anybody to postpone slumber indefinitely. Sleep is a blessing; a welcome respite from sorrow after a disaster. It's an unconscious eight hours of ignoring the crisis and sedating demons, at least until waking up.

Crossing a bridge and passing through Eau Claire, he spotted a Sleep N Save© hotel and exited the highway. He pulled into the parking lot filled with out-of-state cars packed with pillows in the back windows and maps strewn across the front seats. After a moment, Hunter crawled out of his car, and opened the trunk where he stashed two bags packed for a honeymoon. Stumbling inside to the front desk, considering his fatigue, mental state and the late hour all he wanted was a bed. Hunter was not prepared to deal with the happy, young front desk clerk.

"Hello sir, may I help you?" she asked.

"Can I get a room, please?" he mumbled.

"Yeah, you bet'cha," she pronounced with a thick Wisconsin accent. "Looks like you had a big day, eh? Where's your bride?" she asked.

"I'm...not married," Hunter replied.

"Oh, I'm sorry sir, I assumed what with the tuxedo and boutonniere and all," she apologized. Too tired to explain, Hunter forced a smiled, but could barely muster as much as a grunt to answer her.

"Okay then, I'll need a credit card, and if you'll fill this out, you'll be good to go," she resumed in her exuberant tone.

He handed her the card and started filling out tedious paper work while she punched a keyboard. When he finished, she returned his card along with a plastic key card.

"Okey-dokey, here ya go, then. Have a super night then, eh?"

Her silly practiced grin displayed an unsympathetic immunity to any negative vibe. He couldn't help but assume this peppy college-aged girl had been brainwashed by the universal corporate mentality stressing hackneyed public relations mottoes at training seminars held by mid-level human resources managers. Sayings on motivational posters like 'There's a U in the middle of opportunity,' or 'The best customer is a repeat customer.' That night though, Hunter Damon was the antithesis to peppy clerks. In short, he didn't care about the hotel's complimentary continental breakfast. The most positive sentiment he could utter was 'whatever?' After all, 'whatever?' is first cousin to 'what the hell?'

With an overnight bag in each hand, he lethargically ambled down two long corridors towards the room. The bags weighed down his already tired arms, pulling them down so that each step created a 'vheerrrp' sound on the carpet.

Goofy from fatigue, he wondered if — by controlling the speed of his steps while timing the lifting or lowering his bags to adjust the drag against the carpet — he could 'play' *Smoke on the Water* using the 'vheerrrp' sounds.

Using trial and error, he walked fast then slow, then slower, then fast again using a combination of a bent knee, a half-goose step, a near genuflect, and straight up with his shoulders pulled nearly to his neck. It wasn't until reaching his room when he realized that, his spastic walking while dressed in a tuxedo must have made him look like the Monster in the big dance finale of *Frankenstein – The Musical!*

Opening the door and stepping into the sterile chill unique to hotel rooms, he mustered just enough consciousness to undress, running into trouble right away with the cuff links. While fumbling with the clasps, he assumed the tuxedo rental place might want their tux back the next day. The anxiety flared up until he remembered his new motto.

"What the hell? It's a stupid rental tuxedo," he thought. "Anybody whose life revolves around worrying when cuff links get returned deserves an ulcer."

Finally managing to get undressed, he collapsed onto the bed.

For a moment, he put aside his anguish, thinking about his mother and how she must have hidden huge amounts of grief at the church. Lee was always a strong woman, especially for his sake. She showed great inner-strength when Hunter's father died and before that when his brother pulled his disappearing act. Then Hunter wondered about the brother he hadn't seen in 18 years. A thirteen-year-old address in his wallet listed a rural route somewhere in Mississippi, but nobody knew for sure where Richard lived.

Those thoughts led to memories of his father and how hard he took Richard's leaving. Those were sad days to be sure. He preferred to remember good times with his dad, those things he desperately missed since his father's death. In a moment of self-pity, Hunter broke the monotonous roaring hum of the jet engine powered air conditioner in his room, calling out. "Dad, I wish you were here," he prayed.

As Hunter dozed off to the white noise from the air conditioner, his near delirious mind recalled one more hackneyed inspirational saying; *Tomorrow is the first day of the rest of your life.* With that ironic notion, he let out one final short maniacal burst of laughter. It had been only 24 hours since his rehearsal dinner wound down. Most men would have trouble sleeping if their day included what he'd gone through. Thanks to exhaustion, Hunter slipped into the reassuring void of slumber, securing the final nail into what definitely had been the worst day of his life.

Chapter Five
Sunday

Despite exhaustion, Hunter endured a broken, stuttered night's rest, tossing, turning and fading in and out of sleep —— due in part to the roaring din of the air conditioner, but mainly because of the emotional tempest he'd been dropped into. Finally, he enjoyed a few hours of uninterrupted sleep beginning about 4:30 a.m. and continuing until a dream woke him up.

There's no telling what wisdom his subconscious was trying to pass on with this dream. Under the circumstances, even his cognitive mind churned in a flustered stupor, as it searched for even the most hidden answers. What better opportunity for his inner self to reveal truths than when his guard was down and he faced himself?

In it, Hunter is a character in his own dream; like a home movie. He's wearing baggy clothes from the 1920s, riding an old rickety, clumsy bicycle around the edge of a small, still lake. Thirty yards from the lake rose a steep hill overgrown with waist-high grass, where at the top, he witnessed a single grazing lamb. Circling the lake was a road that had been paved at one time, but had eroded into small loose black chunks of gravel from the broken-up asphalt surface.

The dream depicted a sunny day with a young couple, also dressed in 1920's garb, picnicking a hundred yards away. The woman held a parasol while the man poured Champagne into fluted glasses. It was a Gatsbian scene, except for a high-performance sports car parked on the road that places the scene in the present. Hunter rode his bike until he stopped, inspired by the idyllic scene and how it mirrored his carefree satisfaction.

After a minute of admiring the exquisite landscape, he glanced down and saw the rubber on the bike's front tire had dried up. The rubber chipped off easily as he ran his finger along the sidewall. Unconcerned, he climbed back on and resumed his ride. Moments later as he was nearing the hill, the bike tire blew out, and the rim scraped against the gravel.

Hunter didn't completely wake up. Instead, he lingered between slumber and consciousness in that phase of sleep where fantasy ruled with a paper fist. With his eyes shut, hoping to stay in the pleasant ethereal limbo, he heard a voice.

"Hunter. Get up, we're going to be late."

Not sure if he was awake or sleeping, he almost answered. It seemed so real.

The voice called out again.

"Hunter. C'mon. Are you up? I'll meet you in the car."
This time, habit kicked in.

"All right, all right, I'm up," he yelled. As soon as he answered, he bolted straight up. Fully aware of being awake and alone, he questioned himself for answering a voice in his head.

Waking up in a strange, uncomfortable hotel bed, his first impression was how cold it got with the turbo-powered air-conditioner roaring on 'high' all night. His next thought, however, was the memory of the night before. So much for the nice respite during sleep. Back to goddamn reality.

Scanning the room for clues to where that reality was, he spotted the guest services brochure with the hotel's address on the bedside table.

"Eau Claire? Oh yeah," he groaned with a rough morning voice. He turned the clock on the bedside table to see its display and regain his bearings. 7:52 a.m.

His initial instinct was to drive back to Minneapolis. Then it came back to him. He remembered why he went driving in the first place; there was nothing to go home to. But if he didn't go home, what could he do? Never one to contemplate much in an early morning daze, he jumped in the shower to regain his senses. When he hopped out, he wrapped the tiny hotel towel around his waist and started to get dressed. Opening his bags, he peered down at his clothes, reminded that he expected to be married the next time he saw them.

Before he knew it, he was dressed and staring at the tuxedo

crumpled on the floor, trying to remember what he looked like wearing it. He picked the tux off the floor, pulled the envelopes out and stuffed it and the shoes in his garment bag. Looking at the envelopes tempted him to peek inside, but that would only force him to relive the night before. Denial told him there would be time for that later. His immediate concern was figuring out what to do or where to go. Resigned that he had no reason to go back, the other alternative was driving on and delving into the unexplored where there was little he could control.

Back at the lobby front desk, a different annoying peppy desk clerk greeted him.

"Good morning, sir," the clerk exclaimed much too excited for an early Sunday morning.

"I'd like to check-out, please," he asked in a depressed, yet polite monotone voice.

"And which room were you in, sir?"

"I dunno, 2-2-something," he replied, handing over the key card.

The clerk punched his keyboard. "Mr. Damon?" he asked.

"Mm," he grunted in the affirmative.

"Okay. That's $108.65," the clerk informed him. "Keep it on your card?"

He grunted in the same gruff confirming tone. Waiting for the receipt to print, the clerk made public relations small talk. "Have a nice night?"

"Yeah, fine," he answered. The morning clerk was one more smiling corporate zombie in the public service sector. One more casualty of well-meaning inspirational posters and management training manuals that stress phrases like 'customer satisfaction' and 'guarantee' to feign quality customer relations.

"We have an excellent brunch if you'd like a bite before you leave," the clerk offered in a fake voice learned at a seminar and perfected in front of a mirror.

"No, thank you," he replied, signing the bill and keeping his sullen attitude in check.

"All righty then sir. Have a nice day, eh?" the clerk offered.

"Where does this highway go?" Hunter mumbled, pointing

outside.

"That's Interstate 94."

"Where does it go?" he repeated, almost losing his patience.

"Head west and you'll hit the Twin Cities..."

"Yeah, I know that part," he responded.

"...and east gets you to Milwaukee. Follow it around Lake Michigan, and it'll take you to Chicago."

Hunter didn't know why he asked where the highway went, since even a rudimentary knowledge of geography told him that traveling east through Wisconsin would lead him to Lake Michigan.

The sun hung low in the early morning sky as it burned off the dawn's dew. In spite of his understandable melancholy, the day presented the promise of another perfect spring day. Perfect temperature, perfect humidity, and just enough clouds to break up the monotony of an endless blue sky. Thankfully, the fresh air did wonders to wake him up.

He popped open the car's trunk, tossed his garment bag in, then threw his overnight bag in the back seat. Sitting behind the wheel, he gazed at the sky and squinted from the first real brightness he'd seen since September.

That day turned out to be the first opportunity in months to take advantage of owning a convertible. He flipped a couple of latches, pressed a button and started the automated removal of his ragtop. The canvas made its slow smooth mechanized trip over his head, allowing the first rays of sun into the car's cabin in months. Hunter glanced into the rear-view mirror to confirm it was settling into its resting place between the back seat and trunk.

The split second his eyes scanned the rear view mirror, he thought he saw a blur in his back seat. It took another split second to realize the blur seemed familiar, and yet another split second to establish whom it resembled.

It looked like his dead father.

In the brief moment before his mind had a chance to register that he'd noticed something, his eyes had already looked away. Quickly returning his gaze to the back seat's reflection in the mirror, he saw nothing. Whoever...or whatever might have been there had disappeared. He jerked his body around, seeing nothing except his overnight bag.

The idea of seeing the form of his dead father surprised him. He knew he'd seen something. At least he was pretty sure he assumed he might have possibly seen something that almost could have been the vague familiar form of something. Maybe, anyway.

Unless you're Hamlet, seeing your dead patriarch's spirit is not an everyday occurrence. And, unless you're Hamlet, seeing your dead patriarch's spirit is not a sign of trouble. But Hunter relished the notion of his father's love transcending time, space and even death to show support in his hours of uncertainty and doubt. Again, if he had indeed seen something.

Rubbing his eyes, he convinced himself that whatever it was must have been the manifestation of his waking dreams or some kind of deja vu; a simple chemical reaction jumping some random synapse in his brain, which made him want to see his father.

Sitting in his convertible, he reminisced about his father. He'd always had a deep admiration for him; well, maybe not always since every child goes through a 'my father embarrasses me' phase. But one day he noticed how his friends were drawn to his father's modest nature and all-around charm. They saw something he couldn't see. It took Hunter's friends to help him realize how admirable his dad was.

No matter what year it was, Peter Damon always dressed as if it were ten years earlier. Thankfully, he somehow managed to keep sharp about contemporary issues, which was not only impressive for a 50 and 60-something year-old engineer, but it's perhaps the only thing important to most image conscious adolescent sons.

As the years passed, however, his pride in his father grew, especially when his friends complained about their own fathers. He remembered how much they hated them and their hypocrisy. How they would throw their lives away just to spite them. Hunter knew he'd been blessed to have had such a good father. With divorces and affairs plaguing his friends' families (and eventually his own friends), he appreciated the growing rarity of having the same parents from day one until his father died. Like opening a familiar desk drawer and discovering valuable treasure, it was there the whole time, even if he wasn't aware of it.

Peter Damon was also as brilliant as a rocket scientist. Literally. Before Hunter was born, the Damons lived outside Houston, where Peter served on the Mission Control team during the Apollo space missions. Before that, he began his career in aeronautics as a jet pilot in the Air Force. After landing men on the moon for a sixth time with Apollo 17, the senior Damon figured the sky had become the limit. With no more challenges left in Houston, he retired from NASA, moved his family to Minnesota and became an engineer with a small weapons company pioneering the concept of non-lethal weapons.

His father's uncanny ability to break down and examine problems to their simplest terms, combined with his realization of the brutality of war, led to an intrigue with non-lethal weapons. Peter understood first and foremost the importance of a weapon's effectiveness to complete the user's objective — but that raised a valid question. He wondered about situations needing weapons when 'effective' didn't exclusively mean 'lethal.' Weren't there circumstances when an enemy, prisoner or adversary was worth more alive than dead? How could the violence variable be reduced while maintaining maximum effectiveness and safety? These examples of Peter's penchant for breaking down problems let him re-examine their foundation and build it back up; an amazing resource Hunter missed since his dad's demise.

He often remembered an off-handed comment his father made.

"You know son, most fathers can only offer their sons the moon. I helped deliver the real thing."

In the five years since his father's death, not five waking hours had passed without Hunter thinking about him. Perhaps this admiration was extreme, but it was a fair trade-off. His father taught him everything about being a decent man with sincerity, integrity, and principles. And with so many things he could learn from a brilliant man like Peter, those ideals were worth the most in Hunter's mind.

Chapter Six

Pulling out of the hotel parking lot and approaching the highway ramps, he had a choice: west would put him back in Minneapolis by lunch — but why? So he could enjoy the Sunday afternoon following the day his life crumbled in chaos? Could he face all those pitying people, hearing the same sympathetic words over and over? Summoning his new found 'what the hell' attitude he took the on ramp heading east. Why not? No obligations or a job to be at Monday allowed for plenty of time to kill.

Traffic was light on I-94 Sunday morning, and he liked it that way. He figured the success of his driving depended on reducing as much stimuli as possible. The fewer cars on the road, the less he had to think about driving. He could just follow the asphalt like an automatic reaction. No distractions, not even his radio.

This strategy backfired, however. Driving past dairy farms repeatedly reminded him how Hope took half-half in her coffee. Past one farm, sheep in the distance resembled tiny cotton balls in the grass. Cotton Balls? Hope used cotton balls to remove her makeup? Hope? Makeup? Is there any hope to make up with her?

He wasn't ready for that yet. It was too early to heal. Still in pain, his thoughts zeroed-in on losing Hope, but without distractions, his brain offered no opportunity for even a small reprieve.

The initial shock of being dumped and humiliated had somewhat dwindled, but not the confusion. He became tortured by the night before. Sunday was supposed to be the morning he woke up next to his new bride, smile, look into her eyes and say, "Good morning, Mrs. Damon." With five minutes alone with her, he was positive the fractured, disordered fragments of his former life could reform with a synergy making it stronger than ever. Their relationship could easily be restored. This 'event' would simply be an expensive, very public temporary breakup. She didn't even have a reason other than she 'couldn't go through with it in her heart.' What the hell did she mean by that? Was it getting married she didn't want? Did he do something wrong? Was there another man?

If he wasn't tortured enough, that last presumption was an epic mistake nearly causing his brain to implode. Like a train wreck, the more he tried to ignore it, the more he felt compelled to examine the carnage. If he didn't shift back into 'denial mode' quickly, his cerebellum would have melted down and oozed out of his ears.

Finally admitting a desperate need for distractions, he wanted music. A few miles outside Madison, he switched on the radio, barely giving each station a chance before punching the next station up the dial.

"...siiiiiiiing to the glory of the Lord..."

No.

"...but how can she say she loves me, when she can't stand my dawg?"

No.

"...I'm the King of the Gothic dead, a cancer on your lover's head..."

No.

"...ooooh-oooooh-oh baby, you pirouette in my heart..."

No.

"...we drank wine in my pick-up truck, a little later on we began to..."

No.

"Today, we're discussing new Canadian Parliamentary trade initiatives..."

No.

"How can radio be so bad so close to a college town?" he wondered. Approaching Madison, he spotted a shopping mall off the highway. Since all malls are cut from the same cloth, there had to be at least one music chain in it; a perfect chance to pick up classic 'dinosaur rock' CDs.

Except for a cluster of several cars parked in the best spaces, the mall lot appeared deserted. These were the cars belonging to the teenagers and college students with the unenviable jobs of opening stores Sunday morning. Glancing at the dashboard clock, he guessed the mall wouldn't open for another fifteen minutes or so. He parked in one of the remaining prime spots beside a car with bumper stickers stating *Fur Is Murder, Don't Eat Anything With A Face, If Killing Is Wrong, Why Is Execution Legal?* and *Keep Your Self-Righteous Morality Off My Body*, and felt a wave of relief that he wasn't the only person entrenched in denial.

Stepping inside the entrance, enjoying the novel prospect of being the mall's first customer of the day, a wafting aroma of fresh baked goods greeted him. Cookies, cinnamon rolls, croissants, muffins. He stopped, tilted his head back, and sniffed the air. The scent of dark and semi-sweet chocolate, cinnamon, sugar, real butter and blueberries mingled around his head like a baked halo. They were enticing smells of safety; reassuring reminders of simpler days when the solution to any problem could be found in kitchen cabinets. An inspiring idea that the ingredients to life's answers were ordinary and hid in plain sight, waiting only for a catalytic recipe to create baked panacea. The individual parts were there — all that was needed was the right combination.

Except for his footsteps and the different pitched hums of vacuum cleaners, the mall was quiet. Little happened on his side of the store fronts, but behind each gate, a flurry of activity from serious looking workers gave the appearance as if their store meant the world. Passing one gated store after another and another, a series of generic workers on display prepared each separately themed zoo; the book zoo, the shoe zoo, the lingerie zoo, the sunglasses zoo, the computer zoo.

Maneuvering his way through the retail labyrinth, he found a music chain anachronistically named 'Needles' — a reference to ancient days when music came on vinyl records requiring a stylus and turntable. He doubted if any of the young staff had ever seen, much less heard, a vinyl record.

One worker noticed him at the door, checked her watch then shrugged off the remaining few minutes. She slid the partition open and met him with an uncommitted 'good morning.'

"Good morning. You guys open yet?" he asked.

"Yeah, sure. Don't mind the mess, we're a little behind. Can

I help you find anything?" Hunter scanned her name badge. Jenny was an assistant manager.

"If you display your CDs alphabetically like other stores, I'm sure I can manage," he responded in a sarcastic tone he regretted as soon as the words left his mouth. It was unfair to hit this well-meaning girl with an attitude, but Hunter got annoyed when sales clerks asked if he needed help, inferring that their display techniques were much too sophisticated for him to comprehend. Besides, his cross demeanor had spilled over from the previous evening.

Since his trip had no plan of action or ultimate destination, he assumed it could take some time. How much, he didn't know. At least he could control the element of music. Marching up and down the aisles, he grabbed some CDs consciously and others at random, until his arms filled up. At the Easy Listening section, he decided to end his spree. Ready to check out, he lined up the couple dozen or so CDs on the counter, and Jenny's eyes lit up like a vintage Wurlitzer jukebox — back when they played vinyl 45s. Her attitude got more pleasant and professional.

"Did you find everything all right?" she asked as if suggesting one more couldn't hurt.

"Apparently so," he chuckled, sweeping his arm across his new music library like a game show model.

Ashamed by his initial rudeness, he went out of his way to appear friendly. As Jenny scanned the merchandise, Hunter glanced at a poster promoting a new recording of inspirational religious messages by the Supreme Pontiff.

"The Pope has a new release?" he asked, making small talk.

"We'll have it Tuesday. You can reserve a copy," she answered.

"I heard His Eminence blew the roof off the Sistine Chapel in his last concert." Jenny didn't get the joke but smiled anyway. Hunter continued, hoping it might help her understand it. "Of course, I liked him better when the Cardinals played back-up. They had real soul."

Still no show of reaction as she scanned.

"It's a joke," he started explaining. "See, the Pope has a CD, but he's not...a musician. Get it? Real soul?" His explanation started strong, but tailed-off badly near the middle with Jenny's indifference.

"Never mind," he conceded.

Jenny wasn't being rude; she was concentrating on a huge sale. Hunter listened to scanner beeps and watched the total rise anywhere from $10 -$20 a beep.

"Okay, that'll be $389.70," she exclaimed, unable to hide her excitement while Hunter's eyebrows arched from sticker shock. He debated taking some back but whipped out a credit card. It was penance for his initial rudeness. So far, this odyssey had cost him over $500.

Hunter tried one more time to be nice. "Good way to start out the day," he joked.

"Oh yeah," she replied. "Takes the pressure off making sales for the rest of the day," she answered in the same corporate animated tone he heard back in Eau Claire. "Thank-you. Have a good day," she droned, reverting back to a customer-friendly robot voice as she handed him three bags filled with discs.

Back in his car, he began the tedious task of tearing hermetically sealed plastic wrap off the CDs until his stomach started grumbling. Wondering if it was a result of stomach acids boiling from the frustration of opening CDs, he realized he hadn't eaten since lunch with this mother almost 24 hours earlier. Even then, he didn't eat much. Before he could regret blowing off the free hotel breakfast, as luck would have it, he spotted a Waffle-Rama® across the street. He pulled into the parking lot, taking a space between a pick-up and a big rig.

Inside the Waffle-Rama®, he was met by a Chloe, an attractive waitress despite showing fifteen years of hard experiences written all over a 30 year-old face.

"Sit anywhere ya wanna," Chloe muttered.

Surveying the restaurant for a seat, there was a tattooed trucker in flannel at one table and two hunters in camouflage at the counter. Other than that, he had his pick of any table. Seconds after sliding into a booth, Chloe brought him water and asked him if he knew what he wanted. Scanning the menu, he ordered bacon, sausage links, blueberry pancakes, hash browns, an English muffin, orange juice and a cup of coffee.

He'd earned the right to ignore cholesterol for a day.

In the next booth, the remnants of a Sunday paper lay scattered on the table. Suspecting it may have been the 'community newspaper,' he didn't want to risk being busted by somebody laying claim to it. He glanced around and grabbed at sections. Nobody gave him a second look. In fact, nobody gave him a first look. He soon realized why nobody gave a damn about this paper. It had already been rifled through with the good sections taken and many of the coupons torn out. Even so, he tried salvaging something from the few miscellaneous sections pages left behind. Picking up a random section from the middle, he scanned the headlines. Nothing interesting. On page two, however, were wedding announcement of couples that got married in Madison. This was not what he needed. His mind started racing, reliving the events of the prior evening, or more precisely, the lack of events.

"There's not going to be a wedding. My Hope doesn't want to get married. Not to you anyway...I mean, anymore."

It was a conspiracy having a cruel joke at his expense, and the Madison newspaper was in on it. He slammed that section down and grabbed the next section, if only to get his mind off what he had seen, like eating something to get a bad taste out of his mouth.

It didn't matter that he started reading the Gardening section. He didn't have an interest in tips for aphids or care about some woman's passion for tulips, he just told himself to read. But it was too late. The gates had been ripped open. He told himself, "keep reading, don't think about Hope. Don't think about Hope. Don't think about Hope..." His eyes continued moving over the words, as he asked himself, "Why are my eyes still glancing over the page, if I'm not concentrating on it?" His eyes continued racing over words he wasn't reading, when he heard someone ask.

"Excuse me, are you reading this section?" asked the intrusive voice.

Without looking up, he replied, "No, take it if you want."

After a few awkward seconds, Hunter was aware that the man was still there.

"Mind if I join you?" the voice asked.

The interruption annoyed Hunter, but he wanted to remain polite while demanding his privacy. He lowered his paper to tell the stranger that he'd rather be alone.

"Listen, if it's all the same to you, I'd prefer..."

It took a couple seconds to process the face fully. This time, there was no doubt.

It was his dead father.

Chapter Seven

Peter Damon was standing right in front of his son in complete violation of every law of existence. And being dead for five years had agreed with him. He looked just as Hunter remembered: canvas sneakers, khaki pants, a casual dress shirt with a sports coat and a blue ball cap on a balding head.

The son sat stunned, his mouth wide open in disbelief. There was no way this could be a random freak chemical reaction in his mind. There was a real person in front of him. Or at least a real something.

"How ya doing, boy?" his father asked, giving that moment less reverence than something so inconceivable deserves.

"Uh..." Hunter stammered.

"It's me Hunter," his father said, introducing himself with excitement.

"Uh, yes it is," Hunter answered, unsure how to respond. "But you're dead."

Of the hundreds of sentiments he could have uttered upon seeing his father again, most would have been more heartfelt, poetic and meaningful. "But you're dead" seemed the most obvious. So obvious, he repeated it.

"You're...dead."

"Yes, I am son," his father confirmed. "Glad to see you have a firm grasp on the obvious. It's good to see you, too. Mind if I sit down?" he asked, motioning to the seat across from him. Hunter stared at the apparition, wondering if he had a firm grasp on anything.

"You...you, you're...you're dead."

"Okay, this is going to be fun," Peter murmured to himself. "Yes, we're both aware that I am deceased. Can we get past that now?"

"How...what?" In a flash of denial, he sat up straight. "You're not here.
You can't be here? You can't be real."

"Do I look real?" his father challenged.

The son paused, examined his father's face, and in a confused tone answered, "Yes."

"Do I sound real?"

He calmed down even further before answering. "Yes."

"Do you want me to be here? I can leave if you want."

Calmed down, yet still quite confused, Hunter replied. "No, no, stay. I ordered breakfast." Again, *I ordered breakfast* understated the moment, but seeing his father's ghost left him dumbfounded. If he told his father to leave, he might not see him again. He had to get a hold of this situation.

Chloe the waitress and the three other diners witnessed this scene without the benefit of seeing the spirit. All they saw was a guy stammering and nervously motioning for thin air to join him across the booth.

"You all right over here?" Chloe asked, keeping a safe distance.

"They can't see me Hunter," his father informed him. "They only see you talking to the other side of this booth. If you think you're crazy, imagine what they think," he said waving his arms around like a lunatic swatting at an imaginary swarm of bees.

"This kind of thing doesn't happen to sane people," Hunter whispered to his father.

"Breakfast doesn't happen to sane people?" Chloe asked confused.

"What?" he answered annoyed, turning to her.

"You sure you're all right?" she asked, concerned more for her safety than his.

"Yes, I'm fine...I think," Hunter quickly recovered. "I didn't get much sleep."

"You an actor? Rehearsing lines or something?" she hoped.

"Yeah, something like that..." he answered to appease her curiosity so she would go away.

"Heh-heh. Nice recovery," Peter chuckled.

"Your food'll be out in a minute. You want one plate...or two?" Chloe's question revealed her suspicion that he wasn't stable.

"One...will be fine," Hunter answered. Chloe took a long

look at the opposite side of the booth and squinted her eyes, trying to see if she missed something. When she left, the combination of an isolated corner booth and holding up a newspaper section created some privacy for the pair.

"How...how is this happening?" he asked in disbelief.

"It's quite simple. You called."

"I called?"

"You called."

"That's it?"

"Well, it is a bit more complicated than that," his father conceded. "You can't just traverse over whole dimensions on a whim. You want the short answer?"

"Sure," Hunter answered with a touch of skeptical resignation.

"I'm not really-really here-here. I'm hooked into your brainwaves. We've got a psychic connection and you see what your subconscious wants to see right now. But, since I'm dead, as you so emphatically, repeatedly and unnecessarily pointed out, I have no material existence. No body to put a spirit or soul into. So I'm borrowing yours and have become an extension of what you want to see. As a result, I'm in tune with your senses; I see what you see, which is me, I feel what you feel, I hear what you hear, I smell what you smell and I taste what you taste — which is convenient, because here comes your breakfast. I'll explain it better later. Mmm, smells good."

Chloe brought the plates over with caution, maintaining a safe distance from her strange customer. The only thing open wider than his gaping mouth were his eyes.

"Do me a favor," the elder Damon asked excitedly. "Put your face up to the bacon and smell."

Hunter complied but felt self-conscious about it. He didn't know whether it was because Chloe and the others were watching him or because he was talking to a ghost.

"What do you care what they think?" Peter continued. "You'll never see these people again."

His face contorted with confusion and doubt not seen since the Apostle Thomas. It was an expression as bad as the facial expression he made the night before at the church. Being visited by a ghost should be enough to send even the sanest man to pieces, but Hunter began feeling content and safe.

"Eat, eat. Don't mind me, eat your breakfast," his father told him. "Pretend I'm not even here," he remarked absurdly. Hunter grabbed a fork, dug into his hash browns and took a bite. "Oh yeah, those taste good," his father commented as if he savored them. "Put more ketchup on 'em?," he begged.

As Hunter struggled with a new stubborn bottle of ketchup, the apparition began small talk, "So, how are you doing? How are you holding up? I saw everything. I'm sorry about what happened."

"You were there?" the son asked shocked.

"I wouldn't have missed it for the world. I was sitting right beside your mother. She looked beautiful, didn't she? At least, up until your announcement. I tell you son, I've seen every shade of grief in that woman's eyes, but I never saw anything like that. She was strong, though. I'm proud of her."

"What am I going to do? Hunter asked. A small part of him slowly began accepting what was happening. "Stood up at the altar, I lost my job, I've got nothing..." he lamented.

"Well, being on this side, I do have a little insight on some subjects. I'm afraid this is one of those things you're going to have to figure out yourself. All I can do is a father's obligation and offer advice and guidance," he said with a comforting voice.

"Okay, what kind of advice do you have?"

"Those pancakes need more syrup."

"More syrup?" Hunter repeated, expecting more substantial insight than the quantity of condiments needed on flapjacks. Chloe, still within earshot and hanging on his every word, mistook this as a request for different flavors.

"All the syrups we got are on the table," she answered.

Hunter shot her a look that left no doubt that she was violating his privacy.

"Do you mind? I'm having a conversation with the spirit of my dead father. Is that okay with you?" Hunter protested, invoking his new 'what the hell' attitude. As Chloe backed away, Hunter realized he must have been over any embarrassment he'd ever harbored about his father. Their conversation appeared one-sided to everyone else, but he didn't care.

"The nerve. She didn't even offer me a cup of coffee," Peter joked.

"You have a pretty good sense of humor for a dead man," Hunter observed, feeling more comfortable about the situation since it was out in the open.

"You have it all wrong my boy," his father corrected him. "I have a good sense of humor because I'm dead. The opposite of humor is seriousness, and people with no sense of humor are too serious." He paused a bit to enjoy the second-hand flavors and aromas again, and then continued his ruminating.

"They're concerned with material matters and worry about details like jobs, bills, love, possessions and ultimately...death. People love to think about death. Death, death, death. It's the big serious concern everybody worries about. But I don't have to worry about all that, especially death, because I've been there and done it. It wasn't much fun for a second, then it's over and there are no more concerns. Remove the concerns and you remove the worry. Remove the worry, and you eliminate the seriousness. No seriousness means lots of humor. Ergo, I have a good sense of humor, because I'm dead," he added with a wink.

Hunter approached this insight as if solving an algebra equation. If A=B, B=C and C=D...then A=D. He furrowed his brow, nodded his head and accepted the answer with agreeing ignorance, as if it made as much sense as anything else. He wasted no time steering the conversation back where he needed it.

"So what should I do?" he asked.

"What do you feel like doing?" Peter answered with a simple question.

"I...I don't know. Just feel like driving."

"Okay, and how will that help your situation?"

"I guess...when I'm on the road, it gives me an opportunity to think," the son answered with his mouth full.

"That was easy," Peter decided. "See? It's starting already."

A comforted smile came to the son's face as he appreciated his father's simple evaluation. As he motioned to Chloe for the check he added, "Something tells me it's going to take more than just wanting it to be all right."

"Really...?" Peter asked as Devil's advocate.

"Still, I don't remember ever seeing you this...easy minded. It's as if you're not actually you. Death becomes you," Hunter joked as he turned to take the check while ignoring Chloe's disapproving stare.

"Hold that thought, son. Hold that thought. You're halfway there."

Hunter took a few seconds to look in his wallet and pull out $20 for the check and tip. When he looked back up, his father was gone, disappearing with no warning. Panicking, he wondered where his father could've gone, ignoring the fact that he was a ghost. Hunter glanced around the restaurant but saw no sign of Peter. He missed an opportunity to spend more time with his father and tell him things he'd wanted to say. Even though Hunter had been given a remarkable opportunity to see and talk to his dead father, he couldn't help but feel cheated. It was like losing him for the second time.

Chapter Eight

Back on I-94, Hunter contemplated the extraordinary event at the Waffle-Rama®. Did it happen or was Chloe's uneasiness justified? Is an extended conversation with a deceased loved one unprecedented? Could a pan-astral visit over flapjacks be considered a miracle? If his dad took the effort to do something so spectacularly phenomenal, why did he just vanish without warning or wisdom? Even Ebenezer Scrooge got more from Marley than 'Mmm, smells good.' And what did he mean by 'hold that thought, you're halfway there'? Hunter reached the only sane explanation available: he'd gone nuts. Sadly, as real and visceral as his father's visit seemed, lamenting about Hope's flight still took priority in his mind. At least he had proof of that happening.

Cruising down the highway, he inserted a random CD in the stereo and set the volume just loud enough to drown out the constant 'whooshing' of wind cascading into the car's cockpit. Like in the movies, Hunter now had a background music soundtrack to complement his thoughts and influence his mood.

> *Let me tell you 'bout a woman that I knew*
> *Said she hoped I wouldn't kiss and tell*
> *Got me hooked, then told me we were through*
> *Thought she was salvation, but she left me in hell*
> *Yeah, my love for her was strong and she knew it all along*
> *Got her kicks by tearing me down, left me broken on the*
> *ground.*

Being alone with his introspection forced him to ruminate on his situation. Hunter was the most despaired he'd been in his life and had no clue for a solution. His mind meandered; randomly jumping from theoretical reasons Hope had left to hypothetical destinations she might have retreated to. He loved her so much, he didn't know how to live without her? Did he do something wrong at the rehearsal? Replaying Friday night over and over in his head, he couldn't remember anything to show any doubt in Hope.

For a half hour, he compared the connection between his love for Hope and his success. 'Behind every great man, is a great woman.' Hunter agreed that it's true. Unsuccessful men rarely have great women behind them, or anywhere. Most times, the single motivation a man needs for success is to just be wanted, appreciated or understood. If a man is consistently unwanted, unappreciated and not understood, then what would be the point?

Almost on cue, his father appeared in the passenger seat.

"Hey son, how are you doing?" Peter asked popping in from nowhere with a giddiness to be expected from someone who had not traveled in a while.

"Ahhh! Where'd you come from?" Hunter replied startled.

"Wouldn't you like to know? So, where are you headed?" Peter inquired.

"We're not far from Milwaukee," the son answered calmed down.

"I didn't say we," his father corrected.

"Huh?"

"Milwaukee?" Peter resumed, "You know someone in Milwaukee?"

"No. Why?"

"Because I can't think of another sane reason someone would voluntarily drive there."

"Just the next place on the map," Hunter explained.

"Where to after that?"

"Maybe Chicago. I don't know."

"You don't know?" Peter asked stunned.

"Nope. That's the plan. Just keep driving."

"So your plan, is having no plan?" his father deduced with a touch of skepticism. "I'd say that has a kind of understated, ignorant, bullshit quality to it. My God, that's brilliant. It's so crazy it might just work!"

"Maybe. Maybe not," Hunter replied with a tinge of

sarcastic regret. Peter sensed this tension and didn't speak for several seconds while they kept their faces forward, quietly studying the road. Then Peter spoke.

"At least tell me this. Okay, there's no plan — but are you looking for something, or are you running?"

"I don't know," Hunter answered perplexed. "What do you think?"

"You sure don't know much do you? C'mon, you don't want it that easy," Peter asked, starting the ball rolling. "I never handed you anything on a silver platter. If you needed help, I gave you the tools, advice and lessons I've learned."

Hunter sighed, not out of annoyance, but because he did want an easy solution.

"There's a big difference between learning how to use a slide rule and dealing with a major life altering catastrophe," he rationalized.

"My demise changed your life. You did fine. You even did a good job with your mother," his father countered.

"You know what I'm talking about," Hunter challenged.

"I know what we're talking about. I'm not sure if you do." Peter retorted, hitting a bulls-eye.

Neither one spoke for several more seconds while Hunter searched within. First thing was first. The losses hurt the most.

"How do you deal with loss?" he asked his father.

After a moment of careful consideration, Peter sighed and replied, "Loss is personal; it's different for everybody. There's no precise answer and there are varying degrees. It has to feel right."

He'd already assumed that, but his dad's vagueness confused him more. Peter recognized this dilemma and continued with an example. "How did you deal with the loss after I passed?"

Hunter smiled and chuckled. "There wasn't time to mourn. You died, there was the funeral..."

"By the way," Peter interrupted, "thanks for the eulogy. It was very eloquent."

"It came from the heart," Hunter added sincerely, then continued. "Anyway, there was too much going on with interviews. I had no idea you were a semi-celebrity. We had dozens of well-wishers, even several astronauts.”

“Yeah, those guys were good men.”

“After all that, I had to focus on taking care of mom. She never got over Richard leaving, so when you died, I was all she had left. I stayed strong, provided a shoulder and kept my best face on.”

“Again, good job.”

“After several months, I just got used to you being gone. Mourning wouldn’t have been the same. All I could do was hold onto memories of you, helping me with homework, flying kites, teaching me how to drive, and telling me to get out of bed at noon on a Saturday,” Hunter rattled off as a matter of fact. Suddenly he smiled, remembering one poignant moment in particular. “You remember throwing a baseball over my head? But when I turned around, it ricocheted off a pipe and smashed me in the mouth?” he brought up laughing.

“Yeah, that was funny,” Peter reminisced. The atmosphere in the car developed an air of tender fondness as they reflected upon good times they shared in silence. Then Hunter spoke up.

“After you died, a few times I thought I heard you calling me and I answered out loud. I felt stupid.”

“Don’t.”

His eyes welled up with tears, but he shut them and wiped them with his sleeve, hoping his father didn’t see it. Peter respected the moment before continuing.

“So the question remains. How will you deal with the loss this time?”

Hunter sniffed and cleared his throat, eliminating the telltale signs of getting choked-up. “I don’t know,” he chuckled. “That’s why I asked you.”

“Again with the ‘I don’t know.’ Alright, what do you think you’ve lost?” Peter asked, breaking it down to the core.

“I lost the woman I love, my job, my future. I lost my dignity at the church. I lost people’s respect...”

“You think people lost respect for you?” his father asked shocked.

“It’s been replaced by their pity. I hate that. Everything’s spiraling downward out of control.”

“You think all is lost? You don’t have what you had a

couple days ago, so life has no redeeming value?" his father smiled. Then the tone of his voice developed an edge. "Son, what you don't understand is you're as free as a person can be. You have everything you need. Your consciousness. Your spirit. Your soul. Who you are, the real you, is a prisoner of your body. No man can be totally free because his soul, this amazing soul, is held captive in this package of flesh, blood and bones. So to compensate, you have five senses to experience the world. Your senses tell you what's real, but even those sensations — they're only electric impulses traveling to the thick mass of gelatin you call a brain. A man is simply a 4-dimensional extension of the soul," his father added.

"Four dimensions? There are only three dimensions," the son challenged.

"No, there are four," Peter corrected. "True...height, width and depth measure space and physical dimensions of matter; but space and matter, as you understand it, cannot exist without time. Time is the dimensional measurement of when matter exists. Matter can neither be created nor destroyed, and no two objects can occupy the same space at the exact same time. I do miss science." Peter reminisced.

After Hunter accepted his soul's participation in his life, Peter tried to rebuild his son's confidence by listing how his plight wasn't as bad as he feared.

"A job is the least of your worries. You can get a job anywhere," his father proclaimed proudly. "Now, your future," he continued after a short cadence, implying there was much to say. "You didn't lose your future, son. It's impossible to lose your future because it was preordained and set into motion long ago. What happened was, you had several attractive, convenient and logical pieces mapped out, and you assumed it was your future. That life and set of situations allowed you to eliminate some questions, so you felt secure knowing what might happen to a certain degree. Now, you've still got a future — the future you're destined to have. You just don't know what it's going to be." Peter took a long breath and sighed, "As for losing the woman you love, there are dozens of clichés about that. You'll land on your feet," he added with pride and confidence.

"But where? I don't want to go back, and I don't know where to go."

"Son, look at the white lines in the middle of the road. Those lines are there to control you and give direction. They tell you when to turn the wheel or go straight. And each line is a small part of a larger ongoing series of lines. Now the faster you go, the less they look like individual lines and more like one long continuous line. Go fast enough and they blur into one another so you can't make them out as separate. But if you slow down or stop, you can scrutinize the lines clearly. The problem is, if you've stopped to take too much time examining individual white lines, you're not going anywhere. That's when the lines stop guiding you. It's just white paint on asphalt. As long as you're moving, you're making progress, even if it's in a downward spiral. If you're not moving forward, you're just standing still. Keep your momentum, follow your heart, listen to your head."

The sound of his father's words resonated with wisdom, calming him. That calm was tendered with disappointment, however, when Hunter looked over at the passenger seat to discover his dad had vanished. Instantly, Peter Damon returned to his normal place as a series of memories. Less awestruck with this visit, Hunter began to understand that his father had become an integral part of his hard earned lesson. As a teacher, Peter's job was to plant a seed and let the student work it out.

His work cut out for him, Hunter figured the time was right for more serious reflection. Without looking, he grabbed another random CD and slid it in the stereo console. Unfortunately, a dangerous and doleful pattern was being established as his crowded, unguided thoughts became victims of a 'train wreck of consciousness'.

Looking backwards hurts, but it's clearer to see
The good breaks and bad mistakes and what happened
eventually.
Looking ahead is simple, but nothing comes into view
So the future trends and dead ends remain a mystery to you.

Sunday afternoon passed quickly as he approached the fringe of the North Chicago suburbs. With the sun heading down on his right, he thought about spending the night in Chicago. Remembering the point of this trip, he decided not to tempt himself and lose focus. With over an hour of daylight left and absorbed with his objective of finding answers, Hunter couldn't rationalize the inevitable Chicago distractions and merged onto the I-294 toll road, circumventing the Windy City altogether.

As dusk took its time consuming the sky, the flat grasslands of Illinois proved conducive for deep thought. A couple of hours had passed since his father's visit, and he revisited the probability that at least a part of him had lost his mind. Another part of him, however, felt guilty that he may have been treating these visits too casually. When a loved one dies, survivors always fantasize of things they'd say if given another chance. The reality is if the dear departed would 'pop' in, the living would be too shocked to pull up their mental list of 'things I gotta say to the dead.'

As comforting as the visits had been, Peter's appearances compounded Hunter's confusion on several levels. He was grateful, but the intense emotional surge after their reunions, combined with his existing lamentations from losing Hope, his job and future, left him feeling drained. His whole day was spent overdosing on an improbable variety of emotions that ran the gamut, which the mere fact he functioned at all stood as a rousing testament to his psychological fortitude. While he knew his brain had been sputtering on cruise control, he took a measure of comfort that a lesser man would have cracked under the blizzard bombarding a solitary soul all at once. His subconscious analyzed his options and prescribed an unusual combination of shock, complacency and denial as the best temporary treatment. With his mind chaotically spinning at almost the speed of light in multiple directions for the past several hours, all he craved were a few stiff drinks and a soft bed.

Sometimes, retreating is the best course of action available.

Spotting a Budget-Bed® chain hotel north of Champaign, IL he prayed it had a restaurant where he could get a drink. Maybe a meal, but definitely a drink.

Checking-in, it amused him how similar it was to the evening before. The same peppy desk clerk, same generic lobby and the same paperwork reinforced his theory that, regardless of different product promises, brands are pretty much all the same.

After tossing his bags in the room without bothering to turn on the light, he headed to the hotel's restaurant. It was nothing special — clearly an average afterthought designed by a corporate Research & Development department to appear unique by hanging unrelated novel pieces of Americana and mass-produced faux antiques on the wall. More interested with what was behind the bar rather than what decorated it, he shuffled to the bartender, ordered a bourbon and water, downed it in one steady motion then ordered another.

In less than 20 minutes Hunter finished three drinks and retired to his room, where he felt deja vu all over again. Same generic comforting room layout, same factory produced starving-artist painting, same cheap polyester covers on the same durable bed, neon lights flashing in a window overlooking the highway and another air-conditioner set on 'Arctic.'

As the liquor soothed his tattered nerves, he slouched on the bed and rolled his shoulders, aching from taking the brunt of abuse after an extraordinary day. Taking a minute to reflect, he wondered what in the world could happen next. In less than 26 hours, he'd been left at the altar, lost his fiancée, his job and the future he'd been counting on. That disaster culminated in an impromptu, directionless trek, taken with the motivation of finding unknown answers to unexplored questions. Then he had a most profound conversation with his father who had been dead five years — leading Hunter to question if the next room he checked into should have its own private lithium dispenser. Not a typical day by anyone's standards.

It astonished him how such dramatic life altering events could happen out of nowhere all at once. Regardless of any preparation, a man is powerless to see or stop the momentum of many wheels in motion. Most days, a man wakes up, looks in the mirror and recognizes who he thinks he is. He goes about a normal day, acts how he thinks he should, then falls asleep at night without a full appreciation of what had happened – even the small or ordinary things. One day leads to the next and the next and the next. As soon as he knows it, months and years pass by and he compares his life to the way it was at certain memorable milestones. Most of the time, whole weeks or months get forgotten because nothing momentous happens. Two days earlier, Hunter was nervous, but felt secure with a plan and direction for a new life with a wife. Now he had less direction than a hyperactive blindfolded five-year-old whacking at a spinning, swinging piñata.

Thanks to a potent mixture of emotional and physical exhaustion plus three shots of bourbon, he dozed off almost as soon as he slipped under the scratchy hotel sheets and rested his head on the lumpy poly-filled pillow. Although hardly a good night's sleep, his booze induced slumber promised at least several hours when he wouldn't have think.

Chapter Nine
<u>Monday</u>

Monday morning, Hunter jolted up in bed when his internal clock alerted him of being late for work.

"Shit!"

Remembering he was now unemployed, he collapsed backward onto the thin, flat pillow to try and regain the sleep that had provided sanctuary from the torment.

Too late. He was up.

It was the first non-holiday, non-vacation Monday he hadn't worked in eight years. Technically, he planned on taking the whole week off for his honeymoon, but that was when he had a fiancée and had a job. In a recurring trend, his thoughts returned to Hope. After all, just 36 hours had passed since Saturday's debacle, and the resulting consequences were too painful not to think about.

A small part of him, the latent optimist, looked forward to continuing his adventure; exploring an unknown territorial range while broadening an unexplored mental range. After getting dressed, checking out and grabbing a map of Illinois-Indiana at the front desk, he hopped in his car and made two decisions. One, concentrate on positive ideas to relieve his maudlin emotions — and two, head south. Not only was the flat distraction-free Illinois landscape conducive for thinking, but also a southern heading would gradually lead to Mississippi, the last known address for his older brother.

The first ten minutes on the highway, his thoughts stayed introspective, however, not as bitter as he imagined. If there's a silver lining to age, it's the accumulation of wisdom and patience. His heart was broken, but it still pounded in his chest. Recalling earlier devastating break-ups in his younger days, he snickered, remembering how after each one, he knew his life lay in shattered ruins, never to be complete again. He compared high school and college break-ups to those within in the past ten years, concluding that in school, the men took the brunt of the break-up hit, while the women played it off and moved on. The tables get turned for couples breaking-up in their late twenties, thirties and beyond.

As soon as he commended himself for feeling a bit optimistic, pondering break-ups forced his emotions to turn on a dime. His short-lived stoic facade, exposed as a phony scarecrow, changed to a blank stare as waves of emotional pain surged and his soul tried to escape the spreading poison of dread.

An oppressive deluge of discouragement engulfed him like a dark wet blanket as he was reminded of having nothing in the world defining him as once believed. No fiancée, no job...nothing. Even his house in Minnesota, filled with those material possessions, seemed like a foreign place — a museum dedicated to the spirit of an ancient successful life, furnished with anonymous memories and dreams. Even if he wanted, he couldn't go home. Not anytime soon, anyway. After investing so much effort in controlling life, he couldn't control anything.

If Hope didn't really love him, it was best to find out then, rather than go through a wedding ceremony, go through the motions of an alleged marriage, and then go through lawyers during an ugly divorce. What tortured him, though, was after all the time they'd spent together, the plans they'd made, the times she told him she loved him, she might have been lying the whole time. He didn't know, and with no way of contacting her, he couldn't shake the rejection. The most frustrating part of being jilted and her subsequent flight? Being set adrift with no explanation. He figured, if she set him up for the most humiliating experience known to man, she at least owed him the courtesy of an explanation, if not an apology. "I'm actually a lesbian" or "I'm on the run from the FBI." He would've believed anything at that point to validate the agony. She fell into an abandoned mine. Elvis kidnapped her on a spaceship. Anything.

Three weeks prior to the wedding date, they sat down for a 'full disclosure talk.' He had nothing to hide (nothing to affect a marriage anyway), and wanted to make sure she didn't have a skeleton in her closet that could haunt them. Trust is one of the ten basic tenets in marriage along with faith, respect, forgiveness, tolerance, sacrifice, patience, hope, understanding and love. Trust is arguably the most important, because, without trust, there's no way a couple can evolve to the other nine. Although every woman's heart carries secrets and indiscretions, Hope assured him she had nothing to destroy the foundation of their marriage.

So what in the hell happened? The frustration of her abandonment, cutting-off contact, drove him insane. There had to be a reason. Was there another man? Was it cold feet? Did she accept his proposal months ago because it didn't occur to her to say 'no'? And where could she have gone so fast anyway? He last saw her a few minutes before midnight on Friday. After that, she apparently found enough time to write her rejection opus and catch a plane. Where could she have gone? If he hit the open road to deal with this, where did she choose to lick her wounds? Bermuda? Mexico? Paris? His gut gurgled and constricted with jealousy thinking about his fiancée rebounding in the arms of a pretentious, prissy Euro-creep with long sideburns, a black turtleneck, and rectangular sunglasses. He tried to convince himself that he'd never take her back for dignity's sake, even if she begged. The quivering knot in his abdomen told him otherwise. He still loved her.

That gave him his first answer. If he searched for truth, it was impossible to lie to himself. He knew he'd still take her back if given the chance, but he also knew there was something wrong about that. He feared looking weak and desperate in people's eyes. He feared how it would affect their trust. If the rejection hurt him, the fear terrified him.

Staring at the open road, his mind was starting to meltdown.

"You know, it's going to get darker soon," Peter said.

Shaken from his catatonic gaze in the nick of time, he glanced over to see his father sitting shotgun as if he'd been there all day.

"Huh? What did you say?"

"I said it's going to get darker soon."

"It's early afternoon."

"You know that's not what I meant."

"I know," the son conceded.

Several seconds of quiet followed while they reflected on that last exchange and the significance of admitting that it might be a long road with no quick fix — if there was a fix at all. After an awkward silence, his father spoke up in a contrived tone.

"Ah, the open road. I love it. A great place to contemplate life and talk to God. Of course, you don't have to ask for signs. Keep your eyes open long enough, and they just appear disguised as mile markers, exits and truck stops, providing direction to potential promises. This is a big country with lots of wonderful things in it."

Another long, awkward pause.

"You want to talk about it yet?" Peter offered. "If not, that's okay. I'm enjoying the ride."

"I thought I might get a little understanding...a little sympathy," Hunter admitted almost ashamed. "I get dumped for no reason. So what do I get out of it? What's in this for me? What?"

"Of course I sympathize. I hate to see you hurt," Peter assured him. "But let me tell you, people break up every single day. People also fall in love every day; and sometimes, they get married. So then, why do people get married? Because they think they've found their true soul mate? Fair enough. Now here's where things get interesting. Yes, each soul has one true mate they were literally cut from the same cosmic cloth along with; yin and yang, positive and negative and all that balance stuff. Tell me, what do you suppose are the odds of finding your one soul mate? With billions of souls in the world, you think your mate grew up down the street or even in your hometown? It happens, but most times mates are on the other side of the world and don't speak the same language."

"Why make it harder than it has to be?"

"A good 75% of life is challenge; how you see it, approach it, react to it and live with it. Why is one man's life an unending challenge? Can he overcome adversity day after day after day? If so, how? Challenge keeps existence from getting boring — hopefully without getting demoralizing. I know it's confusing, but stay with me."

On the contrary. Hunter often wondered about souls.

"Suppose there's a pair of soul mates and furthermore, let's assume they've met often throughout the ages. They find one another, get married, grow old, die, and then rejoin on the other side. By design, this process becomes easier, because a soul assimilates a small piece of their mate every time they meet. After enough trips, finding your mate becomes second nature; they become more like each other. Ultimately — and I mean 'the ultimate-ultimate' — these two souls fuse back into one, then get reabsorbed into the Godhead, confirming that all is connected, all is one and all is a part of God."

Hunter's expression turned dumbfounded. He understood the definition of each of the words — and the idea sure sounded nice; the whole concept, however, was too colossal for his brain to wrap around.

"Perhaps I'm getting ahead of myself," Peter quipped, "It might be best to forget that last part. One percent of Reabsorption takes eons and eons and eons longer than the most advanced human mind could ever begin to imagine. Anyway, on the other side, souls who have found each other decide if they want to go back and try it all over again. Now, in the corporeal existence, they have no memory of the whole thing. They just feel an unexplainable force tugging at them. Sometimes they meet, but not always. Back on the other side though, they remember everything. It's quite inspiring. The trick is finding your soul mate in the first place. That, my boy, is a formidable achievement in itself. The good news is once a soul connects with its mate they remain bonded forever, even if they don't meet on later trips. They're rejoined after each corporeal life."

"Why doesn't everybody...or...every soul do it?" Hunter asked astonished.

"You have to find each other first. Most haven't. Of souls who have, some go back. Others are already happy and don't put a priority on trips where they're trapped in three dimensions on Earth. Although finding your mate gets easier, there's never a guarantee. But the reward of soul mate love in the corporeal world is the greatest gift in the universe. It's pure love-squared. Imagine the mental, intellectual, emotional and psychological bond brought together by two bodies. It's truly awesome and much more rare than anyone might think. That's the thing you miss on the other side; the grand prize with a body. The main incentive for coming back. Of course, it's not all about that. Like I said, if you lack a body, you have no five senses. Those senses define you as a human. The wonders you can experience with them. The physical realm is the soul's playground."

"Senses define humans?" Hunter repeated as if committing it to memory.

"Sure. The details from your senses create your reality. What you see, hear, touch, smell, taste. Things unique to corporeal existence.

"What about personality and emotions? Hunter asked. "Why don't those define you as a person?"

"Emotional qualities define the soul. You keep those when you pass over and continue to build on them. Emotions are all there really are and all you'll ever have. When I said I needed to 'borrow' your senses, that wasn't completely accurate. Since I have no body, I lack a nervous system to process information. What I can do through our psychic connection is feed off and share emotions to how you react to your senses. I couldn't smell the bacon yesterday, but I was aware of dozens of your emotions all at once — most of which, you weren't even aware of. Emotions my boy, existence, in any form, is all about emotions.

"You know what a soul is? A soul is that spark of energy. Life itself. The brilliant radiance you recognize in the eyes. The part that experiences, accumulates and learns from emotions. Souls feed on emotions — build on them. Ultimately, a soul evolves from the emotions it harbors. Good souls are kind, fair, patient, charitable, loving. Bad souls become angry, greedy, envious, lustful, mean...you get the point. In a perfect world, souls would always be good. That plan went to hell. Since then, it takes effort to be a good soul. It's all worth it though."

"Senses define you as a person; emotions define you as a soul?" Hunter confirmed to himself in a moment of revelation.

"There you go. Souls are overflowing with emotion. And your emotions become like baggage you take on a trip to the other side. They can be cumbersome at times, but you'd be nowhere without them. And like luggage, some folks need a full set, while others are happy with a weekend bag. A good person will hold onto good emotions, spread them around and evolve into a purely good soul. On the other hand, some nurture negative energy from their emotions and well, it can be bad if you don't get rid of the negative stuff."

"Look, I just wish I could make this pain go away," Hunter lamented.

"Pain?" Peter responded. "Think about this. There are people in the world who never find love their whole lives, and they have to carry that emotional baggage over with them. You try living with that pain, dragging it around everywhere. These poor souls have so many pure, beautiful emotions they're dying to share with somebody, anybody; but for one reason or another, nobody wants to take them. What do you think that does to a soul? They want to feel love, but all they know is emotional failure, destitution and rejection. That pain is hard to imagine."

"It ain't that hard to imagine," he speculated.

"Son, I know you're hurt. That's why I'm here. You can think clearer when you talk to somebody who'll listen. What you're feeling is a blip. It may not get better today, tomorrow or next month, but you know you'll love again. You have to learn that even when you're by yourself, you're never alone. No man is ever completely alone. He holds the spirit of every soul he's ever known locked into his own."

Feeling wanted and needed was the last thing Hunter felt after Saturday. This deflating incident had been so sudden and unexpected, as if a spontaneous void sprung inside of him, spewing an organic death. A spreading void, coming dangerously close to infecting the parts of him he needed to fight it off.

The trouble with emotional pain is, although it doesn't physically hurt, it's dozens of times worse than any physical suffering. But with so many available ways to temporarily subdue emotional pain, he had to be careful not to trade one pain for another.

It comforted him knowing his father shared his pain. Peter

had always been a sturdy rock to lean on; grab a hold of in the middle of a violent psychological or spiritual squall. He wanted to tell him, but by the time he looked back over, his father had already silently slipped away. Hunter was by himself in the car again. Now he had to figure out if he was alone.

Chapter Ten

She promised to teach me the meaning of true love
It was way too late when I had to learn the hard way
She kept her word, 'cause I know now what it was she talked of
Only when she packed her bags — and she moved away.

The advantage to a state of shock is an instant availability of denial. Hunter knew what had happened to him since he'd been obsessing about it nonstop for two days while not allowing himself the luxury of dealing with it. In dire need of a break, after almost 600 miles on the road, time started cooperating. At first, a half-hour dragged on like 60 minutes. By central Illinois, it improved to seem like 45 minutes.

Two hours had passed (according to the dashboard clock) since his father's last visit when he reached southern Illinois. Other than a vague decision to keep a southern course, Hunter still had no direction, and his sole itinerary was an uncertain address he didn't know how to find. A friend of a friend had forwarded Richard's address to Hunter several years earlier, and all he knew was that it was a small Mississippi town about an hour from the Louisiana border.

Eighteen years after his brother's estrangement, and ten years after anybody had heard even second-hand news, nobody could say with any certainty if Richard was still alive. With all the loss Hunter had experienced, an urgency tugged at him for contact with his brother, even if it was superficial. An urgency similar to the connection loved ones of the terminally ill develop. The fear of too many things needing to be said in case they never got another chance.

It had been so long since they had any contact, Hunter wondered about the extent of their relationship. If he needed one thing at that point, it was confirmation of his connections with others. Could the ugly strain that made Richard leave have tainted their ties? Stretching itself so thinly over time and space it turned invisible, yet still impermeable? He feared that one cold day in those 18 years, Richard simply tuned-out his family for good. Out of sight, out of mind. He suspected this might be the truth, but couldn't begin to prepare himself for that probability. The farther he went, the queasier he felt about finding his brother's conditions. He feared Richard might not accept him. He feared being disappointed in his brother. Most of all, he feared losing a fiancée, a job, a future, and a brother in less than a few days.

Driving on I-57 South, he passed the small towns and farms that define America's soul. Unassuming communities filled with both praiseworthy deeds and unspeakable horrors. Small towns no better and no worse than big cities, only smaller. Towns where folks in bathrobes jump-start a neighbor's car on cold Sunday mornings, and where teenagers sell drugs from behind the Creamy Treats®. Towns where half the population can't wait to get out and the other half could never imagine living anywhere else. Places where patriotic bunting decorates the courthouse every national holiday, and a nativity scene graces the church between Thanksgiving and New Year's Day. Places filled with God-fearing people who get along with just about everyone except racial supremacists and 'trouble-makers in the ACLU.'

"Have you figured out what you're running from?" his father asked, appearing in the passenger seat.

"I'm not running," Hunter answered defensively.

"Sure you are. I don't mean you're a coward. You just don't want to face the demons in your head."

"The past couple days have been a little weird, okay? I've earned a right to avoid a few issues."

Ignoring his son's request for denial, the wise apparition promptly proceeded to his point.

"Ask yourself, what are you afraid of? What do you fear about all this? Loss? Pain? Loneliness?"

"How'd you know I was thinking about fear?" he asked astonished.

"Fear's a double-edged sword," Peter continued without missing a beat. "An effective motivational tool. Fear can kick survival instincts in gear to show what you're made of or fear can paralyze you into doing nothing. Both are useful reactions in different situations. It's a kind of instinctive knee-jerk response. Fear kicks in, then you feel that ominous wave consume you like you're not sure what's going to happen. You're not in control and that's when things go downhill fast. Now, another side of fear is, after enough time, you look around and you're still there. You ever hear about the skydiver whose parachute didn't open? For the first, 5,000 feet, he screamed bloody murder — until he had to stop screaming just because he ran out of breath. With another 10,000 feet to go until he hit the ground, it seemed anti-climactic to start screaming all over again. What do you do? Say a prayer? Admire the view? Aim yourself towards a big damn haystack?" Peter assumed he'd made his point. Ten seconds of confused introspection proved otherwise. Hunter needed clarification.

"So what happened?"

"Hm?"

"What happened to the skydiver?"

"He smashed into the ground. I don't know. It's an allegory. I made it up," Peter replied a little annoyed. "The point is, there's always a measure of time between your feeling of fear and the outcome of what you're afraid of. What if you see a rattlesnake? You've only got a couple seconds to assess danger and react to what you're afraid of...being bitten. Or if your boss gives you one month to improve, then you have more time to assess danger and react. And what if you're diagnosed with cancer and only have nine months to live? That gives you that long to prepare and accept what you fear — death. All these dilemmas create fear. What you have to figure out is, 'what danger are you afraid of in a situation and what realistically is the worst that can happen?' Then ask yourself, 'is the worst that can happen really that bad?' Fear can be the bullet you shoot yourself in the foot with, or it can be the whisk that makes omelets from your broken eggs."

Hunter listened until cutting to the chase. "All I know is, I'm miserable. I had this whole happy life mapped out in front of me and it's gone. Tell me, where did my marriage and my happiness go?"

Again, Peter dipped into his deep well of philosophies, drawing his son back to perspective.

"Hunter, happiness is relative, you know that. It ebbs and flows; tiny pieces of satisfaction. Small victories with momentary peace of mind. Take two couples. One couple, married 45 years – but only happily for 20. The other couple, blissfully married for just two years, before one spouse dies. Now, was one couple more successful than the other? Is percentage important, or is sheer numbers important? You had 18 months with her. It's all relative. Look for happiness from within. And what about misery? Suppose a man is miserable for 70 years, except for the last ten minutes of his life when he's ecstatic and happier than he's ever been in his life? He dies on a high note. If you're honestly, truly happy for your last moments of life, even if the rest was miserable, who's to say it wasn't successful? Tragic? Maybe. Ironic? Certainly. But successful. People reminisce about the past, dream about the future, but they live the present. The past has a fixed value for lessons learned and memories. The future has unknown, potentially unlimited value for preparation. But the present is the only time you can feel. The only time you can feed your senses and emotions, and that's what matters. Remember your past, plan your future, live your present."

Starting to get inspired by his father, Hunter hung on every word, expecting him to continue. Noticing a longer than usual pause, he glanced over and saw, once again, the ghost disappeared.

"Why does he do that?" he thought to himself.

Time still passed slower, while mile markers counted down at an accelerated pace. Nearing a highway intersection at Mount Vernon, Illinois, he lost his nerve and swerved his Mustang over two lanes to catch I-64 East, postponing his reunion with Richard. Unlike Peter, Hunter wasn't prepared to just pop in on a relative he hadn't seen in a while.

Hunter's mind needed to decompress after being hit with such a heavy perspective; a rest from himself and his intense introspection. Reaching in the back seat, he grabbed another CD and slid it in the dashboard player. The sun was shining, the top was down, and good tunes played. He sat up straighter in his seat than he had in hours and relaxed to rock 'n roll.

Sometimes shutting down, rolling along and taking life for granted is far better than pursuing answers.

> *My hometown, it ain't much for glamour*
> *And my hometown it don't care about fame*
> *The church is across the courtyard from the slammer.*
> *And guys I've known thirty years have stayed the same.*
> *The city's only big 'cause it's filled with too many strangers*
> *And most of them I would never give the time of day.*
> *But friends in my hometown keep me safe from danger*
> *With folks like that there's no sane reason to move away.*
> *So why should a guy who considers himself so lucky roam?*
> *When everything I'll ever want is in my old Kentucky home.*

Hunter found solace on the open road. The interstate symbolized an empty page, free of thoughts and opinions corrupted by the pressures placed on a delicate psyche. It's the guarantee of unlimited choices and scenarios, where tiny details hold potential to change an intended direction. It's a place providing as many or as few distractions as any situation dictates, allowing the mind to wander as far down the highway's constantly shifting horizon as it likes. The wind and the hum of the motor create a constant, hypnotic blank background inviting the subconscious to the surface to breathe sweet possibilities of obtainable options. The road is a clean canvas resting on an easel made up of landscapes; bordered by fences, but defiantly running beside those stymieing confines, as a reminder of America's spirit of individual destiny.

To Hunter the road typified New Year's Day, Holy Confession and a vast untouched blanket of snow fused into an unknown promise; where the path to serenity and supreme salvation lies between tall green stalks of corn on one side and a sea of golden grass on the other. It's an asphalt passage to promise where the price of adventure and the cost of relaxation is the current exchange for a tank of gasoline. It was a benevolent route where even the middle of precious nowhere took him somewhere.

It's been said the difference between Europe and America is, in America, a hundred years is a long time, and in Europe a hundred miles is far away. America may not have an ancient history of architecturally grand churches reaching to the heavens, but there are four million miles of cathedrals stretching across its patchwork patterned landscapes, inspiring more hallowed thought and spiritual renewal than ever imagined in the Old World; an extensive route spurring humble proposals into world shaking innovations. Although America had become the foremost country in the history of the world decades before, it wasn't until its holy roads were built that it fulfilled its destiny as a haven to rouse and nurture even the smallest notion from the most common man.

Samuel Miller

Son

Chapter Eleven

For survival, sometimes it's best to go into hiding.
Jump in a car, with little regard... and do some riding.
'Cause if one detail goes wrong, it's easy to lose control
Lucky is the man who finds that he can...be free to roll.
When destiny has lost its direction and nothing seems to make
much sense.
Hop on the open road and pray — for Interstate Providence.

The next two hours or so was an intermission for Hunter as he cruised east on I-64. With the sun beating down into the convertible, he pushed the pain to the back of his mind and delved into the music. Tuning out consciousness was not without effects, however. By losing himself in songs about other people's problems, he didn't notice the changing landscape across southern Indiana. The miles of flatness he'd traveled so far had led to a gradual increase of gentle hills, rising like air-filled bubbles on a baked pastry crust. Hills with inclines so moderate, their presence were only realized upon reaching each hill's apex.

As soon as the final chords on the CD faded, he ejected it from the player.

"So, where are you now?" Peter asked casually, like he'd been there the whole time.

"About 15 miles from Ferdinand, Indiana," Hunter replied nonchalantly. He was getting used to the spontaneous pop-ins.

"Indiana? Why are you going east now?" Peter asked.

"I don't know. Spur of the moment decision, I guess."

The apparition didn't buy that for a moment. As Hunter got closer to seeing his brother, his panic about finding inevitabilities festered. But if he didn't want to talk about it, there were ways to force his son's hand.

"What's the latest from Richard?" Peter asked, not too subtly.

"I know the same as you. The last I heard about him, you were alive."

"Is he still with that girl?"

"I told you, I don't know any more than you."

The tense silence lit a necessary fuse. After several moments of anticipation, Peter spoke up.

"He left because of her, you know?"

Hunter sat up, raised his eyebrows and sternly asked, "Are we going to talk about this now? I will. I held it in for years. When you died, I figured I lost my chance. Do you want to talk about this now?"

"Yes," the father meekly replied.

"He left because he thought you were a racist who didn't like the black woman he fell in love with."

"I didn't hate her because she was black," he assured his son, "I didn't like her because she was crazy and dangerous."

"Are you going to deny that you noticed that she was black?"

"Of course not. I had eyes, didn't I? Your son comes home from college, and without any warning says, 'Mom, Dad, meet Chantilly.'"

"Chaniqua."

"What?"

"Her name was Chaniqua."

"Whatever. That's not important. You meet somebody, anybody, and your brain processes thousands of pieces of information in the first second. Yes, I noticed. Yes, it shocked your mother and me at first, only because it didn't happen much. But it wasn't because she was black that we didn't like her."

"Why not then?" Hunter challenged.

"She was crazy, Hunter. She hated white people. Spouting off about wealth redistribution, land seizures, publicly executing politicians! You don't go into someone's home and tell them you hate them and what they believe. She was so angry, with that shaved head. She carried a gun in a holster and wore the damn thing to the dinner table. Minnesota is liberal, but we never sat around the dinner table conspiring revolution and peasant uprising. We certainly never went into a stranger's home and called them fascists. It wasn't her race; we didn't like her hateful politics or how she manipulated your brother like some perverse social status pawn."

"She was a revolutionary because she was black."

"Now, how am I supposed to respond to that?"

"Richard loved her and he resented you for rejecting her. And I resented you for making him leave."

"I didn't make him leave, son. He said he never wanted to see my face again, then stormed out of the house; I suppose to impress his girlfriend. You know, that's the last I ever saw of my son? My last image is the back of his head shaking in resentment and disapproval. After that, he probably thought he couldn't come back without losing face. He was always too proud."

"Would it have been so bad? Having your son marry a black woman and having racially mixed kids? I mean, compared to never seeing him again?"

"I told you that didn't matter. You boys could've come home with women out of Picasso paintings with barber pole striped children and we would've loved you the same. He left us. We didn't disown him. You want to talk about pain, son? That was pain. The loss, the guilt, the emptiness. Do I regret that night? Yes, I regret everything about that night. But he left us."

After a long discomforting silence, the father reiterated to accentuate his point. "He...left...us!" With that exclamation, Peter vanished again.

Without a chance to respond, Hunter felt cheated. He didn't know what he would have said, but one thing was certain — Peter Damon was a man of high principles, integrity and honesty. He couldn't remember his father telling a lie and figured he wouldn't start when he was already dead. Besides, his dad had never shown an iota of racism before. It might've been that Hunter knew the truth the whole time, but assigning blame to the basest of motivations made it easier to grasp. Too many times, the dynamics of a dichotomy force disputants to point fingers instead of searching for truth on both sides. Conflict is an ugly part of life, and ethics, justice, and restitution are not commodities exclusive to one side of any argument. For that matter, neither is understanding, cooperation, compassion and responsibility.

I'm looking for a Missouri redhead
A distinctive fiery woman from an ordinary place
A Midwest girl who will gaze at me in bed
With seductive eyes and scarlet tresses in her face
Show me the angels' bridges spanning into Heaven's bay
Watch her come quick as I'm calling out her name.
Independence is near and she's not far from peculiar
A wild heart born behind a picket fence, ain't never gonna be
the same.

After another hour east on I-64, Hunter crossed a bridge over the Ohio River into Louisville, Kentucky. Admiring the skyline Louisville impressed him as a handsome, charming city. The traffic, however, was heavier than a medium-sized town might merit. Recognizing an inordinate number of out-of-state license plates, he chuckled and wondered if Louisville was some kind of karmic crossroads for adventurers on soul-searching treks.

The road signs offered him new directional options: continue on I-64 to Lexington, hop on I-71 to Cincinnati, take I-65 north to Indianapolis or south to Nashville. Traffic slowed, but he needed to decide quickly. There were four available routes, but without guidance, he felt lost and frustrated. Free of responsibility, there was nothing to lose with whichever choice. So why this sudden angst? Complete freedom scared the hell out of him, as if he needed direction forced upon him; something to control him for a change.

After all that build up, he opted for the I-65 route because it had the lightest traffic.

Since bypassing Chicago, Louisville had been the first city of any considerable size since following I-94 into Milwaukee. Admiring the skyline and its surrounding layout, Louisville presented itself as a proud town with a confident, cosmopolitan attitude kept well hidden in plain sight beneath a surface of protected antiquity. A city where elegant Victorian brick facades blend in with modern steel and glass towers. Inviting and unpretentious, as if Louisvillians knew they lived in a town better than most, but kept it a secret.

Thirty miles south of Louisville, the hills started rising steeper. As the highway snaked its way through the shortest distance between the narrow gaps between hills, it was no longer a matter of realizing an elevation only upon reaching their summits. All he had to do was look left or right. Even the hills where the tops had been sheared off for coal were more dramatic than the monotony of the Midwest.

Several minutes later, Hunter spotted a hitchhiker. It wasn't his habit to pick up strangers, but this hitcher appeared clean-shaven, had short hair and a sports coat of all things. Even guys thumbing a ride from Louisville looked elegant. Since Peter hadn't popped-up in a while, he decided it might be nice to have a conversation with someone with active Alpha waves. Pulling to the shoulder, the twenty-something ran to the car.

"Your car break down?" Hunter asked.

"No man, I just need a ride," the stranger answered.

"Where are you headed?"

"Nashville. You going that far?"

"Hop in."

The dapper man jumped in the car with a small weekend bag and immediately expressed gratitude. "Oh man. You will not believe my story," he bragged.

"What's your name?" he asked.

"George Smithson," he replied extending a hand.

"Nice to meet you. I'm Hunter. We've got a couple hours to Nashville. What's this story of yours?" he asked.

"Okay," George started, "I'm a law student, right?" Instantly, Hunter breathed easier about picking him up. Lawyers may be criminals, but not the violent kind. George continued. "Some buddies and I decide to blow-off steam and go to Louisville for the Kentucky Derby weekend."

"That explains the out of state license plates," Hunter thought.

"So, we go up and have a great time, right? Man, I won $300 at the track, and I don't know squat about horses. Just lucky I guess. So Saturday, we meet friends of my buddy's and I hook up with this girl, right? It's like, you have no freaking idea how hot-hot-hot Louisville babes are. It's a damn secret city of hot chicks with big, huge beautiful...heh-heh...trust funds. I'm telling you, they grow on friggin' trees there."

"Trust funds grow on trees?" Hunter interrupted.

"Yeah, those too. So, I'm out to impress this high-society girl that I won this cash, right? And she's like, 'Really?' while her eyes light up like the Vegas strip. She says she hasn't eaten all day and was seriously craving food. I'm no moron; I'm like, 'see you dudes later.' I ditch my friends and the girl and I end up at some pricey steak house. It's all smooth. So I'm this sharp-dressed, lucky, debonair guy with $300 burning a friggin' hole in his pocket and she's, like, this hot debutante, right? I figure, show her a good time, impress the lady, okay? Blah, blah, blah, we go out. I spend my winnings — and more. Blah, blah, blah, we end up at her apartment, blah, blah, blah, etc., if you know what I mean. So now, get this. Dude, not only do I spend all my cash, but also Saturday night and all day and night Sunday," George exclaimed, emphasizing his good fortune. "Long story made short, since I ditched my buddies, I got no freaking idea where my ride back to Nashville is. I'm stranded. So this morning, she's all like, 'I gotta go to work and you gotta leave.' And I'm like, what's that all about?' So I've been walking on this goddamn highway since she dumped me here this morning. Isn't that some bullshit? And oh yeah, I got a paper due in an hour."

Hunter smiled. Not only could George's ordeal not hold a candle to his own story, but it seemed the art of courtroom litigation was doomed. Taking advantage of the first real human contact since Saturday, he began his tale when he met Hope at the Christmas party. By the time he realized he started too far back, he'd committed himself. Too bad; if George wanted to be a lawyer, he'd better get used to listening to people rattle off long stories. Prudently, Hunter left out the part about talking to his dad's ghost. No matter how highly esteemed a man is held, people feel uneasy if he claims to have seen a UFO or had a comprehensive dialogue with someone from another dimension or astral plane.

But Hunter didn't limit himself to just vital facts or 'blah-blah-blah' over anything. At first, George seemed interested, listening as the plot developed, waiting for the other shoe to drop. Soon though, his participation dwindled to a series of sporadic approving and sympathetic grunts and moans. Near the end though, George understood his role as 'quiet listener'... After finishing his story, the next forty-five minutes were spent in an awkward virtual silence, until they crossed over into Tennessee and Hunter pointed out a billboard he hoped wasn't an omen of Southern mentality.

**Fireworks Next Exit
Beer Sold Sunday!**

"Nothing good can come from that," he observed with a sarcastic sneer.

Upon reaching the Nashville city limits, the only words an exhausted George spoke were directions to his home.

"Oh man, I never thought I'd make it back. Listen, you wanna come in or something?" George asked. "I know you've been driving awhile."

"No," Hunter declined. "But thanks for listening," he replied.

"Oh yeah. Hey man, it's like, we've all been there. I guess. If anything, you made my story that much more...interesting, you know?" George chuckled, then continued. "Listen, I hope everything works out, okay? I hope you find what you're looking for, or get away from whatever you're running from, or whatever. You know?"

"Yeah, I know, I know," Hunter replied, mocking George with a smile.

Back on his own, Hunter drove toward the downtown Nashville skyline. After beginning the day in central Illinois and driving nine hours, Nashville seemed as good as any place to spend the night. The farther he explored, the more he discovered a cache of vibrant energy. The bustling nightlife for a Monday surprised him. Music City, USA was attractive, contemporary, trendy and smart. Its one-time down-home, country-fried, pickin'-and-a-grinnin' identity was still evident, but that bucolic image had been reduced to a charming secondary characteristic blending nicely with an urbane, sophisticated impression. The image of the hillbilly rube wearing overalls with a blade of straw between his four remaining teeth had been replaced by business savvy professionals in smart designer clothes. Billy Bob done got himself some fancy book learning and became William Robert.

Passing a high-end Imperial Hotel©, he figured, "what the hell?" After two nights in budget conscious, no-frills, dry-wall hotels, he deserved the luxury of a hotel chain that relied on reputation instead of flashing neon; a hotel where dinner didn't come from vending machines, but a restaurant where he could enjoy a sumptuous, overpriced, meal.

The hotel's first-class attitude added a new dimension to his adventure, and the flurry of activity in the lobby furthered his new positive view of Nashville. An abundance of guests in the lobby made him worry if there were any vacancies. Still, he strolled through the tony lobby, admiring the marble and crystal decor, to the front desk where he was greeted by a front desk clerk in a tight tailored uniform. Like the other desk clerks, she was a product of a corporate mentality. But it was the subdued 'cool-as-a-cucumber' attitude found in large confident companies and not the annoying 'go-out-and-get-'em-tiger' aggressive sales pitch attitude.

"Good evening sir, may I help you?" she asked.

"I need a room, please."

"Okay, sir. Are you with the anesthesiologists' convention?"

"No, I'm just here for the night."

"Great. I'll need you to fill this out and I need to see an ID, please?"

After three nights in a row, the hotel check-in procedure had become predictable. The desk clerk gave him his key card to a room on the 11th floor and recited her memorized monologue of hotel information. Upon finishing, bags in hand, Hunter dodged his way through the thick crowd like a running back to the glass elevator, and spotted the hotel's gourmet steak restaurant on the mezzanine level. Craving a feast, as if to make up not only for lost time, but lost meals, he cleaned up, changed clothes and headed back down the elevator, anticipating epicurean ecstasy. A superior steak dinner would provide an apropos end to a long, eventful and memorable day.

But just because it was near the end of the day, didn't mean it had to stop being eventful and memorable.

Chapter Twelve

The elegant Pleasant Colony Steak House was decorated using British Imperial styles as the theme. Its primary impression mimicked a deft blending of territorial elements from former African colonies and India, using dark, rich mahogany, polished brass, mirrors, linen and luxurious leather furniture. This lavish ambiance was detailed with additional accessories unique to Australia and the West Indies. Low lighting provided a warm, ethereal glow, accentuated by flickering votive candles on each table creating a potent 'Hemingway' atmosphere that no doubt made this spot ideal for a romantic rendezvous.

Facing a twenty-minute wait for a table, Hunter left his name with the hostess, hopped on a stool at the bar and ordered a drink. Scanning the milieu, he appreciated the parallel the restaurant made with its 'exquisite taste.' By stark contrast, many of the diners dressed as though they shopped exclusively at The Abergappy Republic[©]. He didn't want to presume, but he wondered why they didn't make an effort to dress nicer if they knew the restaurant held specific ideas and precise concerns about its refined appearance. Clarity revealed itself after overhearing a patron (wearing a cowboy hat at the table) ask a waiter if he could 'get that steak tartar done medium-well?' Hunter smiled, thinking how entertaining being bourgeois could sometimes be.

Waiting for his name to be called, he heard a woman's voice behind him.

"Excuse me, you aren't with the convention, are you?" she asked.

Turning around, he saw a woman with a rare combination of qualities; beautiful, confident, yet discreet and cautious.

"I'm sorry, what?" he answered stunned.

"The convention...are you with the convention?"

"No, I'm...just me," he answered, disappointed not to have

been with whatever convention she was referring to.

"I hope I'm not bothering you," she apologized, "I saw you put your name in for a table and was wondering if I could join you for dinner. I'm here for an anesthesiology convention and I don't..."

"Oh, sure," he interrupted. "Please, join me."

"That would be great," she sighed, relieved. "I don't want to impose; it's just that I'm so hungry."

"It's no imposition at all. In fact, it shouldn't be much longer," he assured her. "My name is Hunter Damon, by the way," he said, raising his glass as an introductory toast, then adding a slight nod.

"Hi, Faith Byrdsong," she replied, perhaps expecting at least a handshake introduction.

"Faith Byrdsong?" he repeated lyrically. "That's got to be one of the most poetic names I've ever heard. Faith Byrdsong," he recited, waving a finger with a flourish like a conductor's baton, accentuating the music in her name. "Nice to meet you. Please, have a seat," he motioned to a barstool beside him. "You're an anesthesiologist?" he asked.

"Yes. Sorry for the inquisition. I was hoping you weren't one of them."

"I didn't go to medical school long enough to be an anesthesiologist," he confessed.

"Oh," she responded surprised, "how many years did you study medicine?"

"None."

Faith cracked a wide smile and put her hand to her face, not believing she'd walked right into his joke.

"It's funny" she exclaimed, "all these men are professionals until they become conventioneers," she remarked with a cynical sneer. "Being one of the few single women here, they automatically feel entitled. The drug reps took the men out on the town. I didn't feel like being in that circus."

"Well, Faith Byrdsong," he repeated her name with exaggerated bravado, "you don't have to worry about me," he resumed in his usual voice, taking a sip of his drink.

"Are you married?" she asked, staring at his ring finger.

He held up his left hand to offer Faith a better view. "No,

I'm not. I am not married."

"There's nothing wrong with being single. I like being single," she replied unconvincingly.

"No, you see — it's just, I was supposed to be married Saturday night."

"And?" she asked fully expecting the rest of the story.

"And, she didn't show up."

"She didn't show up?" she echoed, intrigued.

"She didn't show up. So when I left the church, I didn't feel like going home and I went for a drive. I'm still on it."

"My God, that's horrible. That's just horrible. Why didn't she show up?"

"I don't know. She left me a note...but she didn't say why."

"What a bit...bit...uh...big disappointment!" she censored herself. "Where are you from?"

"Minneapolis."

"Minneapolis?! Well, Mr. Hunter Damon from Minneapolis, you made good time."

"Yeah, I suppose so. How about you? Where are you from?" Hunter asked.

"Scottsdale, Arizona. I didn't drive though," she chuckled. Her joke made him grin, setting the mood for the evening.

Faith Byrdsong was as lovely as her name suggested. Her big brown eyes radiated a soft, intense concern that was both unsettling and comforting, and her long chestnut hair reached past her shoulders to the middle of her back. A cotton dress revealed golden brown skin that hinted of a trace of Mexican ancestry, and its plunging neckline exposed a thin necklace complemented by a silver charm crucifix dangling from it.

Their dinner conversation began with those polite, safe fundamental points strangers discuss: weather, school, jobs, food, movies, pets, etc. But when a foundation was established, Hunter felt safe to narrate the story he assumed Faith was dying to hear. Women love scandals and tales of broken hearts, especially if they make other women look bad.

Telling the story again, he maintained a stoic facade, trying to make it seem less pathetic as it sounded a few hours earlier. Faith saw through it, and to her credit, didn't question anything.

Since implying earlier that she wasn't interested in a one night romantic dalliance, the understood ground rules had been silently set, removing the pressure to impress; liberating their evening of those traditional defenses, which sabotage sincerity and mask motives. As a result, Hunter was compelled to be himself. Their evening began as polite strangers, but by the time the two and a half hour meal ended, each successive glass of merlot melted inhibitions while shared stories amused each other. With their guards down, they had gotten to know each other much better than expected.

"I'm curious about one thing, though Hunter," Faith continued. "You made it here from Minneapolis in two days. Do you mind if I ask how far you intend to go?"

"You know," he reflected with a furrowed brow, "I've never been on a cross country trip like this before. I've traveled — I've just never done the whole 'explore America' thing," he answered, making air-quotes with his fingers. Although he didn't answer her question, she didn't press the issue.

"What about you, Faith," he asked. "Have you done much traveling?"

"Not as much as I would like. I did tour Europe three years ago."

"Europe?" he asked, recognizing a new topic for discussion. "Where'd you go?"

"Places different than the same old cities. I started by visiting a friend in Norway, where I met their monarch. Oslo is so relaxed, the King walks around like an ordinary citizen," she cited as a matter of fact. "Then I went to Copenhagen, Düsseldorf, and visited friends in Baden-Baden..."

"That is definitely not one of the usual cities."

"No it's not," she laughed. "Then to Zurich; and the Alps are simply bea-u-ti-ful," she declared, stressing each syllable. Hunter wondered if it was possible for her to be any more animatedly, and then quickly got his answer.

"Then...I went...to Italy!"

Upon mentioning Italy, she backed up in her chair, stood up straight and smiled with a distant reminiscence.

"Italy...was...fabulous," she reflected, emphasizing each word. "Milan, Florence, Venice. There is no other place like

Venice. So relaxing. So scenic...romantic. I wish there was some place in America that did things the Venetian way."

"I've always said there's potential in the untapped gondola market here in the states," he joked. Faith laughed and lightly touched his arm. It was their first contact.

"Hunter, I bet you're a very romantic man." she flirted gently.

He took the red carnation from the small decorative vase in the middle of the table gave the flower to her with a shy 'aw-gee-shucks' boyish charm. It wasn't a seductive move, but more of a relevant complement to her compliment.

"I have my moments," he said cracking a wide smile and cocking his head.

With the heartbreak of losing Hope still fresh in his mind, the idea of another woman was not even considered. Instead, he enjoyed talking honestly with a stranger he would never see after that night — bonding with an attractive woman he'd just met without letting the motive of 'how-to-get-intimate' get in the way.

Something, however, clicked in Faith's mind between the strawberry cheesecake and espresso. Hunter's involuntary veiled vulnerability intrigued Faith and her Florence Nightingale compassion kicked-in. She'd found him smart, funny, charming and handsome; most importantly, they'd hit it off pretty well. Add three and a half glasses of wine, and she figured 'why not?'

"I don't want to give you the wrong idea," she hinted, running a finger along the rim of her wine glass. "But I was wondering if you'd like to come back to my room for a nightcap?" She smiled and glanced away like a shy high-school girl.

For that brief moment, she relinquished her confident image in favor of an unguarded, though adventurous woman. Hunter's eyes widened. "Uh, wow." His delayed reaction put Faith on the defensive.

"Oh. I'm sorry," she interrupted apologetically, sensing rejection. "I normally don't do things like this. It's just that I think you're..."

"No, hey. You don't understand," he assured her. "The

thing is, I really...I mean you have no idea...you're a beautiful, fascinating woman," he expressed with gratitude and regret, trying to assuage her with the right words. Instead, all he could utter was a jumbled series of incomplete thoughts. "It's just that...you know, I'm out here, the point of this...trip...and if I were...go back, I mean, only been two days and...you know, for better or worse, it might, it just wouldn't be..."

Stopping for a breath, he composed himself and found the exact words. "Whatever happened could destroy the reason I'm out here to begin with. You understand what I mean? You understand what I'm saying?" he pleaded.

Faith's eyes opened almost as wide as her mouth. "My God," she paused, "a man of principles. You're a man of principles?" she uttered, astonished.

"I just can't believe I'm passing up..." Hunter started to reply.

"No, no, no!" she interrupted, "Stop! Don't...say...another word. Shut up!" she exclaimed, raising her hands to accentuate her sentiment. At that moment, Hunter had become her image of an ideal man. She didn't want to risk him spoiling the moment by probably saying something stupid. "Let me have this, please," she pleaded. Smiling, she closed her eyes, committing the previous five seconds to memory. When she opened her eyes, she explained.

"Do you know how rare men like you are? Do you have any idea?"

"You're very kind," he said. "Listen Faith, I hope you understand why I can't. I'd like to thank you for a much needed evening. I haven't had much company these past couple days except for my..." he stopped short of mentioning the visits from his father. If she thought he was crazy, that could nullify the points won for being principled.

"...my thoughts." he continued. "I needed this. After talking to you..." he trailed off, trying to conjure the exact words. He settled on saying the first complete thought to come to his mind.

"Thank you for taking some of the pain away," he finished sincerely.

"Hunter," Faith smiled, "I'm an anesthesiologist. Taking

pain away is what I do."

Rising from her chair, she fought a sly smile, hiding her embarrassment of such an overt proposition. But Hunter didn't reject her and he didn't judge her. She kissed him innocently on the cheek and headed for the door. After ten feet, she stopped and turned around.

"I found a man of principles," she chuckled. "It's funny how the reason I'm attracted to you, is the same reason I can't have you," she confessed. "I hope someday your ex realizes what she threw away."

Hunter raised his glass and toasted her. She bowed her head, clutched her purse, turned back around then slowly slinked out of the restaurant into the brightly lit portico.

Hunter paid the bill and stayed at the table for a few minutes to finish his drink. His spirits felt lighter, as if a burden lifted. However, the relief was comparable to anesthesia. He couldn't feel the pain at that moment but knew it would return if the cause wasn't removed soon.

Even with a large dinner, that last drink nudged him over the edge of sobriety. Back in his bathroom, he splashed water on his face. When he came out, his father was waiting.

"I tried to raise a noble son," Peter said, "but do you understand what you just did?"

"What do you mean?" Hunter asked as if he'd expected his father to be there.

"She was an attractive woman; a doctor no less. That's high-cotton."

"How did you..."

"I'm everywhere you are. Just because you don't see me, doesn't mean I'm not there."

"How does that work exactly?"

"Have you ever seen a six-legged dog?"

"No."

"Have you ever considered the possibility of a six-legged dog?"

"No."

"Do six-legged dogs exist?"

"Not that I know of."

"Have you ever seen me?"

"Of course."

"Do you ever think of me?"

"All the time."

"Same principle."

"What in the hell are you talking about?"

"Besides," his father said, "you have lipstick on your cheek. Why didn't you go with her?" He wasn't chastising him. He was just curious.

"You think I should have? And destroy the whole reason I'm out here?" he asked, checking his cheek in the mirror, rubbing at Faith's lip imprint.

"I'm playing Devil's advocate," Peter reassured him. "Are you drunk?" he asked.

"A little," the son replied, holding two fingers an inch apart, then opening them wider as if to admit 'maybe more than a little.'

"Good, then your answer will be honest. Do you still love her?" Peter asked.

"What kind of a fucking question is that?" Hunter shouted as he sat down at the foot of the bed.

"A damn good one judging by your reaction," Peter replied. Hunter calmed down and sighed.

"You don't plan a future with someone, then two days later forget about her because she rips out your heart and humiliate you in front of 500 people. Even if she wasn't even there to do it," he said, slurring a bit.

"This better not be about humiliation," his father questioned him.

"No, it's not," Hunter assured him.

"And it better not be just about rejection," his father continued.

"Well, it is," he snapped. "Not entirely, I guess," he corrected himself.

The drinks compounded his stress, confusion, and exhaustion. He buried his face in his hands, rubbed his eyes and grunted loudly in frustration. Calming down, he continued his tirade while getting undressed for bed.

"I'm in a hotel room in Nashville, Tennessee, and you ask me if I still love her. I'm a thousand miles from home, but a thousand miles has lost all meaning, because it's like I don't even have a home. I had these great plans for this new life, and now, with no explanation, they've turned to dust. Not even dust...they've vanished into thin air. I have nothing. Can you understand what I'm saying?" Hunter pleaded as if stuck in limbo.

"Son, listen to me. When you turn the light off tonight, and you fall asleep, the sun will rise tomorrow and you'll wake up like you have thousands of times before. Yes, you're a thousand miles from home. Yes, you're in pain. But tomorrow you'll be a little closer. I can't say how much, I don't know. You may not know yourself for a while. Somehow though, a little distance might make it seem closer," Peter expressed before vanishing while Hunter's back was turned.

He knew his father's insight held truth in the long run; it was the present that needed a cure. His face contorted in a way that had become all too familiar the past couple of days. His eyes squinted slightly with a far-off stare, as if locking away truths he tried to ignore. After his psyche snapped that lock closed, keeping his mind safely in denial a little longer, he fell backward onto the bed.

Less than thirty seconds after his head hit the pillow, he fell asleep, beginning another well deserved, much needed respite from the drama, far from the reality he so wanted to escape.

Chapter Thirteen
<u>Tuesday</u>

Hunter woke up Tuesday morning from not only the best night's sleep since his trip began, but since getting engaged in the first place. Feeling strangely rejuvenated, he showered, dressed and headed downstairs for the breakfast buffet.

In the hallway, hung-over doctors scrambled over themselves, begging each other for aspirin. The irony of anesthesiologists going overboard with the numbing effects of booze amused him. "Physician, heal thyself," he mumbled.

Going through the buffet line, he glanced over his shoulder and spotted Faith seated alone at a table. Wanting to eliminate any self-consciousness she might have felt from her 'end-of-night proposition', Hunter strolled over
like he'd known her all his life and then some.

"Good morning," he cheerfully greeted her with a wide smile and open arms.

Impulsively excited to see him, she turned distant, masking her jittery embarrassment from her ill-fated seduction.

"Oh, good morning. Did you sleep well?" she asked.

"You have no idea," he replied. Hunter sensed her uneasiness and decided to bring it out. "Listen, about last night, I had a great time at dinner, but..."

"Please, no explanation needed," Faith assured him. "I understand. But I want to apologize for such a forward pass," she confessed, "I want you to know I've never done that before."

To Hunter, her mask was unnecessary. "No, don't apologize. You know, I don't think I've never turned down an offer for..." he stopped just short of saying 'sex,' letting his facial expression do the work. He knew how people see each other very differently in the light of the next morning. "You know what? I think the world would be a better place if more women made the initial advance," he fantasized.

"And I know the world would be a better place if more men turned down the offer," she countered.

The awkward ice shattered and their comfort level had not only been repaired, it strengthened. They resumed their breakfast, picking up where they left off the night before. After more conversation, Hunter realized he had only fifteen minutes to check out. Staring at the greasy remains of hash browns and sausage links on his plate, he started getting up but found he couldn't.

"Listen Faith, it's been nice talking to you, but I..."

"Hunter," she interrupted. "I know I was a little tipsy, but I meant what I said last night." Faith wasn't being desperate or seductive. Her sincere tone was one only two people with nothing to lose or hide could appreciate.

"I know," he reassured her. "You are an incredible woman."

"Let me finish, please," she begged, "I barely know you, but I do know some important things about you. You're a man of principles and integrity, and that's rare these days. Trust me. I know you're hurt, and you're searching for something, but please don't change," she pleaded, revealing just half of what she planned to say.

"We can't be that rare," he responded with a playful tone, filling the strained silence.

"Most men want to be, but they're only concerned with keeping accounts and a high standard of living. You're different. I don't know what happened with your ex, but I feel better knowing there's at least one man like you out there."

Embarrassed by her praise, he smiled and looked away. Faith knew what Hunter didn't understand. Trouble accepting a compliment exposed him as an honorable, humble man.

"Thanks, but I don't deserve such kind words." He turned back to her, smiled and continued. "It's not like I try to have principles," he answered in a 'throw-away' tone.

"And yet you still have them," she confirmed, gazing with a helpless gaze that Hunter saw, but didn't notice.

In a near exact reenactment from the evening before, she stood up and walked halfway to the door. She turned around, gazed at Hunter one more time, smiled and nodded her head a few times, displaying the unique feminine quality of being consumed by one emotion, but concealing it with another. Her eyes cloaked her loss, accepting that, like many other times in many other lives, it was the wrong place at the wrong time.

"Good luck Mr. Hunter Damon from Minneapolis," she offered him.

"Thank you, Dr. Faith Byrdsong from Scottsdale," he answered, saluting her, this time with a juice glass.

As Faith walked away, she suspected he'd be watching her leave. It took all her will to keep walking and not turn around. Once outside the door and around the corner, she was happy she had the discipline to not turn around, yet disappointed she didn't get that one last glimpse of the extraordinary man she found.

Hunter remained at the table for a few minutes, not realizing how badly Hope had damaged him. His integrity was admirable. His principles were noble. But his heartache over Hope left him blind to a once in a lifetime chance encounter.

Checking out of a nice hotel dosed him with sticker shock, even though paying a premium for high quality was a familiar concept. Besides, he still had a fair amount of cash and traveler's checks in his 'honeymoon stash,' not to mention the large severance check from Paul Jones.

Waiting for the valet to deliver his car, he reflected upon Faith's view of integrity. Hunter had always put a great deal of stock in integrity. It meant setting a higher ethical standard and sticking to it for better or worse.

Some people blinded by ambition and greed set lofty goals, then mold themselves to achieve them. They prefer not to define themselves by who they are or what they believe, but by what they want and how to get it. People with integrity, however, establish their beliefs in the beginning, and then make their journey from there. They get intended results, perhaps not as quickly or as gratifying, but they're rewarded with a clear conscience. It's honorable to have goals, but integrity is essential for honesty. The encouraging truth about integrity is, it's self-perpetuating and self-verifying. Those who value integrity will always have it and will always want more. Their integrity won't allow them to lose it.

When the valet delivered the Mustang, Hunter jumped in and headed to the highway. Sadly, as soon as he hit the on ramp, his mind reverted back to its conditioned somber disposition of the previous two days.

Pay your money and you take your chances
But a dime don't buy too many dances
So you're stuck thinking maybe true romance is
The heat you feel from anonymous glances
It takes a lot of work in this world
If the boy's gonna get the girl.

A sudden sense of rejection tinged with guilt sprouted in him. It was a Tuesday — normally a workday. While former co-workers kept their noses to the grindstone, he'd been improvising a tour that had taken him to Dixie. Only two days removed from his job, and he missed it. He missed the banter with friends, the conspiracy theories from the weird guy in the mailroom and the receptionist's gripes. He even missed the pretentious babbling from the phony, backslapping account guy. The office atmosphere probably seemed more tense than usual, with Paul Jones displaying compassion to prove he wasn't totally heartless, yet adding a touch of dictatorial rule to justify his strength. Business continued as usual at the office, but it hurt knowing that in a week, he'd be reduced to nothing more than a few pleasant memories to colleagues he'd developed a corps d'esprit with. The years of friendship equity would be replaced by some new hack with half his talent. But hey, that's the business.

The more he studied it, the more he appreciated adaptability as the main defense helping humans evolve and strive. A man adapts to a situation, gets used to it, and then comes to depend upon it, until being thrust into a new situation where the entire process repeats itself. Lacking foresight, he equated this adaptability to his work and life in general rather than his situation. Of course, Hunter didn't have a clue what his new situation was yet.

My buddy, he was just hired to be the company mule
Now on weekends he's too tired to go out and play the fool
My baby sister was put in charge, of the company store.
They told her she'd be living large, but they only keep her poor
My next-door neighbor, you know he's, keeping all the
company books
Makin' him lie 'cause he's got to please all of the company
crooks.

The Interstate change splitting into Huntsville or Knoxville was approaching, forcing another quick choice. Taking Knoxville could delay seeing his brother even longer, but he'd afforded himself that luxury long enough. On to Huntsville.

"Wow, you are tense," Peter said as he popped in.

"I'm not tense. It's a great day."

"Look at that death grip on the wheel," he said, pointing at Hunter's hands.

"I'm concentrating on the road. And you're not helping me with that."

"Bull. You're tense and nervous. You're not in control and you hate not being in control."

"So? It's predictable. There's less chance anything can go wrong," he rationalized.

"No. The more in-control you try to be, the more you open yourself to vulnerabilities."

Peter could almost count the beats as Hunter mulled over his latest truism. Suddenly, the son's jaw fell open and his eyes glazed over with a look of innocence and discovery, as he gazed ahead in awe of this revelation.

"There we go," Peter confirmed, noting his son's comprehension. Happy his insight struck the intended target, he expounded. "When you try to control things, you're trying to eliminate or minimize certain unfavorable outcomes. Nevertheless, many of those outcomes are inevitabilities in many cases. So, since you're in denial — and those inevitabilities are not the results you wanted — you end up in even more trouble."

"How do you know all this?" Hunter questioned.

"I'm the dad. That's my job. Plus, dying opens up all kinds of new doors. Besides, you already knew that, you're just in denial." Neither one spoke for the next half-minute while Hunter grappled with this concept. Could he deny that he was in denial of being in denial? After enough time reflecting on that concept had passed, Peter initiated the next issue.

"So, where are you now?"

"On my way to Alabama," Hunter answered. "Where are you?"

Ignoring his son's poignant sarcasm, Peter responded by getting to the point they'd been avoiding.

"You're still heading to your brother's?"

"That's the plan."

"You know I can't go there. Richard told me he never wanted to see me again as long as he lived."

"He didn't mean it."

"Yes, he did."

Deep inside, Hunter knew his brother meant it.

"Let me tell you what being a father means," Peter began. "One day, you bring home this perfect little person, and you've got a blank slate. It's exciting and frightening at the same time. You think about the virtues and values you want to teach; provide the character that defines the man you are and instill qualities you want him to have. Honesty. Integrity. Courage. Compassion. Ambition. You remember lessons your father taught you, and remind yourself that it's your responsibility to pass them on. Your mind races into the future making plans for trips, ball games and how to answer the tough questions someday. But what strikes you is, he's a small version of yourself. A legacy. A piece of you to continue. A guarantee that long after you're gone, someone will remember you and who you were. And all this validates you. Life suddenly has more meaning than it did before you were given this awesome responsibility. Time passes, and you can see how your teaching makes a difference, but you still let him become his own person. That's where trust comes in. I tell you, there's not a better day in the life of a father than when he can lean back in his chair, look at his child and know that he did a good job raising him, regardless of his success. You gave him freedom to make his own decisions — first with small choices, then larger decisions. You don't expect him to be perfect, but you know every mistake is a lesson learned to make him better. So somehow, it means more to you when he comes back after making those mistakes than if he never lived. You let him go, let him make mistakes, and if he comes back, that's love," Peter said, emphasizing the last two words.

Stunned by his father's sudden reflection, Hunter couldn't remember his father ever showing much of an emotional side. He'd started taking it in, when his father continued.

"Now, imagine him telling you he hates you and rejects what you've taught him, what you stand for and believe in. Imagine him telling you he never wants to see you again. As much as you don't want to believe it, it's as if he's not your son anymore. As much as you want to be bitter, you love him unconditionally and would take him back under any circumstance. All he has to do is ask. But until he does, the wedge gets bigger and harder to ignore." At the moment he finished, Peter vanished.

There are few things possessing the power to transcend time, space, and energy. Love and rejection are two of them. Listening to his father lament, he knew some bonds formed are there forever. For a moment, Hunter felt the pain of a dead man.

Chapter Fourteen

A smile is more than just a mouth up-turned
A kiss is more than simply touching pursed lips
A soft caress is something that can't be learned
And making love is more than moving 'round hips.
It's all in the eyes. Your hellos and good-byes
How lovers see your soul, the truth and the lies.
You'll find, the deeper into her eyes that you look
The easier it is to read her sighs like a book
Examine your lover from the inside out
And she'll only love you more, no doubt.

Not quite an hour and a half later, Hunter was welcomed to Alabama by a highway sign with the three consonants scraped off the state's name.

Welcome to A a a a!

This screaming sign appealed to his penchant for word games, but he prayed it wasn't an omen. Although Alabama's image has always been a little arcane, he didn't know much about the last three states he'd driven through, either. If what he assumed about Alabama was combined with popular stereotypes, Alabama promised a lifestyle alien from anything he'd known.

Past Huntsville, further into the state, the austerity of rural Dixie exposed itself with each successive farm. Run-down homesteads with rusted silos and dilapidated barns couldn't mask the obvious poverty. Along the sides of the highway, fences in disrepair tried to protect proud farms while broken down shells of heavy machines sat lying and dying in the middle of fields. Every few farms, barefoot children played in dusty front yards, mingling with barnyard animals. But before he could adopt an attitude of Northern condescension, he remembered the abject poverty up there. The difference is that Northerners prefer to contain their squalor in dismal, dreary violent city projects.

So far on this trip, the farther he got from a city, the higher the grass grew and the lonelier he felt. For some reason he couldn't grasp, this time the withdrawal calmed him.

"I'm starting to recognize that look," Peter remarked as if he'd been sitting shotgun all day instead of pulling one of his pop-ins. No longer shocked by the novelty of his dad's appearance, Hunter barely took his eyes off the roadside scenery. Even though Peter had been dead five years, it hadn't been much longer than a couple hours since his last visit.

"What's Heaven like?" Hunter asked with the innocence of an eight-year old.

"Sorry. That question is against the rules," his father responded.

"There are rules now?" he asked bewildered.

"Of course. There's always going to be rules. Without rules there's anarchy, and the only people who like anarchy are undisciplined malcontents who can't follow rules," Peter answered playfully. "I can tell you it's all relative. Just keep believing what your vision is and you'll be fine. No big surprises."

Hunter digested this latest insight and decided to test the boundaries of the newly imposed rules.

"Then what was death like?"

Peter struggled a moment, trying to think. "I remember the split-second right before — knowing it was my time to go. Thinking, that moment was the culmination of my entire life," he reflected then paused. "And I remember the split second right after; being aware it happened — and it was not only all right, it was wonderful. For the life of me though, no pun intended, I don't remember dying."

"It can't be that bad. I mean, here you are, and you seem well adjusted," Hunter observed.

"Death is different for each person. It only has as much or as little meaning as you want it to have. But no man is the Alpha and Omega. If you understand that, you have nothing to worry about," his father revealed.

"You say that like you're preparing me for something, like you know the future." Pausing uncomfortably, he waited a foreshadowing hint. "Well?"

"Well what?" Peter asked.

"Do you know the future?" Hunter pressed.

"Inconsequential things, small events already in motion the living don't know yet."

"So what can you tell me?" he asked staring at his father, looking for any sign.

"I can't tell you anything," Peter answered. "What? You want to know when you're going to die? I have no idea," he conceded. "If you want to increase your odds of living though, I suggest keeping your eyes on the road."

Hunter corrected his steering and started to ask, "You're saying..."

"Son, I don't know what's going to happen," Peter interrupted. "This is your trip. I'm just along for the ride. You want reassurance of the future? I can't do that. You need insight into the mysteries of your mind? That's not my job. You need advice and wisdom? I'm here for you. But don't ask me what's going to happen, because I don't know."

Hunter showed his disappointment. What good is a relationship with the dead if they won't tell you what's going to happen? To complicate matters, his already unstable state of mind combined with Peter's vague answers made him snap.

"You're telling me these things, but I feel like...frankly, I don't know what to feel. I'm trying to find answers to questions, and I don't even know what those questions are yet. You're confusing me more. It's too deep...too profound."

Peter stared straight ahead and thought for a second.

"Maybe a demonstration will help," he postulated, reaching in his pocket to pull out a quarter. The coin, like his father, was not a part of Hunter's dimension.

"All right, keep an eye on the road, but watch and listen," he instructed.

Peter held the quarter in his right hand between his thumb and middle finger. Immediately Hunter recognized it as the same stupid slight of hand coin trick his father had performed for years. To be honest, the trick never failed to amaze him; it was only stupid because his father never divulged the secret.

"Okay. Time goes on, and you live your life, right? You have experiences, feelings, wants and desires. After enough time, life becomes so real, you can almost feel it or touch it."

Peter ran a finger around the coin's milling, stressing the near-tactile quality of life. "Then one day, life gets tangled up and confusing," he said as he cupped his left hand and led it towards the quarter. "Maybe you head down a path you never thought you'd go down. Maybe you start believing in things with opposing views."

His cupped left hand covered the coin then closed, giving the appearance that the quarter had been taken by his fisted left hand. He dropped his right fist to his lap and raised his left fist to Hunter's face in a move of misdirection.

"And when you look at your life," his father said, opening his left fist to reveal an empty palm, "you find nothing. So you begin searching for it, only to find it right where you left it to begin with."

With a comical flourish of his right hand, Peter revealed the quarter, and made his point.

"You are who you are, and you will always continue to be who you are. Sometimes you may stray and try to be someone else, or somewhere else. But if you're looking, you'll find yourself exactly where you left yourself. The moral? Life is only as confusing as you let it be. It's how confusing you let it be that becomes the perplexing part."

The atmosphere in the car grew thick with tension. His father hadn't used that particular tone of voice in over a decade. It wasn't a lecture; he had too much respect for his son to be condescending. It was more of an annoyed reaction to what should have been obvious. To lighten the mood, his father did offer a nugget of truth.

"In case you haven't noticed, there is a loophole. I can't reveal things you have no way of knowing. However, I can lead you to answers you could figure out — if you just took the time to sit down and think. Truths you may have forgotten that are already deep inside yourself, so it's not giving anything away. All it takes is stripping away a few layers. Do you know why people are afraid to die? Two reasons. First, they don't want to leave behind what they have. Family, friends, experiences, rituals, and possessions. The second reason is, people don't want to lose their potential. What they can become, potential things they can do, see or have. Nobody knows what the future holds, so nobody wants to give up their imagined potential. And nobody wants to die before experiencing more potential. There you go. People don't want to give up what they have, and they don't want to give up what they might have. Now, if you accept that nobody really owns anything...that everything always did and always will belong to God, including your soul, that makes the first part easier. And if you understand you're here to fulfill a purpose...even though you're not supposed to know what it is...well, that makes the second part a moot point.

Suddenly, Hunter knew it made sense. Death is about loss.

The faces of loss represent the most tragic events in the human experience. Lost time, lost potential, lost loved ones, lost souls...lost hope. With so many things to lose, there has to exist an equal number of things to gain. While many times it appears the things gained don't nearly equal the things lost, there is an elegant, delicate symmetry directing life as relentless as the forces of nature seeking equilibrium.

While Hunter pondered these new revelations, Peter sat in the passenger seat nurturing a satisfied, smug smile, arms folded as he gazed over the side of the car into the sun. Strangely, even with the top down, the wind had no effect on him. His clothes didn't ripple, and what little hair he had stayed in place, unaffected by the wind. He didn't even cast a shadow. Hunter almost pointed this out, but Peter was enjoying the ride to himself. Besides, there was nothing that could add anything important to what was said moments earlier.

Closer to Birmingham, the road signs alerted to the next highway interchange approaching. If he followed the route to Mississippi, he had to take I-20/59 to Tuscaloosa.

"You know, son, instead of this aimless driving, running or chasing, there are other options," Peter piped in. "What if you just keep going south all the way to Florida," he pleaded. "There's no better place to get your head together than a beach.

Take a vacation. Enjoy frozen blender drinks with girls in bikinis."

As attractive as the beach proposition sounded, running away would chain him up in a smaller, darker, colder cell located deeper in denial and more isolated from humanity. Denial had afforded him the luxury of time and apathy, and now that bill had come. He mentally prepared himself for a myriad of reactions from his brother. The farther south he traveled, the more old familiar feelings resurfaced and the more difficult it seemed. Ultimately though, Hunter knew if he took another detour, he would never get there.

Firmly bent on heading to Mississippi, he turned to tell his father. As had become Peter's annoying custom, he'd already vanished without a word or trace. Perplexed, Hunter wondered if it was possible to affix a rhyme or reason to his father's impromptu entrances and exits. Was Peter so in-tune with Hunter's psyche and soul that he knew the precise buttons to punch at which time? Somehow, his father exited on a dramatic note every single time, like a tertiary Shakespeare character who delivers the line that opens limitless contemplations. Peter had become a messenger of his son's thoughts, and just as the deepest parts were prodded to the surface, the I-20/59 turn-off to Tuscaloosa shifted his priorities. This stretch of road could reconnect a part of his past to his present.

When the bells and whistles become thorns and thistles
Luxury becomes like a prison cell
You can pay a high price from a single roll of dice
It was a pretty good life until you fell.
But when the arrow and chains are what bring you gains
Take comfort 'cause torture only lasts a while
Just remember all along, 'what don't kill you makes you
strong'
Then it takes a lot less to make you smile.

Stubbornly unaware of it, every mile of his journey became less about losing things he held dear and more about self-discovery and exposing issues within himself. However, since he still grappled with those top-of-mind losses, including his brother's estrangement, it remained easier to delude himself that it was about what he'd lost.

After contemplating the meaning of the current mile markers, he tried spending time reflecting upon his father's latest wisdom. Peter's insightful perceptions proved better than any knowledge of the future from the great beyond. It was a common sense approach to solving mysteries of human nature that history had ignored. The significance of life and death has been a puzzle perplexing the best and brightest for eons. As substantial as those concepts are, perhaps philosophers had scrutinized them too seriously. The most mysterious events become the easiest to grasp when the distracting scenery is ripped away, making it possible to inspect with the clearest honesty of the heart, mind and soul.

For whatever reason, a random thought about Hope entered his mind, triggering a wave of anguish. Hunter tried to assuage the pain by applying his newfound philosophy to the very thing tearing him up inside, but it grew harder to focus past the darkening cloud fogging his judgment. Besides, he still didn't know the reason all this happened. His repressed poisonous frustrations began bubbling over, brimming with bane in the core of his fragile psyche until finally, his retreating reason shut out all semblance of constraint and sanity. With bursting anger, he flew into a frenzy, exploding with pent-up pressure, pounding the steering wheel, and yelling into the apathetic dusk.

"Why?! What the fuck do You want?! What am I supposed to do?! Tell me!" he shouted in desperation, rage, and confusion.

Almost immediately after his brief cathartic emotional detonation, Hunter calmed down; laughing at himself for screaming at the empty twilight with such vehemence and still expecting a response from the darkening isolation.

Casanova, when are you ever gonna learn?
The hotter you want your women, the more you're gonna burn.

Ladies love to look into your confident eyes
Too bad they're blind to unavoidable lies.
And hey Romeo, thou art not much better
It could be true love, but man, you just met her.
You got a charming way with words, but don't know their
power
They put out a love spell after only one hour

Focusing on his obsessions, his pensive pondering, and subsequent emotional release lasted him well into Mississippi, past Meridian, and just outside Hattiesburg.

Exiting the highway after spotting a row of hotels, he pulled into the parking lot of an Econo-Stay® and sighed deeply. He understood why people who've had breakdowns spend so much time in bed; dealing with an intense emotional release is physically exhausting. Drained of most of his energy, he leaned forward, resting his forehead on the steering wheel while he composed himself. Shoulders slouched and eyes closed, anxious tension collected in every burning muscle of his back and neck, as if a searing dull blade sliced him up from the inside with every movement. Part of the strain had been three straight days of driving, but most resulted from his losses and the restless anticipation of seeing a brother he'd had no contact with for 18 years. Approaching the end of his rapidly fraying rope, Hunter finished his intense ruminating session with one final plea.

"God," he chuckled, "I could use a sign about now."

Raising his head and opening his eyes, he saw the hotel's marquee.

Join Pastor Cleo Natuscan's
Christian Brotherhood Prayer Service
Tuesday Nite!

Reading the marquee, Hunter addressed Heaven.

"You've got to be kidding," he pleaded with God. He glanced at the marquee to check if anything had changed. It hadn't. Hunter gazed back to Heaven as if to give Him a second chance.

"C'mon God, any kind of sign. Anything at all," he joked.

Admitting it's not good form to ask the Almighty for a figurative sign, then see a literal sign, and still ignore it, he looked to Heaven a third time and conceded.

"A deal's a deal."

Chapter Fifteen

It was just another in a popular hotel chain, but for whatever reason, this Econo-Stay® seemed larger than others. Most he'd passed were three or four stories, but this one had an impressive six floors. Regardless, he checked-in while scores of the Divinely devoted dressed in their Tuesday best milled about in the lobby on their way to Pastor Natuscan's Christian prayer service. Hunter intended to keep his promise of attending, but held reservations. For all he knew, that night's service was graduation for a suicide cult, followed by a tainted 'juice and cookies social.'

At the front desk, he remarked, "You guys look busy tonight."

"We've got prayer services on Tuesdays," the clerk replied.

"Where can you hold this many people?" he asked.

"The grand ballrooms. Take a right at the elevators, and around the corner."

Swinging his baggage across his back, he headed to his room. Tempted to call it a night after another long day, he reconsidered reneging on his promise, but instead compromised on a shower to soothe his aching muscles and rejuvenate himself. He took his time part in due to the 'driving grime' covering him, but mainly because he suspected these fundamental prayer services didn't actually start until an hour into them. Changing into clean clothes, he addressed Heaven once again.

"Twenty minutes," he told God, informing Him that part of the deal for keeping an open-mind was not staying one minute longer than his comfort level allowed him. On the way down, the juxtaposition of having religious services in a hotel ballroom amused him. A church is God's home visited by hundreds of people once a week for an hour. This hotel is home to hundreds of people a week, but was apparently visited by God for an hour or so.

The Christian Brotherhood didn't bother to decorate or make any changes to signify a transformation into a place of worship. In the ballroom, there were about 600 folding chairs set up, (two sides with thirty rows of ten chairs each) like it would be for a meeting of the South district middle management of GeneriCorp©. Surveying the room, he couldn't help but think a hotel ballroom lacked the elegant, respectful, reverent feeling he got from his own church. It looked better suited for a bake sale or a child beauty pageant than a place of worship.

There was no stained glass, no statues, no altar and a conspicuous lack of a crucifix or cross, an important icon to any group with the word 'Christian' in its name. There was, however, a lecturer's podium, a five-piece electric band and video cameras set-up in front to broadcast the service to six monitors along the sidelines to help folks in the back see the 'action.' Immediately inside the room was a table with various Christian books, CDs, DVDs, t-shirts, knick-knacks and baubles for sale. By the looks of the cash box, business had been brisk. Several items offered asked, 'What Would Jesus Do' — a reminder to disciples to conduct themselves as instructed by the Lord. Remembering that Jesus was not pleased upon finding commerce in the temple, Hunter figured the first thing He'd do, was unleash His wrath on the vendor's table and their trinkets.

The motley crowd numbered over 600. Most of them were standing with their hands waving in the air, hypnotized, while the band played and the singer sang an up-tempo contemporary gospel song, which also lacked reverence when compared to traditional hymns. As soon as Hunter looked to Heaven to presumptuously inform God that this counted towards his 20 minutes, the music stopped and Pastor Cleo Natuscan bound on the stage with a zeal and enthusiasm that scared the hell out of him, which may have been the point.

If Hunter was a skeptic before, the affluent appearance of Pastor Natuscan didn't help. Dressed in stylish clothes and designer shoes, the good Pastor accessorized with a large, expensive wristwatch and gaudy gold and diamond rings. His thick black hair was shiny and slicked back and his perfect, straight, white teeth looked like they were carved from ivory. Hunter couldn't be sure, but Cleo Natuscan's taut face, free of wrinkles and imperfections, was consistent with having a little 'work done' to help complete such a pleasing appearance. Pastor Natuscan looked the part, and charm flowed from his soft eyes like a lazy brook. There was no doubt about it; he was quite charismatic. But something important was missing. Hunter couldn't shake the idea that this man of God resembled so many other Christian evangelists. They reminded him more of glorified car salesmen and garish game show hosts than pious shepherds of the Lord.

After a few hallelujahs and amens, Pastor Natuscan grabbed a microphone and started his holy roll.

"Who here knows what Murphy's Law is?" he asked the congregation. Building to a crescendo, he answered himself. "Murphy's Law states, 'If anything CAN go wrong...it WILL go wrong!'"

That prompted a reaction from the crowd, including laughs and lots of amens. The most alien aspect of this service was the complete absence of order or quiet reverence. Perhaps that too was the whole point.

"Now, Ol' Murphy sounds Irish-Catholic. I'm guessing he's in hell right now; and he's just sitting there in the pain and the flames and the torture, thinking, 'Yep, it sure did go wrong!'"

A red flag shot up in Hunter's mind. The Pastor continued.

"Do you know what Murphy forgot that caused everything to go wrong?" he asked. Murmuring ensued, and a few members shouted out, but the Pastor ignored them. Instead, he struck a precise, prepared and practiced regal pose at the front of the stage. "Lord, Murphy forgot his FAITH!" he shouted as the crowd went wild. Pastor Natuscan had worked the audience up so well, he could have said 'Lord, Murphy forgot his FRENCH TOAST' and the congregation would have reacted the same.

Hunter imagined Jesus working His audience this same upbeat way, like a comedian, during His Sermon on the Mount.

"Welcome to 'The Mount.' I'm Jesus, and I'm going to save your soul by dying, hopefully not tonight though! (Bada-Boom) Thank you. Hey, do we have any peacemakers in the audience? No sir — not pacemakers, although some of you seem to need one. (Bada-Boom) Peacemakers? Anybody? You guys over there? Oh, you'll go over big here in the Mid-East. (Bada-Boom) I'm just kidding. You're children of God. Hey, how about the meek? Anybody feeling meek? You sir? Feeling a little meek, huh? Good job, you inherit the earth. Now may be a good time to get assertive. (Bada-Boom) Uh, excuse me sir? Sir? Yes, you. Excuse me...do I come to your work and tell you how to stoke the fires of hell? (Bada-Boom) Seriously folks, love and serve God, be nice to people and accept Me as Lord and Savior of your eternal soul. Hey, you've been a wretched, sinful audience, but I love you anyway! I'm Jesus Christ and I'll be here all eternity! Thank you, good night! Please tip the staff when the buckets come around."

Thinking of that scenario, Hunter sincerely prayed that Jesus has a good sense of humor. After all, most funny comedians are Jewish.

Still, he knew it shouldn't be the way the message is conveyed that's important, rather it's the message itself. Meanwhile, Pastor Natuscan's sermon continued without missing a beat.

"Now how can YOU, show GOD, you have faith in His word? You give MORE money to His ministries! In Mark 4:31, it says faith; 'Is like a grain of mustard seed which when it is sown in the earth, is less than all seeds that be in the earth: But when it is sown, it groweth up and becometh greater than all herbs.' Faith starts small but it's GOT to grow tall. And it's ONLY by faith that we're saved! PLANT your SEED! Put it ALL in and eat and drink with the Lord! And if you give more, God will REWARD you! All you have to do is ask. He's gonna do it for you. He'll bless you ten times over! Not 1-2-3-4-5-6-7-8 or 9...but 10 times over!"

During Pastor Natuscan's impassioned plea for money, large plastic buckets, reminiscent of those used in casinos were circulated, and the flock dumped checks and large bills into it with a fervor he'd never seen. This huge emphasis and unsubtle appeal for money concerned Hunter. The idea that Pastor Natuscan's attire and jewelry exhibited an allegiance to style over substance bothered him. The image of a man of God driving a luxury car seemed contrary to Jesus asking His Apostles to take only one pair of sandals when they went out to minister.

When the bucket reached Hunter, he passed it on acutely aware of several judgmental stares coldly scolding him. Even so, when the buckets were marched to the back, they contained enough cash to renovate even the largest cathedral. To Pastor Natuscan's delight, the flock had given their fleece freely.

"NOW, how do you show GOD, you want a closer relationship with Him? You FREE yourself of sin that imprisons your SOUL. Get RID of drugs! Get RID of demon alcohol! Get RID of pornography that not only stands in the way of your relationship with your spouse, but with God. Get RID of your foolish pleasures. You STOP the devil, so before the deceiver has a chance to knock on your door, you can say with the power and glory promised to you by Jesus Christ, "Get thee BEHIND ME Satan! Not TODAY! Not NOW, NOT EVER!"

Once again, the crowd erupted as if he scored the winning touchdown.

SCORE: Satan – 666 / God – INFINITY.

Suddenly, it dawned on him. Pastor Natuscan wasn't saying anything new, and apart from 'Catholics going to hell,' nothing was said he didn't already believe. As the service continued, Hunter noticed Pastor Natuscan only really had two or three things to say; he just kept changing the wording so they sounded like different messages. However, when these positive messages were delivered with his enthusiastic, fervent speech, no wonder the flock handed over enough cash to keep him excited.

Scanning the congregation's faces, Hunter knew these were good, honest folk. Some may have even been in dire straits, searching for help or answers, like himself. What better place to seek help than where it's promised in the first place? God. There's no better way a man can invest his entire stock of faith than in God. God should be a force in everybody's life, at the very least, for the sake of civility.

Somewhere along the line, however, some ministers decided to change the dignified reverence of Christ's sermons in favor of their particular Pavlovian technique to the mob mentality. Politicians have known it for years. P.T. Barnum knew it before that. Christian pastors had become God's ringmasters, directing the audience's attention here and introducing the dangers of this and that, using plenty of vocal flash and pizzazz, all the while keeping the congregation comfortable, entertained and excited.

"...but you got to-got to-GOT TO have faith. And when you have the kind of faith I'M talking about, you will be FILLED with the Holy Spirit, and God will GUIDE you to righteousness through His Almighty door to His table where you will eat and drink and be filled with His blessings!"

The service was exotic compared to his experiences, but Hunter was careful not to persecute different Christian views. He was in no position to judge, and to be honest, they inspired him. Even if Cleo Natuscan was exposed as nothing more than a Christian mountebank with a pleasant cadence that reduced God to a mere enterprise, the heart of the believers remained sincere. The flock received its daily bread; they believed and they had faith. And it was good.

Hunter's main bone of contention was the lack of formal liturgical rituals. A show of solidarity that the congregation stood together, knelt together and prayed in unison as a sign of reverent exaltation. There was no participation in the holy sacraments that Jesus demanded believers to do as a remembrance of Him. Frankly, they weren't doing anything they couldn't have done at home while watching television, which was exactly what the folks in the back rows were doing anyway.

"And when you let Jesus Christ into your heart, He is your SAVIOR! He is your SALVATION. He is your BELOVED, majestic Prince of Peace, and the KEY to life everlasting in the kingdom of GOD! And glory be when He comes BACK to claim His throne. In Acts 26:16, Jesus says, 'But RISE and stand upon thy feet: for I have appeared unto thee for this purpose, to make thee a minister and a witness both of these things which thou hast SEEN, and of those things in the which

I will appear unto thee. To OPEN their eyes, and to TURN them from darkness to LIGHT, and from the power of Satan unto God that they may receive forgiveness of sins, and inheritance among them which are sanctified by FAITH that IS IN ME.' And here is where you come in. It is YOUR responsibility to take God's message to the world. TAKE it to friends. TAKE it to family. TAKE it to souls in dead religions. Take this news to the Jews and TELL them about Jesus, because we owe them a great debt. STAND in the gap! Go to EVERY corner and in a loud, proud clarion voice, exclaim to all that their SOUL is at STAKE!"

Thirty minutes of high energy stimuli and Hunter was spent. The intensity of the service made him feel as if he'd OD'd on God, which again, may have been the point, and the Pastor's frenzied plaudit got the fervent congregation excited, which was inspiring. It wasn't that the service was a sham, not at all. If anything, the rousing worship provided an incredible energy to initiate a spiritual renewal. Hunter was no theologian, but this experience made him wonder.

Did the Christian Brotherhood's display of devotional excitement make them more favored in God's eyes than believers who chose a more subdued, dignified, solemn and reverent approach to worship? Does He prefer people who practice an aggressive, public profession of praise? Or in His omniscience, does He judge the purity of the heart of the most quiet, humble and pious man with equal impunity? Is salvation a simple matter of using a universally issued 'Get Into Heaven Free' card, or is it necessary to practice faithfully the sacraments Jesus demanded his followers to remember? Perhaps both approaches are two sides of the same coin; they look radically different, yet each possesses the same value. The difference between Saints Peter and Paul. One is no more legitimate or crucial than the other. One is hot; the other is cold; neither is lukewarm.

The idea that Jesus chose Paul, a depraved hedonistic lecher, to travel and minister in a recruiting drive for His fledgling Church, is no more improbable than picking Peter, the unorganized weak link of the 12 Apostles and a coward, as the vanguard in charge of setting up His new base of operations headquarters in Rome. But both choices were Divine strokes of genius. If either Peter or Paul succeeded, despite massive credibility problems given their respective tasks, then His Catholic Church was destined to be the ultimate force of good and love it was preordained to be. One was a traveling salesman responsible for spreading ideas, while the other was tapped as Chairman of the Board to take care of business at the home office. Both Saints had done their job well. And, again, it was good.

It's common for religious newcomers to use God as a quick fix; a spiritual bandage to halt an emotional hemorrhage of the soul. But many times the intensity of a novice's initial piety creates unrealistic levels to sustain. Regardless, religion wasn't going to save him. Religion was invented by men and developed by men who harbored squabbles with other men, who split-off from still more men who held separate interpretations of God. Religion is men wearing hats and other men sitting in judgment of men who wear hats. It doesn't matter who shouts the loudest, who has the largest vocabulary or who has the nicest buildings — unless the shouting, the vocabulary, and the buildings are designed to inspire and glorify God. Religion shouldn't be about agreeing with someone on Point 1-A, then damning them for disagreeing on Point 1-B. And this talk of 'dead religions'? How can any true Christian refer to a denomination as dead, if its traditional core of beliefs revolves around the teachings of Jesus Christ?

Hunter believed in one, holy, universal and apostolic Church that teaches about Christ. Denominations are only cultural differences. One tree with many branches. God is supposed to bring people together, not rip them apart. No, religion wasn't going to save Hunter Damon. It was something more simple. What he believed and confessed to believe was going to save him. His creed and how faithfully he practiced it held the key to his salvation, and no man, whether he wore a big hat or an expensive watch, could shake his confidence about that. At the same time, a healthy dose of religion may have been exactly what he needed to reconfirm who he thought he was and who he wanted to be. Religion couldn't save him, but religion could inspire him to believe and do things that would save him.

Back in his room, sitting on the bed, he opened the bedside table. Sure enough, the Gideons hadn't disappointed him. It had been years since he'd opened a Bible, but for the next couple hours, Hunter gleaned more spiritual nourishment than he could have gotten in ten Pastor Natuscan services. Then it dawned on him. Maybe the congregation was on to something. Maybe it's not enough to assume you're saved because you haven't killed anybody or committed adultery. Maybe God doesn't care about weekly attendance if it's become about spending an hour for obligation's sake without showing conviction.

After reading far into the late hours, he clicked off the light, settled into bed and thought briefly about the possibility of seeing Richard the next day. He accepted it might be impossible to change things, but filled with his renewed spirit, he asked God for guidance to help do His will.

Salvation comes from faith and performing good deeds and contrite acts as further shows of faith. Hunter knew what was inside of him, even if he wasn't completely aware of it. As soon as he confirmed that in his mind, unbeknownst to him, one more vital tumbler fell magically into place.

Chapter Sixteen
<u>Wednesday</u>

Checking out Wednesday morning, the Econo-Stay© bore little resemblance to its environment the night before. There was no trace of the enormous crowd, no placards in the lobby, no fliers taped to the walls and no rows of chairs in the ballroom, which had been rearranged to accommodate the 'Dixie Hog Farmers Consortium.' Barely a reminder existed suggesting the Lord God made even as much as a cameo appearance. Hunter's outlook had improved after perusing the Bible the night before, but was it enough? Without complete faith, the Bible has little more meaning than a second-rate pulp-fiction novel. Still, the proverbial mustard seed Pastor Natuscan referred to had been planted.

At a Stars N Bars© Convenience Mart, he gassed up his car, grabbed a map of Dixie and headed back on the Interstate. The oppressive mid-morning heat and humidity in rural Mississippi engulfed and smothered him, sapping his energy to the point that even shifting gears posed a major toll on his efforts. No wonder Southerners take life a little slower; it's like living underwater.

> *Between the Rocky Mountains and the swamps of Louisiana*
> *The Dakota Badlands down to Alabama*
> *From Alaska down to the Everglades*
> *And Appalachia up to the Cascades*
> *From Ellis Island to the Golden Gate.*
> *That Canyon's Grand, those Lakes are Great*
> *I'd kiss every square inch like sacred ground*
> *From Miami Beach to the Puget Sound*
> *From San Diego all the way up to Cape Cod*
> *From 1492 to our future date with God.*
> *From port to port and sea to shining sea.*
> *I love America...but she forgot about me.*

Forty minutes later, he exited I-59 somewhere near the edge of obscurity bound for Derby, the town listed on a 10-year old piece of paper as his brother's address. Noticing the sign welcoming him to the Derby city limits, he thought 'city' was a generous term.

For 18 years, Hunter figured he'd eventually see his brother one day, but like many things, it became comfortable to push it aside and assume 'one day' would come in the distant future. With no more exits available for a bailout, he was forced to face the inevitable. What if Richard had transferred the bad feelings he harbored toward their father onto him? Did he estrange himself out of shame? Did he hate the family the whole time, or did his contempt slowly manifest as an equation of spite plus keeping face multiplied by years? Maybe Richard didn't hate anybody at all, but wanted his family to offer the olive branch first. One thing was certain. Hunter wasn't about to face his brother on an empty stomach. Besides, stopping off for a breakfast would put it off for another hour.

Not far down the road, he spotted Lieut. Gibson's Cafe, a greasy spoon with a popular reputation, judging by the number of cars in the gravel parking lot. Assuming this eatery's proprietor was a retired Marine, the outside of Lieut. Gibson's resembled every Southern roadside diner he'd seen in movies set in the rural South. The restaurant's name, painted on the building's weathered bricks, had faded, and its old neon sign had chipped paint on the glass tube. It's outward appearance offered a reassuring authenticity to the cafe, but upon entering, he'd stumbled upon something far from common. Lieut. Gibson's was a military theme restaurant exhibiting memorabilia and paying homage to American wars — a tribute to battle, like some kind of TGI D-Days[©].

An evolution of service rifles and side arms decorated the tops of the walls around the entire dining area, and a display case beside the door held a collection of mortar shells, hand grenades, and bullets. In one corner, mannequins dressed in battle fatigues and surrounded by camouflage netting, kept a faithful, protective vigil over diners. In another corner, a Navy porthole framed a faded photo of famed sea hero of the Second World War, Admiral Chester Nimitz, and beside that a wooden shelf showcased a colorful array of war emblems from numerous Army divisions. Bringing it all together were dozens of historical war photos hanging on the walls. Most of them were Normandy beachheads labeled Juno, Gold, Omaha, Utah and Sword, but a few were blurry photos of artillery cannonades from World War I. If the South ever carried out its threat to rise and rebel again, this restaurant would make a strategic rallying point and arsenal.

Several diners enjoying their breakfast, including a mechanic with the name Zevadiah on a patch on his shirt, glanced at him with subdued suspicion. Hunter tried being casually inconspicuous, but nearly everything exposed him as 'not bein' from 'round here.' It didn't matter. Chances were, everybody in this town already knew everybody else.

At the counter, he took a seat, picked up a stained menu and waited while the waitress, Thalma, talked on the phone.

"Be right with you, hon," she assured him.

Scrutinizing the menu, it all looked pretty good, but he wasn't sure what grits were.

While waiting, he couldn't help but hear Thalma's side of her conversation.

"Okay...okay. Not many, a few. Okay. Yes. No...yes...no. Okay. Alright, see you then, Alfonso." She hung up the phone and bellowed to the chef over the din of the diners, "Hey Gibby, the exterminator cain't come 'til Friday."

The burly chef spun around, shot Thalma an annoyed stare and pointed at Hunter with his spatula. "Thalma, we got an out-of-towner here," he chided her, shaking his head and cursing under his breath. Hunter assumed the chef must be Lieut. Gibson. Not because he answered to the obvious 'Gibby' nickname, but because of the 'Semper Fi' tattoo on his forearm.

"I'm sorry honey," Thalma apologized. "What can I git 'cha?"

"How about coffee, toast; what's the difference between ham and country ham?"

"Y'ain't never had country ham? Ya need to git you the country ham," Thalma assured him.

"Country ham it is. Hash browns and...orange juice please."

Thalma relayed the order to Gibby who delivered it in less than five minutes. Hunter enjoyed his Southern-style breakfast, all the while realizing that Lieut. Gibson's Cafe in Derby, Mississippi, was another world, far away from anything he knew in Minnesota. He had been on the road four days, and while each state he'd passed through had unique differences, rural Mississippi was like a foreign land; a place where the native language resembled English, however, it required some concentration to understand more or less — like Canada. He'd discovered a whole new culture.

After finishing every last delectable morsel of breakfast, he figured the secret to country ham involved a curing process of burying it in salt for about five years.

Thalma gave him the check. "Everthang all right honey? Can I git you anythang else?" she asked.

"May I have a large glass a water, please?" he pleaded.

She fetched some water and Hunter gulped it down in one long tip. Rehydrated for the moment, he pulled out his cash and paid the tab.

"Anythang else I can git you?" Thalma repeated.

Hunter left the change as a tip and asked, "Yes, I need directions for an address on Lookout Road."

"Honey, there ain't no houses on Lookout Road. It's jes a gravel road leadin' to Stone Street. Maybe you need Stone Street."

"Hm," Hunter reacted condescendingly. He pulled the worn, faded paper with his brother's address from his wallet. "No, the address says Lookout Road."

"Well, who you looking for?" Thalma inquired sincerely. "We all know everbody here in Derby."

"Richard Damon."

Gibby let out a cackle. "What you wanna see ol' Richie Damon for? You with the govment or something?" he asked giggling. "You know Richie Damon don't take kindly to surprise visitors. 'Specially not govment folk," Gibby continued.

"I'm not with the government. Richard is my brother."

Thalma swooned, backing away slowly in fear as if Hunter were the brother of the devil himself, which apparently for

Derby, Mississippi, was not far from the truth. Suddenly, the dozen or so diners all stopped chewing and stared at Hunter in silent amazement, like deer caught in headlights, unsure of what to do.

She put her hand to her gaping mouth and her eyes glazed over in terror. "Oh my dear sweet Lord. There're two of 'em," she uttered in fear.

Gibby stepped in front of his waitress to shield her, and took control of the situation.

"You ain't here to start trouble are you, boy?" Gibby asked menacingly.

Caught off-guard and dumbfounded, Hunter once again felt conscious of every eyeball focused on him.

"I'm just looking for my brother," he rationalized.

Gibby pointed down the road with a forceful finger "Head down this road, Middleground Road, for five miles, turn right and go down old Lookout Road about four miles as the crow flies. You can't miss it."

"Are you sure I can't miss..."

"You can't miss it," Gibby reiterated, leaning forward with his enormous fists on the counter. "Trust me," he emphasized with a cynical chuckle.

Hunter nodded, confused and grateful thanked them, turned and headed to the door — a little insulted and a bit scared. At the door, Zevadiah stopped him and asked, "Hey son, you really Richie Damon's brother?"

"Yes."

"And you gonna try and get into his compound, past all that security?"

"Uh...I guess."

"Well good luck. And remember to duck. That sonuvabitch is crazy."

Pulling out of the lot, he hadn't driven a mile down Middleground Rd. when a police car sped up behind him — siren blasting and lights flashing. Hunter pulled over and watched as the southern cop, complete with mirrored sunglasses and toothpick, swaggered to his car.

"Morning sir, license and registration, please?" the officer asked.

"What's the problem, Officer?"

"Jes yer license and registration...please," the cop reiterated forcefully.

He complied, but a bad feeling developed in his stomach and his mouth went dry. The country ham didn't help either condition. Sitting in the Mustang, Hunter felt psychologically inferior; his face was only inches from the officer's barrel chest. The gold badge on his uniform read 'Officer Riley'. If Derby was as stereotypical a Southern town as he had seen so far, having Minnesota plates could not have been a good thing.

"I'll be right back sir," Officer Riley mumbled with a thick, twangy accent as he headed back to his patrol cruiser. After several uncomfortable minutes of watching the cop in the rear-view mirror, Hunter's fears were being validated. Eventually, the officer strutted back to the car.

"Sir, you Hunter Damon?" he asked.

"Yes."

"I'm gonna need you to git outta the car, please sir."

Things hardly improved, but his already limited options had been reduced to having to 'git outta the car.'

"What's this all about?" he asked concerned.

"Sir, yer gonna have t' come with me back t' the courthouse."

Fearing this was a southern county that time and progress forgot, he tried making excuses why he couldn't go with the officer.

"But my car? I can't just leave my car..."

"I'll have Zev drive it back. He'll like drivin' a nice car like this," Officer Riley added.

On the quick ride to the courthouse, Hunter assumed it was smarter to keep quiet, lest he rile up the officer's ire. Passing Lieut. Gibson's Cafe, the diners stood with their noses pressed against the windows as if they fully expected to see him. Did he insult Thalma or Gibby? Maybe asking for water was bad manners in the South. Maybe he didn't leave a big enough tip.

At the courthouse, the officer pulled him out of the car and roughly escorted him inside to a cell. This unnecessary aggressive demeanor pressed Hunter's buttons, calling up his newly acquired 'what-the-hell' attitude to test the waters. Since he was already in a cell, there was nothing to lose.

"You mind telling me what this is about? Do I have any rights in this town?" he challenged. In retrospect, it may not have been a bright strategy.

"'Scuse me, sir?" the cop answered, not believing he'd heard correctly.

"You people ever hear of Miranda? Am I under arrest? What's the charge?"

The cop backed Hunter up against the wall of the cell.

"The charge could eas'ly be assault of a po-leece off'cer, if'n you catch muh drift," he countered with a scary intensity. The cop backed away, then continued. "Now you jes settle y'self down and cool-off in here while I call for Judge Himes to come on down."

After shoving Hunter down onto the bunk the cop shook his head, disgusted that his authority had been questioned, then slammed the barred door. "Miranda? Heh-heh, that's a good one. You are from up north ain't cha?"

"Oh my God," Hunter thought to himself, "I'm going to die in a jail cell in rural Mississippi for being a Northerner."

"I'll be back," Officer Riley said. "Make y'self at home," he cackled.

Hunter leaned back on his cell bunk. "Great. Held hostage in evil Sticksville by an inbred hillbilly with a badge," he said out loud to himself.

The officer poked his head around the corner. "'Scuse me sir, you say sumthin'?" he asked, hand resting casually, yet poignantly, on his butt of his holstered gun.

"No...no, I didn't say anything," Hunter retracted. "I'll just wait here until you get back."

"I didn't think so," the officer added as he left.

Hunter's mind raced. Nobody knew where he was. He had visions of being one of those forgotten work farm prisoners wearing striped jump-suits, breaking rocks and building roads for a corrupt 'Boss Man' who rode a horse, held a shot-gun and got kick-backs from the state highway commissioner. He'd live in a dilapidated aluminum barracks, sleep on wooden bunk-beds, drink from a ladle and mix with a bunch of convicts, including the barracks leader, Slim, and their slow-witted mascot, Mouse, who didn't talk, but played the harmonica with virtuoso skill.

As he sat in the jail cell, he had never felt so alone in his entire life. Not even losing Hope and his job made him feel quite this lonely.

Chapter Seventeen

The first hour in the cell, Hunter's initial fear of doom diminished. After two hours, the boredom turned excruciating. The highway rock pile started to seem like fun. Sitting alone, his eyes traced the cracks on the ceiling, imagining them as lines on a map.

"You remember the heartfelt talk about the joys of fatherhood?"

At the end of his bunk, he saw his dad.

"This is the exact opposite of that," Peter added.

"I didn't do anything," Hunter protested.

"Let me get this straight," Peter resumed, ignoring his son's plea. "I was a jet pilot in the Air Force to protect the world from communism. I pioneered extensive research resulting in a revolutionary update and upgrade of my country's defense systems and weaponry. And, with all humility, I was somewhat instrumental in landing multiple men on the moon. How am I repaid? Disowned by one son who is hated by an entire town and lives a hermit existence, and my other son is locked-up in redneck hell by backwater Wahoos. This is not the legacy I expected."

"I think this has something to do with Richard."

"Oh, do you think?" his father asked cynically, "If you get out of here, your mother must never know about this."

"Damn," he remembered. "I haven't talked to her since Saturday night at the church."

Peter buried his face in his hands. "Son, if I weren't dead right now, then you would be."

Immediately, he flashed back to facing his father's no-nonsense, yet fair code of morals and responsibility. Fearing for his safety took a backseat to the guilt of not contacting his mother.

"I...I just forgot. She must be worried."

"Once again, your power for grasping the obvious is truly

awesome," Peter added to get his point across.

"I could use less sarcasm and more support right now. I have to figure out how I'm going to get out of this and find out what the deal is with Richard. God, I'm thirsty," he pleaded.

"Ah, you had the country ham? Good, huh?" Peter confirmed.

"How come you were so much comfort and smart up until today, and now you're a pain in the...?"

"You talkin' to y'self, boy?" the returning cop interrupted. "Do I have t'put you in our psycho cell?"

The cop's intrusion surprised Hunter, causing him to glance away. When he looked back, Peter was gone.

"What's this all about? I'm sure I have rights, even in Mississippi," Hunter protested.

"Jes come with me, please," the officer said, unlocking the door.

The officer led him down a hall, around a corner to a stereotypical southern courtroom, complete with slow-moving ceiling fans and a fence with a swinging gate separating the gallery from the bench. The only thing missing was a crowd of 50 sweaty women fanning themselves and lawyers in seersucker suits.

"Now who ya got there, Riley?" the presiding judge asked from the bench.

"Well, Judge Himes, y'honah, this here's a Mr. Huntah Damon."

"What's the charge? And where's his council?"

"He ain't broken any law in town, y'honah." Riley said.

"So why in the name of Aunt Fanny's cornbread biscuits did you call me down here for? I ain't got time for this," the annoyed judge reacted.

"He ain't zactly under 'rest, but I figured ya might wanna meet this fella."

"You brought me down here for a social call?" the judge asked stunned.

"Y'honah, this here's Richie Damon's younga brutha."

Almost instantly, the ruddy color drained from the judge's face.

"Oh my deah Lawd, there're two of 'em?" the judge sighed.

"Judge," Riley continued, "I received a call from Gibby's, sayin' a man claimin' t'be Richie Damon's brutha was in town. I stopped him, ran a check of his plates and it came up with this report," the officer filled in as he handed the judge a piece of paper. Confused, Hunter's mind raced, unsure what he could've done to warrant a 'report'.

"Your honor, sir..." Hunter broke-in.

"Mr. Damon, please let me read this papuh," the judge interrupted.

"But your honor..." he interrupted again.

"Mr. Damon," the judge warned as a final reproach without so much as raising his eyes from the paper, "I'm known 'round these parts for my compassion and great wealth-a patience, but if you say one mo' word, or even half a syllable, you are takin' a genuine risk with your liberty down here in Derby, Mississippi."

After reading the report the judge glanced up. "Mr. Damon, are you aware there's a missin' persons report out on you from the state of Minn'sota?"

Now it was Hunter's turn to lose the color in his face.

"Your honor, sir, I can explain," he pleaded.

"If'n I ate a sugar cube fo ev'ry time I heard, 'Y'hona, I can explain,' I'd be shootin' cotton-candy out my backside and sellin' it at the state fair. This will be jes swale. I been-a hearin' explanations from yer brutha fuh years. Now, I git to hear one from the junyah membah of the Damon fam'ly. My heart's jest a-poundin' under this heah robe."

Given the judge's attitude, Hunter estimated he already had two strikes against him. Perhaps more prudence and diplomacy was in order.

"Well, your honor, Saturday was my wedding day..."

" Well congratulations Mr. Damon. Wait-a-minute. Ya got marrd Saturday, but ch'own kin wasn't there? And where's yuh bride?"

"Ch'own-kin sir?" Hunter repeated, making it sound like a Chinese entree.

"Life'd be so simple if'n Yankees stayed up Noth," the judge sighed.

"Ya kin. Ya brutha, Mr. Damon?"

"No sir. To be honest, I haven't seen my brother in 18 years."

"That makes sense; lucky you. C'tinya."

"Sir?" he asked puzzled.

"C'tinya, c'tinya. G'won with your story boy," the judge replied exasperated.

Hunter retold his story. However, each time he told it, the more edited it got.

Upon hearing the story, Judge Himes sat back in his high leather chair, rubbed his eyes and let out a long, sympathizing sigh.

"That is some story ya got there, Mr. Damon. That just ain't right. That's as wrong as fishing with a skillet. My wife's cousin got left standin' at the altar up in Jackson some years back. You 'member that, Riley?" the judge asked. "It came out like a mean dog on Monday that he was...a little funny; and he weren't no joke teller neither if you unnerstan what I'm saying. Hell, th' bride knew it 'fore he did," the judge whispered as he leaned forward. "Last I heard, he got in touch with his softer side, moved to New York City and been living with one-a-them artsy-types; some kinda foppish gallant, fox-trottin' northern, dancer dandy artist," he continued with a near whisper. Then he sat up in his chair, resuming his normal composure. "Now, I'm a good judge of character Mr. Damon, and I think yaw're a good man..."

Getting anxious and impatient, Hunter interrupted. "Excuse me your honor, why exactly was I stopped and why am I being held? Is there a fine to pay or something?"

"Mr. Damon, I'm gonna be frank. We may do things diff'rently down heah as in Minn'sota, but we do know what we doin'. Regardless of what they tell y'all, we are quite edgecated."

He nodded acknowledging that the judge understood that this situation was hardly by the book.

"Now, Ah'm sure yaw're aware we had some... racial disharm'ny several years back down here. Admittedly, it was not Dixie's brightest time. However, there's been much change in folks, and for the most part, everbody respects everbody else. Race is a non-issue with most us down heah. Most 'us anyway. There uh still a few dull-witted morons who insist on segregation," the judge said glancing towards Riley. "No, you're not being charged with any citation, and I unnerstand this is unusual as snow in July, but we have us an unusual sit-che-ation. Y'see, I only bring up the issue of race, because ya brutha has forced the issue. He's uh...alienated himself from the rest of Derby. Fact is, they refer to him as "Damon the demon."

"Your honor, I haven't seen my brother in a long time, but I know beyond a shadow of a doubt, he's not a racist. Richard had a black girlfriend the last time I saw him," he pleaded.

"Oh, that's not the problem. It's actually the opp'sit. I'm sure you know all 'bout northern lib'rals — them folks who val'date themselves by being crusadahs for whutevuh cause of the week. Well, ya brutha and his girlfriend, Ah don't know if she's the same girl you knew or not, but they'uh ten times worse 'n that. They'uh some kind of self-styled revolutionaries. Th' problem is, everbody gets along real fine here in Derby. There is no racial problem; not much anyway," he again directed towards Riley. "So ya brutha has, on occasion created trouble so he can put out the fires. Now, he's been quiet fo 'bout the past, three years or so, but that jes makes resdents even mo nervous. He's managed to get everbody mo riled up than usual by doin' nothin'. The whole county's on edge just-a-waitin' fo his next move." The judge sat back, tapped his finger on the bench and let out another long sigh.

"So now, his baby brutha comes to town. Mr. Damon, I have t'make sure as flies on pies, that you're gonna behave yourself and respect the good people of Derby an' our hospitality. I don't know ya politics. I don't know if ya recent traumatic nuptials, or lack thereof, and job dismissal pushed-jova the edge or whut. But if ya came down here to start trouble, ya got two choices. Keep on driving out of town, or we can put 'cha up in our Hotel Pokey for an undetermined amount of time. It's my job t' blow out the match 'fore it reaches the powder.

"Yes, your honor."

"All that bein' said, there is another issue regarding ya brutha Ah should tell ya'. Y'see, Ol'Richie lives several miles from the populous of Derby, an he's built himself a protective compound surroundin' a trailer. It is something t' see. But, Richie Damon hasn't had a job or means t' support himself and his lady friend fo years. True, he's been quiet, but people ah sure he's up t' some kinda malfeasance. 'Course, as long as he's not causin' s'much trouble as a few years back...," Judge Himes tailed off.

Listening with incredulous indifference and fueled by an instinct to defend family, Hunter responded with indignation. "What if he's not actually involved in anything illegal? You people ever think about that?"

Judge Himes lowered his chin and glared over his glasses, reminding Hunter that although he sympathized, he still demanded the respect due to a judge.

"...your honor...sir?" Hunter added.

"Mr. Damon, Ah'm gonna talk to ya man to man. Richie Damon is not a boy scout. Ah'm tellin' ya this for y'own good. If ya do decide t' go see him, I offer ya two pieces of advice. One — unnastand he's prob'ly changed a great deal since the last time ya saw him."

"I understand that," he said as he looked deep into the judge's eyes and saw compassion. "And your second piece of advice?"

"Jes 'member t' duck at his front gate. That sonuvabitch is crazy."

Judge Himes let out another sigh signaling the end of one subject and the beginning of another.

"Now, this next part is, shall we say, non-negotiable. One thing we take quite seriously down here in Dixie, is, we love our mamas. You Mr. Damon, you are gonna call yo' mama back in Minn'sota, soon as you leave this court and let her know yer right as punch on Sunday. Do we unnastan' each otha?

"Yes, Judge Himes, sir."

"Well, Riley, I think that took care of everthing. Welcome to Derby, Mr. Damon," the judge added with a friendly tone.

Relieved he wasn't going to rot in a prison camp wearing dirty denim shirts, chained to criminals and swinging pick axes. Hunter's mind raced, wondering about how worried his mother must have been to file a missing person's report. It had become so easy the past few days to concentrate on himself and his problems he'd forgotten about loved ones back home.

Back in the jail, Hunter asked if he could use the phone. Out of spite, Riley hesitated until he was reminded that the call was a court mandate from the Judge. Riley capitulated, but only if the call was collect. Noticing Riley spying over his shoulder, Hunter contorted his face, asking for privacy. Riley relented and retreated to a back room for a moment.

Dialing the numbers and following the automated prompts, he debated whether to tell his mother about his father's visits. He decided the poor woman had been through enough and the shock might do her in. The phone rang twice when he heard Lee's voice.

"Hello?" Lee Damon asked.

"This is a collect call. Do you accept the charges from…"

"Mom! It's Hunter. I'm okay."

"I'll accept. Hunter, where are you? Are you okay? We still love you."

"Yes, I'm fine, I'm fine," he answered, wanting to ease his mother's fears. Then the inevitable. He had to ask about the fallout from the wedding. "So, uh...have you heard from..."

"No. Isn't that just shameful?" Lee interrupted. "But everybody is on your side and very supportive."

"Mom...mom, I don't care. It's okay, it's okay," he lied to placate her.

"Where are you, honey?"

If he wasn't going to tell her about the visits from Peter, he sure wasn't going to tell her about being in the courthouse in Derby and being on his way to visit Richard. Not yet. "Um, I'm in...Florida. Near Orlando. Thinking of going to Disney World or Animal Kingdom," he lied again.

"Do you need anything? We love you," she repeated.

"I know, I love you too. No, I'm fine. I've had a lot of time to think."

"I just feel so...oh Hunter dear, I'm so sorry. You deserve so much better," she said as her voice started to break from crying.

"Listen, tell everybody I'm doing fine. Just getting my head together. And mom, no more missing person's reports, okay?"

There was a long silence, and he knew his mother had begun crying.

"I love you mom."

The silence continued, and he wasn't sure if she was still on the line.

"Mom?"

"Yes, I'm here," she sniffed.

"I'll call you soon. Give me a few days, all right?"

"All right," she conceded.

There was no reason to say 'good-bye' — it would have ruined the intensity of the mood. As he hung up the phone, his eyes got misty. He rubbed them to eliminate any sign for Riley to pick up, but as it was, the officer had been watching and listening the whole time. When he got back to his desk, Riley let his macho cop demeanor down for a moment.

"See, thas why we love our mamas down here," he said in a comforting tone.
"They make everthang jes fine."

Hunter felt his contempt for Riley fade briefly. He patted him on the epaulets of his uniform and nodded with gratitude.

"Thank you," he said.

Chapter Eighteen

True to Riley's word, Zevadiah dropped off his car, with the key in the ignition. From there, Hunter mentally backtracked to Middleground Rd. then reset the odometer. Not long after passing through Derby, Middleground turned to an unpaved, winding road not quite wide enough for two small cars. God help him if a truck came the other way to tax his already low concentration reserves, especially with so many other issues troubling him.

Leaving a plume of dust behind his car, he reached Lookout Road — the only turn for at least three miles in either direction. Remembering he had four miles to go on Lookout Road, it didn't take nearly that long to pinpoint what he suspected had to be Richard's place. That section of Lookout Road, being the highest point of the county, offered an astonishing scenic vantage point, allowing him to scan down the road and spot what appeared to be a large trailer surrounded by layers of barbed wire making some kind of compound. Gibby was right. He couldn't miss it.

"Ohhhhh...shit," Hunter exclaimed as a whole sinister scenario began unraveling in his active imagination. He wondered if he should stop at all, but he knew he would anyway.

All these years, he wondered about the fate of his brother. How he was living? Where he was living? The frightening reality loomed a mile and a half away, and he pictured nasty, vivid and violent visions. His imagination roared into overdrive, besieged by a dizzying barrage of ominous speculation. Within another couple hundred yards, he got a far better view of the entire compound than he wanted.

It was a bigger than usual trailer, a triple-wide, covered by green aluminum siding. A few modifications almost helped it look like a house, like a front porch leading to a deck and an awning over the door, but it still had that 'no foundation' appearance unique to trailer homes. The only other major structure was a large shed fifteen yards from the trailer. Surrounding these two buildings were three concentric perimeters of razor wire with about ten yards between each circle. Greeting him as he pulled into the large patch of dirt meant to be a driveway, were the rusted skeletal remains of an El Camino on blocks, an almost new pick-up truck and a small sedan. He parked on the end beside the truck, and walked to the front gate. It was eerily still until the tranquility was disrupted by the menacing barking of unseen dogs. Several feet to the right of the front gate hung an oversized wooden sign dented with pockmarks, as if it was used for target practice. The message was clear:

Warning: No trespassing.
This means you.

Hunter assumed that being family, he'd be excused from the warning.

As he reached for the front gate latch, he barely noticed a thin wire running along the back of the gate. It sparked a flood of familiar memories he hadn't recalled in years. After a quick series of flashbacks, however, he remembered.

As a teenager, Richard took an unusual interest in stories about booby traps during the Vietnam War. For two aggravating years, his brother engineered and built fairly sophisticated snares mostly inspired by slapstick movies and sometimes reminiscent of elaborate Rube Goldberg machines.

Always annoying, usually ingenious and normally harmless — most times Richard would simply suspend a bucket of water, hidden from sight above the victim's head, or position a camouflaged garden hose nozzle at crotch level. Occasionally the unsuspecting mark might get smacked in the face with sticky substances like jelly or honey. Outwardly these pranks perturbed Peter. On the inside, their dad — ever the engineer — seemed proud and impressed with a few intricacies in the older son's creations; at least until they started getting serious. Richard's appetite for mischief didn't take long to grow hungrier after each successive prank pushed the envelope, until what turned out to be his last trap almost sent a neighborhood kid to the hospital.

That final escapade began by hooking up an unusually powerful boat battery to a wrought iron handle on the inside of a cellar door of a long deserted home. Richard then just had to coax a new neighborhood friend into exploring the scary cellar. Upon grabbing the cellar's outside iron ring handle, the unsuspecting youth shook violently for several seconds, unable to let go until a basketball (released by a lynch-pin when the handle was pulled up) rolled down a track that knocked out a stake, which supported a platform holding a bowling ball. The bowling ball, wound by a cord, then pulled another pin, which sprung the latch to a trap door (hidden by a welcome mat) that Richard built into the opposite cellar door the kid stood on.

Hunter found the trip-wire to the gate. His eyes followed the nearly invisible cable over the driveway and into a clump of trees.

Heeding the warnings from town, he knelt down, hid his head behind his arms, and pulled the gate open. After tripping the wire, in a matter of moments he heard a fast whirring noise, followed by a loud 'thwack'. Looking up, a single aluminum staff arrow, firmly embedded in the wooden warning sign flexed up and down. If the message wasn't clear before, it now had a new lethal meaning. 'This means you' did indeed include him.

"Jesus!" he screamed. "He's nuts."

If that was Richard's idea of a warning shot, it would have deterred the average stranger, but fifteen feet away, at the second gate, Hunter noticed a speakerphone and a mounted surveillance camera. If he could make it to the camera, surely that would help his odds. Treading with great care, he picked up his feet, watching for more trip wires. He spotted one. This time, a wire led to a medium sized wooden box set in the ground about 15 feet away. It looked like an apiary, but it could have been modified into some fiendish box of unknown potential malice. Stepping over the line, averting a potential catastrophe, paranoia set in when he reached the speakerphone. Was the button connected to a speakerphone, or something violently diabolical? He tensed up, pressed the button quickly and braced himself for doom.

"Dammit! What part of 'No Trespassing - This means you' don't you get?" a voice yelled from the speaker. "Don't make me come out there or I'll rip off your damn head and feed it to my dogs."

"Richard! Richard! Don't shoot. It's me...it's Hunter."

Just like the surprise reunion with his dad days earlier, he felt cheated he didn't say something poignant after so many years. After a long pause, he got contact.

"Hunter? Little brother, is that you?"

Thinking he detected excitement in his brother's voice, Hunter soon learned it was anything but.

"What are you doing here, Hunter?" he demanded. "You don't want to be here. You should go," he continued in a threatening, yet protective voice.

The dejection disappointed the younger Damon. After reviewing a variety of reunion scenarios, he forgot to include the 'You-don't-want-to-be-here. You-should-go' option.

"Richard," he pleaded into the speaker. "C'mon, let me in," Hunter begged.

After another extended, uncomfortable pause, he got an answer.

"Stay there. I'll be out in a minute," Richard said, somewhat disturbed. "And don't move or touch anything."

One minute of standing in a potential minefield surrounded by lethal snares passed excruciatingly slow. Finally, the trailer's front door opened, and Hunter got his first glimpse of Richard in 18 years. He'd built up the significance of this moment to the point of expecting blaring trumpets and a choir of angels. Instead, the only noise came from the barking dogs. Richard unlocked the gate nearest the trailer and made his way to the second gate, maneuvering with quick, fluid motions, taking some large steps and some small, avoiding his trip-wires. When Richard reached the second gate, Hunter got a better look. Richard had a little less hair, what was left was a little grayer, and he carried more weight on his mid-section and around his face. Other than an inch-long scar above his lip, his older brother looked much the same as he remembered. With the gate disarmed and unlocked, Hunter greeted his sole sibling with a long overdue brotherly hug, expressing nearly two decades of separation. Richard, initially passive, partially reciprocated with a quick squeeze and three pats on the back.

"What are you doing here, Hunter?" His tone implied more suspicion than welcome. Very anti-climactic.

"It's good to see you too," Hunter stole his father's line, showing disappointment. Ashamed, Richard had trained himself to be leery of everybody.

"I'm sorry. It's good to see you Hunter. Come on in the house for a minute. Tell me what's been going on. I have a couple surprises."

Hunter deliberately gawked at the compound, letting his brother see what he was doing. It created an awkward moment neither of them knew how to resolve, other than Richard guiding him past the trip-wires. It was a good thing, too. Even if he'd gotten past the second gate, there was no way he would have seen a couple of them.

The inside of the trailer revealed a spacious, surprisingly nicer interior than its utilitarian exterior suggested. Decorated with pine and glossy black lacquer furniture, wood paneling and Berber carpet, Richard's homestead hardly typified the common image of trailer homes. One thing bothering Hunter, however, was an entire wall covered with at least a hundred guns on hooks. Unlike Lieut. Gibson's, none of these guns were antiques or collectibles. This modern munitions menagerie contained strictly state-of-the-art automatics, pistols, and rifles. Considering Richard's unpopular reputation, he got an uneasy feeling that these guns weren't on display as much as they were being stored. Richard noticed his little brother's shock but decided the best course was ignoring it. Denial was quickly becoming a family trait. What little optimism Hunter held for his brother's life began to wane, until they passed a partition into the living room section of the trailer.

"Well," Richard said pointing to a couch, "here are those surprises."

To Hunter's surprise, on the couch, were Richard's two children: a girl, maybe ten years old and a boy who looked to be around six. As Peter pointed out, the first thing he noticed was that they were mulattos. He didn't feel bad about that; it was just a piece of information his brain processed upon meeting them.

"Kids, say hello to Hunter."

Hunter? Not 'Uncle Hunter'? The girl came first and presented her hand while the young boy stayed on the couch glaring at his uncle with suspicious contempt.

"This is LaTanyaneicia."

"Hello LaTanyaneicia," Hunter greeted, making a conscious effort to pronounce her overly long, contrived name, "nice to meet you."

"And the little fella on the couch is Bob," he said in a playful voice.

"Bob?" Hunter repeated, baffled by the contrasting simplicity of his nephew's name.

"I know; it's a long story," Richard said hurriedly, not wanting to explain.

As long as that story may have been, it couldn't have felt as long as the uncomfortable pause that followed as he surveyed the living room, validating the town's trepidation.

Along one wall in the room hung a large 'Black Pride' banner. Beside it were two large bookshelves filled with militant literature, several anti-government leaflets, and a few more guns. Adding a touch of ironic civility was a professionally produced canvas family portrait hanging on the opposite wall. The room was uncluttered, but it troubled him that there were pistols, revolvers and rifles lying about instead of random children's toys.

"Wow, kids. So are you married?" he asked, making a half-hearted effort to mask the real question he wanted to ask: 'what the hell are you doing?'

"No, Chaniqua and I aren't married," Richard replied, keeping the charade going.

"Yeah? Still with Chaniqua?" Hunter asked, adding a long cadence. As the woman who instigated Richard's flight, tearing his family apart, the fact that they were still together after 18 years gave the relationship credibility.

"Yeah, still together. She's at work right now. She's a guard at the women's prison," Richard mumbled before turning the tables. "Now what are you up to?" he asked neutrally.

"What've you been doing? How's mom and dad?" he added as if tortured.

The tension turned toxic, not only with each word, but with every pause. Not evil; only uncomfortable. They both knew what had to be said, even though neither one wanted to say it.

"Dad's dead. He died five years ago," Hunter explained, even though he'd seen Peter just two hours earlier. Richard grabbed two beers from the refrigerator in an attempt at bonding.

"I'm sorry," the elder sibling replied with the conviction of a funeral guest; sincere and heartfelt, yet apathetic. Handing his brother the bottle, the atmosphere continued growing thick. Richard told his kids to play in their rooms with a lighthearted tone, suggesting that, despite appearances, he was probably a very good father. That is, except for the arsenal on the wall and the hate literature.

Up to that point, the two were brothers by blood only. Strangers sharing similar genetics, a distant history and an 18-year vacuum. People forget important events they normally would mention had they been talking on a regular basis. Milestones like, 'I bought a house,' or 'I changed jobs.' Hunter's mind stewed in awkwardness as he fought to find the right words to balance diplomacy and his curiosity. Richard didn't have that problem. He'd built a new life and didn't mind cutting through the stifling tension.

"You know, you look great, Richard!" Hunter exclaimed, trying to start a normal conversation.

"Well, little brother, what I want to know is, what're you doing here?" Richard asked with detached interest.

Realizing this wasn't going to be a feel-good suburban reunion, Hunter sighed and told his story. Starting from the very beginning, he didn't leave anything out, particularly details when he and Hope were a hot item. Telling the story had become second hat by then, but had an added element since Hunter felt an innate motive to impress his sibling. Richard listened and didn't interrupt, barely moving except to grab another beer from the mini-fridge beside his chair. He simply raised his eyebrows in surprise at the correct times. Hunter finished the story, and with a long swig, finished his then tepid beer.

"That's uh...that's messed up. Man, I am sorry. You doing okay?"

"I'm hanging in there," he replied unconvincingly. "I'm thinking a lot on the road. You know, just me and...my thoughts," he lied.

"Listen, I know we haven't had much...contact all these years, but if there's anything I can do..." Richard lied too. He knew he had nothing to offer, and the truth be told, he wanted his brother gone before receiving an expected phone call, and definitely before Chaniqua got home.

Curiosity finally prodded Hunter. "Richard, what the hell is all of this?" he asked, making an exaggerated sweeping motion with his arm.

Expecting that question sooner or later, Richard lowered his head and let out a defiant sigh. "Hunter, you wouldn't understand."

"You're goddamn right I wouldn't understand. Tell me anyway."

"No. It caused a wedge between us as a small idea, and now it's much bigger. It's my life, Hunter. No offense, but my life is Chaniqua, my kids, and my work. There's no room for you or Mom or Dad or Minnesota or whatever. And if you knew my work, that wedge would only be painful. You just gotta know, that whatever you think I've become, we're happy."

"Happy? The whole town thinks you're friggin' wacko."

"You stopped in town?" Richard asked suspiciously.

"More like I was stopped. I met Officer Riley and Judge Himes."

"Riley," Richard laughed. "What piece of work he is. Disguised as a cop by day and, disguised in white sheets at night."

"Is that what this is about? A reverse hate group? You're the Kluless Klux Klan?" he added sarcastically.

"You don't need to know what it's all about," he replied calmly. "Forget about me, Hunter. It's been 18 years."

Hunter sat there stunned for several seconds.

"Richard..." he started pleading.

"Jesus!" Richard interrupted in anger. "You'd think you'd

get the fucking point by now. Let it go, man. The less you know, the better it'll be."

Defensive indignation replaced the awkwardness. Their reunion was at a crossroads where Hunter had to choose words deliberately. The guns, plus the racist material, plus a three-year low profile, plus the secrecy added up to a number of possibilities — and none of them were humanitarian. About to ask a carefully worded difficult question, he lost his chance when the telephone started ringing. Richard answered it, making Hunter privy to one side of a conversation.

"Hello? Yeah, it's me. Yeah, we're still on. What do you need? How many? Okay. Okay. Yeah, I can do that. You got cash? No, up front, then we'll decide the drop off. Same place? Okay. Be careful you're not followed. Yeah, I know. Yeah. I'll try to be there. I might be a little late. I can't talk. I'll see you then. Okay."

Richard hung up and turned to his brother. "Uh, listen Hunter, I hate to cut family hour short, but you've got to go. I have to be somewhere soon and Chaniqua gets home soon."

"Can I go with you?" he asked, already knowing the answer.

Richard chuckled, "No, you can't go."

"Let me crash here until you get back?" he offered as a compromise.

"Hunter, I am glad to see you. Really. But you can't get involved."

"Involved? I'll be in this trailer. You go, I'll look after the kids and we can catch up when you're done," he pleaded. "Richard, it's been 18 years. I promise I'll never bother you again, but we can't end it like this," he begged. "C'mon, I came all the way down here. Be my brother for just a few more hours."

The elder Damon rolled his eyes and let out a long dejected sigh. Against his better judgment, he relented and told his brother he'd be back in a couple hours, then warned him that he was on his own when Chaniqua got home. He told his kids to take a nap in their rooms, and as he stepped out the door, Richard glanced back at Hunter one last time, smiled and shook his head with disbelief. He knew nothing good could come from this.

Hunter grabbed a fresh beer and guzzled it inside of three minutes. It helped calm his nerves from these new revelations and quenched the still lingering thirst from the country ham. He sat down on the soft leather couch and read 'Black Power' propaganda, amazed and perplexed.

"How could anyone believe this?" he asked out loud to himself.

Although only the middle of the afternoon, he reflected on the day's events so far, which included a culinary experience at a southern-style eatery, an involuntary visit to a southern-style jail and courthouse and the sudden insight that his brother was a southern-style redneck revolutionary living in a booby-trapped compound. The beer hit him hard, and he felt his muscles ache from increased tension. He closed his eyes put his head on an embroidered pillow that read "Never Trust The White Devil" and fell asleep.

Chapter Nineteen

Hunter napped on the couch until he heard a loud double-click next to his ear.

Click-Click.

As he opened his eyes, the long silver barrel of a revolver no more than three inches from his face startled him. His eyes grew larger as they followed the gun to the hand, up the arm and shoulders to the face of an angry, black woman with a shaved head, dressed in a prison guard uniform.

"Two questions, Cracker-boy. Who the fuck are you and why are you in my home?" she demanded.

He raised his arms, evaluating the situation and his options. Again, his options appeared limited.

"Chaniqua, it's me...Hunter. Richard's brother."

Chaniqua moved the gun away and looked into his eyes. She smiled slightly and scrutinized his face.

"Yeah, I thought it might be you when I saw Minnesota plates," she replied reassuringly. Then she grimaced again and moved the barrel back even closer so it touched his nose. "Now, answer me Cracker-boy. What are you doing in my home...with my kids?"

"I came to see Richard. He let me in," Hunter answered quickly.

"Obviously he let you in. Otherwise you'd be a rotting pile of stinking pasty-white dead Cracker dog meat in my front yard."

"Yeah...," he agreed. "Um, listen Chaniqua, do you suppose you could put the gun away?"

"Not yet."

"Okay," he continued calmly. "Could you take your finger off the trigger or put the safety on?"

"That defeats the purpose of sticking the fucking gun in your pasty-white, thin-lipped, skinny nosed face. Now, answer my goddamn question, Cracker. Who sent you?"

"Nobody sent me. I've just been driving and I ended up here in Mississippi."

After a few extreme, intense seconds, Chaniqua began laughing. "Boy, now I know you're lying or crazy. Ain't nobody just drive down to Mississippi 'cause they want to. Even assholes from Alabama go out of their way to avoid Mississippi."

He sighed loudly. "It's a long story. I'll give you the short version, if you put the gun away," he bargained.

"This'll be good," Chaniqua responded with a chuckle. She uncocked the gun and tossed it on the table.

Telling his story again, this time he raced through basic facts for the sake of brevity to appease Chaniqua. When he finished, she leaned back on the couch in astonishment.

"Wow, that's some fucked-up shit," she expressed to comfort him.

"That seems to be the consensus," he admitted.

"Then you also know you can't be hanging around here."

Biting his lower lip and arching his eyebrows, he conceded he wasn't a part of whatever plan was being conspired. Not content on leaving until seeing Richard again though, he relaxed on the couch — the opposite reaction of what Chaniqua intended.

"Those are beautiful children you have," he mentioned sincerely, changing the subject.

"Does it bother you they're mixed?" Chaniqua challenged him.

"No. Does it bother you?" he returned, smiling. "The way I see it, racially mixed children are God's way of stirring-up ingredients," he said, making a whisking motion. "For some reason, you never see ugly kids from mixed parents."

"Got that right," Chaniqua agreed.

Thinking about her children made her smile. Hoping common ground might ease the tension and bring down some walls, Hunter struck while the irons were lukewarm, emphasizing that her kids were bridges above a deep chasm of ignorance, fear and hatred; nurturing the idea by suggesting they may be ground breakers someday.

"I imagine there's a huge burden a mixed child carries," he

sympathized. "One day, he'll be forced to understand what people haven't accepted for thousands of years. And if he gravitates or relates to one side, he ultimately has to realize that he's one-half another race; race he may have even learned to hate," Hunter offered smiling.

Chaniqua returned his smile as if appreciating his insight. Then she caught him off-guard.

"Get out of my goddamn house, Cracker," she calmly demanded.

"Chaniqua, I...I..." he stuttered.

Grabbing a 9 mm automatic from the coffee table, she pointed it up and fired. The blast was deafening as a bullet pierced the roof, sending debris to the floor and making a small jagged hole in the ceiling.

"Ain't no, 'I...I' about it, just get the fuck out," she screamed.

Hunter didn't see that coming. Startled by the shot, he seriously questioned his odds of surviving. If Chaniqua shot a hole in her own ceiling, she would have had no qualms about putting a hole in a stranger she hated. Stunned and with ringing ears, Hunter could not believe what had just happened. LaTanyaneicia poked her tiny face around the corner.

"Mama, what was that?" the young child asked.

"Nothing, baby. Go back to your room," the mother ordered.

The verdict was in. Chaniqua was nuts, too. Hunter stood up very slowly wondering; if she didn't shoot him, would she at least give him a sporting chance of maneuvering through the booby-trapped compound? Before he could reach the door, Chaniqua continued her rant.

"What the fuck do you know about race relations? What it's like to be a minority? Or even a half-minority? You sit up there on your lily-white throne in Minnesota spouting off your lame-ass can't-we-all-get-along bullshit rhetoric. What we need is action. And I ain't talking 'bout no government subsidized bullshit, I'm talking 'bout a preemptive revolution."

His mind raced back to the Thanksgiving dinner when he heard this vitriolic rant the first time.

"Revolution?" he asked astonished, eyeing the door.

"Yeah, that's right. Soon, and I do mean soon, it ain't gonna be about what the nice, kind liberals are gonna give us," she mocked, "it's gonna be what we decide to take. And we may just take it all."

Her eyes grew maniacal, taking on an inflexible stare. The volume of her voice sounded normal, but the tone grew more threatening and fanatical as she went on.

"You wanna know what this is about? It's about these," she replied brandishing the still smoking 9 mm underneath his chin. "It's about guns. Arming soldiers in the city," she continued with a scary intensity. "They think we're drug dealers. We don't deal no fucking drugs. It's the White Man who takes drugs to the city to keep us down. Then he points to the gangstah on the corner to make himself feel better and get re-elected. They don't have nothing on us. Every one of these is legal. We are taking uprising to the streets and we're not taking anything less. It's about guns, blood, power, revolution. The guns are already on the streets. All the soldiers need are more guns, a little organization, the right leadership and this fucking fascist country will be plunged into chaos not seen since the Stone Age.

"Civil War?" he asked horrified.

"Won't be nothin' civil about it. Happens all the time in Africa," she declared with pride. "And think about this. When the black, brown, yellow and red come together to take on the white, who do you think gonna be the winning colors? A word of advice; when you get back to Minnesota, you may want to go out of your fuckin' way being nice to as many black folk as you can. It may save your pathetic, worthless life," she added as if she'd done him a favor.

Hunter's shock yielded to disgust. Tempted to show his anger with disapproving head shaking, he knew that she still brandished the gun.

"Now, you're gonna get your sorry, lily white, skinny Cracker ass and get out of my house. If you're quick about it, I may disconnect the security." Chaniqua said tossing the gun onto the couch.

At the front door, she flipped a large toggle switch. Presumably, flipping the lever disengaged the traps, probably by giving slack or taking tension off trip-wires. Before leaving, Hunter hesitated. The fact Richard wasn't a drug dealer gave him some comfort, but 'racial revolutionary' and urban guerrilla terrorist' wasn't much easier.

Grabbing the doorknob, he stopped short of turning it.

"Say good-bye to Richard for me, please," he mumbled.

"Don't you get it Cracker-boy? You're dead to him," she exploded. "He gave up on you and your whole white bread Cracker family years ago."

Still unsure of his safety, he was visibly wounded and a little embarrassed. He opened the door, then stopped and turned around again.

"Just tell me," he asked stepping over the threshold. "Are you all happy?"

Expecting an offensive retort, Chaniqua was taken off-guard. She looked away and smiled, taking the time to reflect on his sincere question.

"Just go," she replied quietly.

Their eyes met, exchanging a look of candor not usually shared between adversaries. He nodded, signifying he understood, and closed the door behind him. Carefully following the worn footprints in the yard to avoid the tripwires, he made his way through the three circles of fencing.

In the safety his car, he studied the compound one last time. Like everything that week, his long awaited reunion didn't work out like he'd hoped. His ringing ears and the arrow embedded in the wooden sign reminded him that it worked out precisely as he feared. The fears about seeing his brother had come to fruition. His worst-case scenarios were realized, yet they were anti-climactic. Their shared past had been reduced to a far distant memory with little in common, and Richard was just another stranger he told his story to.

Hunter wanted to feel guilt about demoting his flesh & blood to a stranger, but realized he couldn't. There's an undeniable ambivalence inherent to strangers, and in that ambivalence, he really didn't care. After all, nothing had changed. Nothing had happened. Nothing was different. He was just relieved to get out alive.

After retracing his path back onto I-59, he'd only been on

the highway fifteen minutes when he noticed the sun starting its slow spring descent into the western sky. Road signs told him New Orleans was an hour away, and he figured the Crescent City would be the perfect place to end one of the weirdest days of his life. He'd had his fill of rural Dixie. He needed to get lost among people who had perfected a 'what the hell attitude.'

"Laissez le bon temps rollez," Peter exclaimed, however, Hunter had all but lost the wonderful feeling of novelty whenever his father popped in. He didn't take it for granted. The shock value simply wore off.

"What?" he asked.

"Laissez les bon temps rouler," his father repeated. "Let the good times roll. You're heading for New Orleans, right?"

"Yeah, I guess so. How'd you know?"

Peter sighed. "When are you going to get it? I'm tuned to you spiritually, emotionally and psychically. Plus that road sign says New Orleans."

Hunter remained preoccupied with the ironic guilt of his ambivalence that he ignored his father's joke, a gesture not lost on Peter.

"How did it go?" his father asked.

"Weird. Strange. You were right," he confessed.

"Not what you thought it would be?"

"No...yes." he corrected himself.

"What were you expecting?"

Curiously Peter's first questions were not about Richard's well-being, how he looked or what he was doing. Almost as if he already knew.

"I...I thought it would be more...something. It's like he didn't know me, and he didn't care."

"You haven't been in his life for 18 years, son. His life isn't about you. His life is about him and the people he has in it; as your life is about you and the people you have in it."

Staring ahead, he understood what his father said, but that didn't make it any less bitter. Even with this ambivalence, he wanted Richard's acceptance. Peter sighed as if organizing a thought.

"Okay, a life is defined as a series of sequential events over the course of an existence. It's that simple. The hard part is remembering to live every day and recognize and appreciate the people and the things in it. Overload your senses. Take nothing for granted, the good and the bad — because you never know when it might disappear. Take it all in and hold onto it as memory and experience. Because at the end of the day when the lights go out, it's only you and your thoughts. That's what life is; simply a series of consecutive events. A journey we make as individuals, but share with others — if we choose to share it with anyone at all," Peter ended eloquently.

"That's awfully solipsistic don't you think?"

"Check out the big vocabulary," Peter mocked. "Don't forget," he continued, "you're the one who took to the road by himself."

"I'm not alone, remember?" the son joked, "I'm sharing it with you."

"But I don't exist," Peter replied.

Responding with a wry look, he discovered that Peter had disappeared again. His father's exits were as unexpected and unannounced as his impromptu entrances. He'd pop in, use logic to prove his points; then as soon as those points were understood, he was gone again.

Cause I'm the best boyfriend — that you never had
Baby, open your eyes and you'll see why I'm a treasure
I'm what you've complained for years you desire in one man
Honest, romantic, attentive and I can bring you pleasure
Hey I know your heart and I'll rock it like no one else can

By the time Hunter reached the outskirts of New Orleans it had gotten dark, but the city lights and the smell of the gulf guided him to the French Quarter like a beacon. He followed Pontchartrain Boulevard, took a few turns, and pulled up to a refined Victorian-style hotel in the Vieux Carre district.

The Montgomery Hotel overflowed with significant personality and historical mystique. Its cultured architecture skillfully combined the Victorian, Art Deco and Post Modern eras, exhibiting sleek innovative imagination with traditional Old World elegance. On the lobby walls, mirrors running from floor to ceiling faced each other, reflected upon themselves to provide the illusion of infinity. This endless reflection suggested the Montgomery's popularity defied time with the appearance of hosting guests from both the distant past as well as the distant future at the same time. Broad leaf plants accentuated the lobby, giving it a lush organic warmth, and an ornate fountain in the lounge provided a handsome aesthetic focal point with a relaxing sound of splashing water. Even the elevator was lined in mahogany with intricately carved lattice trim and antique ivory buttons.

The check-in procedure was predictably familiar, but thankfully, it was closer to the Imperial's.

He rode the elevator to the 11th floor, settled in his room and peered out the aging warped window at the wild jungle of antique brick and neo-neon below. All at once, a history and culture of primitive emotions called out, and Hunter had no choice than to explore the Big Easy.

It was 10 p.m. as he strolled along the Quarter. Passing by St. Louis Cathedral in Jackson Square, he stopped to admire its handsome facade. Oblivious to the tourists, artists and commercial elements, he stood surrounded by historic buildings, astonished by the wide spectrum of ugliness and beauty packed into one single day. And what a long, strange day it had been. But in New Orleans, 10 o'clock is just the beginning of every long, weird night.

Chapter Twenty

A cacophonous fusion of music wafted into the street as Hunter toured the Quarter. A combination of music styles, each one emanating from a separate bar, supplied a jumbled free-style soundtrack paralleling his jumping reflections. The closer he got to one bar, the more its music dominated the mix until passing by and reducing its music to a low cumbersome background melody for the next approaching bar. This same Doppler Effect held true for conversations between people, except the dialogue was dominated by drunk tourists slurring loudly, telling each other how drunk they were and where they should go next to get more drunk. A stout blend of smoke, stale beer and high humidity formed a thick consistency hanging in the air; while it seemed to help many inebriated revelers remain upright, it created a challenge to walking for others.

The sidewalk was littered, the back alleys stank of vomit, urine and garbage and vice outnumbered virtue at least 20-1, but New Orleans nightlife intrigued and amused him. He'd experienced his fair share of wild nights and briefly reminisced about college nights he couldn't fully remember. Apart from the bitterly sensuous aspects, New Orleans offered Hunter one quality he hadn't found yet: the chance to be alone in a candid crowd. Here, he could observe individuals – from the privileged elite to the dregs of society – with anonymity; like a god admiring a work in progress. Just beginning to enjoy his solitude, he heard a voice.

"Hey, what you lookin' for boy?" it asked.

Scanning across the street in the direction of the voice, a large black woman stood in the doorway below a blue neon sign. Since she positioned herself on the sidewalk at night, he assumed she was a hooker. Her strong West Indies accent made it difficult to understand her at first.

"You talking to me?" Hunter asked.

"Ya, you be da one I be talking to. I say, what you be

looking for baby?" she repeated.

"I'm not looking for anything; just walking," he lied. He was searching for a lot of things, but nothing a hooker could provide.

"You not looking for nuttin'?" she mocked, "Oh baby, everybody be looking for sometin'. Dey just don't know dey be looking. But baby, you most certainly be looking. You be looking hard, hard, hard. Trouble is, you ain't knowing what it is. Dat's all in your aura, baby."

Aura? What kind of hooker says 'aura'? Intrigued, he paced to the edge of the sidewalk and squinted towards the shadowy figure. She appeared to be in her sixties with long deep lines on her face. To hide her enormous girth, or maybe out of comfort, she wore a loose muumuu with sandals. A colorful scarf wrapped on her head added a foot to her height. Not much to look at, if she was a hooker, she would've needed unprecedented skills. Stepping closer, his eyes were drawn to the neon sign reading 'Fortune Teller.'

"Dat's right, you come over here and we help you find your way. I promise ya. You come over here to Big Mama Aristides," she said in her doorway. "And ya bring ya friend too," she added.

"I'm alone," Hunter answered confused. "There's nobody with me."

"Oh baby, ya not alone. Ya gots the power all over ya," she giggled out loud. "Ya most definitely not alone."

Hesitating at the curb, Big Mama waved for him to come inside. "Aw, come on boy. Open up dat mind. Ya tink da Good Lawd gonna just set ya loose out dere in dis world with no guidance? Tell you what; it be a slow night, I give ya half-off. Ya be doing both us a favor," she chuckled.

Relenting to her sincerity, he walked into her studio, trading one foul stench for another. Inside Big Mama Aristides' Fortune Telling Studio, incense and patchouli burned his nostrils and stung his eyes, but he gave no indication the noxious scents bothered him.

"Besides," she continued, "I love readin' fo ya cleaned-up white boys. Dey gots a look like everting in control, but dey da most bewildered," she laughed again. "Now, let's find out what kind of soul ya are."

Big Mama focused her attention, gently placed her hands on his cheeks and stared inquisitively into his eyes, moving his face from side to side. Wanting to cooperate, he didn't know how to facilitate. Should he stick-out his tongue and say 'ahhh'? Open his eyes wider to make them easier to peer into?

"Lawd yes, ya good soul. A good, good soul. I see it. Mmmm-mmmm, but ya be ripped apart. What happened, baby?" she asked with sympathy in her eyes.

"It's a long story," he told her.

"Dats awright, baby, I tell you what happened," she laughed as she pulled out a deck of tarot cards. They sat down at a wobbly card table on a pair of mismatched kitchen chairs. A worn patch in the vinyl on the table served as a testament to years of working at one table. Big Mama gave him the deck to shuffle while she summoned her powers of discernment.

"Now, what's ya name, baby?"

"Hunter. Hunter Damon."

"Hunter?" she said excitedly. "Dat's a fine name for you, since ya be huntin'."

As he shuffled the oversized cards, one of them fell out onto the table.

"Oooh, da spirits must-a want me to see dat card,' she said picking it up. "What we got here; dat Hermit? Now who you 'spose dis be, Mr. I'm-alone-dere-ain't-nobody-wit-me?" she said with a wink. She set the Hermit aside took the cards and spread them face down with a ceremonial flourish.

"Now, you just clear ya mind and let dem 'ol spirits tell ya what ten cards dey want you to pick," she instructed.

He chose the cards, placing each one face down. After a trance-like concentration, Big Mama breathed heavily three times and started the reading.

"Hmm, da Chariot. Ya not from here, are ya baby? Ya come a long way."

Big Mama's Studio sat in the heart of the tourist district. Everybody passing her door came a long way. Initially unimpressed, he continued out of politeness.

"That's right," he confirmed.

"Ya on a journey, but ya still got a ways to go. See how he's moving?"

She turned over the second card. "De Emperor. Dat's an enlightened man. It also mean a good father-child relationship. You get a long wit your daddy?"

"He's been dead five years."

"But not forgotten, I bet," she winked again before turning the next card.

"Mmm, ten of wands. Aw baby, ya lost ya hope?" she inquired. The idea she mentioned his fiancée's name was eerie, but it could have been a coincidence coming from a typical fortune teller's vague question. Not wanting to admit that he had indeed lost both Hope and hope, Hunter stayed quiet while Big Mama continued.

"Hmm. Three of swords? See how dey piercin' dat broken heart dere. Now, you ain't got no ring, but ya got yourself a girl?" she asked.

Another semi-safe assumption for a fortuneteller, given the desperate mindset of those seeking help. He kept his answers as vague as her questions.

"No. No I don't."

"Awwww, a handsome, smart boy like you ain't got no girl? Das a shame, baby. Deys telling me you had a girl, but ya pay no mind about her. She weren't right for ya never-no-how." Big Mama then drew the next three cards. Strangely, they were the eight, nine and ten of swords. Each card's picture alone looked disturbing She leaned back in her chair, staring at him much like all the citizens of Derby had earlier in the day.

"Baby! What goin' on in dat head of yours?" she asked shocked.

"I'm guessing swords aren't good?" he asked.

"Well dey can be baby, but..." she paused. "We shuffled dem cards and got 'em at random. Dese be da cards da spirits want ya to see." Big Mama sighed heavily. Hunter could tell she was choosing her words carefully.

"Ya overwhelmed wit' grief. Trapped like dis here lady," she said pointing to the card depicting a bound woman surrounded by eight swords. "And da nine of swords; see how he in so much pain and so scared? He havin' nightmares.

As frightening as pictures on the eight and nine of swords

were, the ten of swords told a grisly story. It portrayed a man lying in a pool of blood with ten swords stuck firmly in his back and neck.

"It be dis one dat bothers me, baby," she moaned ominously. "Ya done bottomed out, ain't ya? What say we keep going? Dere bound to be sometin' good here," she prayed as she reached for the next card; the Queen of Cups.

"Oooooh, who be dis? Dis ain't dat girl," she said pointing to the three of swords card that she said referred to Hope.

"Uh, I don't know," Hunter answered dismayed, still reeling from the bad news of the previous three cards.

"Well, ya keep your eyes open. Maybe she who ya huntin' fo," Big Mama breathed a small sigh of relief before turning the next card.

"Hmm. Wheel of Fortune," she whispered concerned. "Baby, dis wheel signifies karma and destiny and how dere be cycles in ya life; good and bad." Hunter could see how grueling this reading was for Big Mama; even more so than it was for him since she had the understanding and experience of knowing each card's deeper meaning. As punishing as it may have been, she tried to hide it; until she turned over the last card.

"Death," she murmured.

"Death!" Hunter repeated alarmed. "I came here to be told my life sucks and I'm going to die?"

"Now hold on baby. Ol' Death's about a...metaphorical death," she struggled unconvincingly. "See here how it follows da Wheel of Fortune? Ya 'member what all I said 'bout karma and cycles?" Just as her expounded explanation calmed him, she continued, "Course, it *could* be a literal death I 'spose," she conceded.

Hunter's head fell to the table in defeat. Big Mama quickly picked up the rest of the deck and fanned them out in her hands. "No-no-no, none of dat baby. Here, ya take one mo card, and I'm sure da spirits gonna be mo kind," she said as if requesting the spirits to be gentle.

"There's no Dismemberment or Go to Hell card is there?" he asked worried.

"Wait-a-minute," she said flipping through the deck. "We

take dis one out, just in case" she explained, discarding the Devil card.

Hunter's hand was trembling, going back and forth unsure of which card to pick. Finally, he picked a card and covered his eyes.

Then Big Mama Aristides smiled. "See dat baby? You got da World card."

Still thinking about the previous cards, Hunter showed his discouragement. Big Mama Aristides, however, was quick with hopeful insight. "Hey, look at me boy," she ordered. "You think you all alone out dere wit ya hunting, but ya ain't," she advised, "ya got dat aura all around ya. I can see it. Ya gonna find it baby, and dey gonna help ya."

"They?" he asked skeptically.

"Ya baby. Don't you be worrin' 'bout who 'dey' are. Dey know who dey are," she giggled. "Ya just gotta remember to stop lookin' under rocks for ya answers. Ya keep looking under dem rocks, and sooner or later baby, ya gonna crawl under one, and ain't nobody gonna see ya again. Dat'd be a shame, 'cause ya such a good, good soul. Ya gonna find everyting ya need to know right here," she tenderly added, touching his chest above his heart and staring into his eyes with compassion. After a few moments of quiet reflection, she continued her reading.

"Okay, now baby ya know about da Phoenix bird? He got himself all burned up, nuttin' left but ashes. But ya know what? He rose up again from his ashes better dan ever. Ya gonna be like dat ol' Phoenix bird."

"Really?" he replied with feigned interest.

"Oh yeah, baby, ya gonna be just fine. See, sometimes ya be living good, but sometimes baby, fate and the Good Lawd got sometin' else in store for ya. But da good Lawd, He don't waste good souls and He don't let good souls waste demselves. He gots sometin planned for ya," she reaffirmed. "But baby, maybe like dat ol' Phoenix bird, ya gotta hit rock bottom 'fore dat's gonna happen," she continued, tapping the ten of swords.

"Rock bottom?" he repeated uneasily.

"Yes, I'm sorry, baby. It won't be fun, Lawd no, but it'll all be worth it in da end. I promise ya. Ya just gotta find ya faith, baby," she assured him.

Hunter showed his disappointment. Not because Big Mama was vague, but because her reading had been an accurate prognosis.

"Well, baby, thas all I got for ya. Ya pretty cut 'n dried as dey come. Can't say I sees many folk as cut 'n dried and sincere like you. Tell ya what; dis one's on Big Mama. No charge on account dat I done told ya nothin' good. I wouldn't feel right, karma and all. But, ya gotta promise me, ya come back to Big Mama when all dem good things find you. Den we settle up. Deal?"

As they got up from her simple card table, Big Mama Aristides unexpectedly rendered a bone crushing bear hug reassuring him that hardships happens for a purpose, then sent him on his way.

Most people consult psychics to validate or search for signs of good news in the near future — a way to emotionally subsidize their spiritual faith while they wait. Hunter's experience with Big Mama Aristides only reconfirmed what he lost. If that wasn't bad enough, this large medium predicted things were predetermined to get worse. No wonder her business had slowed down.

Back on the streets, he tried imagining the madness required to live in the heart of the sideshow of humanity. New Orleans boasted a vibrant exuberance stemming from loud drunkards and a runaway lack of common morality practiced in the Midwest. Anything goes and nobody thought twice. He passed the depraved, the destitute, the disenfranchised and the wealthy degenerates. Partying women danced in the street, wearing not much more than lingerie; inebriated men stumbled about and relieved themselves anywhere convenient. Passing an extravagant nightclub called 'Chateau Gay', amorous androgynous couples in the street showed little restraint and even less shame.

This city exuding so much charm, elegance and mystery seemed overrun by the ambitionless whose garish, depraved motives were limited to consuming blender drinks and screaming out songs about the beach. They bowed to the altar of common hedonism and their insatiable mantra begged 'more–more–more.' That was the way they liked it here, and he was only a guest. He didn't judge them — quite the opposite. He simply knew he didn't belong there for more than a weekend. Of course, the past few days, he didn't belong anywhere. The more he dwelled on it, the more he realized it had been like this his whole life. He'd always been comfortable with himself; he just never felt comfortable in his environs.

Escaping the masses, Hunter enjoyed taking the long way back to the hotel. New Orleans emitted a distinct quality that generated a prime atmosphere for soul searching. It may have been the uneven cobblestones that lent an air of old world simplicity and unpretentiousness. It could have been the abundance of crosses and the extensive invocations of various Saints. It might have been the steam rising from the street and mixing with the fog creating a dense sticky-sweet ethereal uberworld. Whatever the reason, it reminded him of somber backdrops to film noir detective movies.

Back in his room at the Montgomery, he questioned how a place of such beauty could survive, even flourish, in a city famous for its boorishness. Getting undressed and slipping beneath fine linen sheets, he pondered how the integrity and beauty of a pure heart existed while surrounded by temptation and chaos.

Hunter didn't know it, but as the fourth day of his journey ended, many of the answers he searched for would be revealed very soon.

Chapter Twenty-One
<u>Thursday</u>

An unrelenting pounding of housekeeping roused Hunter up early Thursday morning; something he'd avoided the previous four mornings.

"Come back later," he slurred into his pillow. The maid apologized with an indistinguishable accent and proceeded to her next slumbering victim.

The Montgomery Hotel's bed was by far one of the finest he'd ever slept in, however, that night's sleep had bordered on one of the worst. Waiting to drift off the night before, he tried not to harbor on the day's events, including being arrested, nearly skewered, disowned by his estranged revolutionary brother, had a loaded gun cocked in his face, and then finally told that things were most definitely going to get worse. Instead, he concentrated on his luxurious accommodations at the hotel. Unfortunately, it was impossible to control every small random thought in his mind.

"New Orleans would've been a nice place for a long weekend with Hope," his mind ambled.

That pushed the ball rolling in the wrong direction again, and his anxiety rapidly snowballed at the speed of thought. He worried how large a fortune he was spending for one night in that room. Then he reminded himself to monitor his money better since he wasn't making any.

Why not?

Because he got fired by his boss.

Who?

The father of the woman who humiliated him at the altar in front of hundreds of his friends.

Oh yeah.

Furthermore, even the coldest setting on the Montgomery's malfunctioning air conditioner couldn't off-set the smothering heat and oppressive humidity in New Orleans that night. So for a few frustrating hours, flipping around in fine linen sheets, he tried not to dwell on melodramatic scenarios of doom. He flirted with the idea of breaking into the mini-bar and depleting its supply of mini booze bottles, but if a tiny bag of cashews cost $8, there was no telling how much the hotel would gouge him for a shot of liquor. But as the night crept by he managed to doze off, only to be awakened a few hours later by a maid with a knock so loud and resolute, it made falling back asleep futile. For being 'on vacation', he hadn't done much resting.

Deciding what to wear that morning was easy, however, since he was down to the last of his casual clothes worthy of all day driving. Because the past four days were supposed to have been spent on a beach or in a bed, there wasn't much use in packing a lot of clothes. Regardless, if driving all day was going to remain comfortable, getting some laundry done would have to be a priority.

Checking out of the Montgomery Hotel, concerns about spending too much were validated after receiving a second dose of sticker shock in three days. He still had a fair amount of cash. There was no reason to panic, but he didn't see any more upscale hotels in his near future — especially since it was unclear what lay ahead or how long this impromptu journey would take.

Back in his Mustang, he began considering an aggressive approach to finding a resolution to this excursion. He thought about his friends. He thought about his mother; wondering what the right time frame between personal freedom and maternal concern was before calling her again. Still, he knew it wasn't time to stop yet, so back on I-10, heading west.

Some jealous men, they tell a cynical story
To keep you scared, so they can keep the glory.
And other men, you know, they think it's funny
To make you think your job's in their land of milk and honey.
So don't hand me no line about dangers on the road.
Because I'll be fine out there when I find Tom Joad.

After passing Baton Rouge, venturing deeper into rural Louisiana, the swamps and magnolia trees bordering the highway gave off the truest freshness he'd ever smelled. Old, splintered wooden signs along the road advertised 'gator' this and 'gator' that. Hunter scoffed at himself for presuming the South began somewhere around the middle of Illinois. Not even Alabama or Mississippi gave off such a rustic, provincial and unpretentious impression. Still, this backwoods scenery change alienated him, sparking his need for control and further accentuated his worries of no direction.

Like the tires on his car, Hunter's mind spun rapidly with no apparent beginning or end. Perplexed expressions proceeded in perfect lockstep, like Pavlovian ratchets steadily circling the same hub. An unending vicious cycle where the problems create the angst, and the angst invites more problems. His musings ran rampant, like a renegade carnival ride in zero gravity; an M.C. Escher roller coaster mocking reality so that up is down, backwards is forwards and normal is absurd. Like a greased ball bearing on a gyroscope keeping the wheel spinning, defying even the laws of physics demanding that they eventually stop.

But unlike the tires, his ponderings made no forward progress.

"Hey, did you feel that?" Peter asked sitting shotgun again.

"Feel what?" Hunter responded, eyes still on the road. The need to acknowledge the spirit had since faded.

"The weight of the whole world just landed in this car. I bet that screws up your gas mileage," Peter added with a chuckle. Hunter too, couldn't resist snickering before turning serious again.

"Where the hell am I going?" he asked rhetorically. "I have no direction. Why am I even here?"

"You think you're different from anybody else?" Peter retorted. "Everybody asks, 'Who am I? Where am I going?' The only difference between you and them, is you don't have any distractions to keep you from obsessing about it."

"That's another thing. When did you become so philosophical and profound?" Hunter asked. "You never talked like this when you were alive."

158

"Death has its advantages," his father replied.

"It's just...I've lost everything important to me," he continued.

"So," Peter queried, "you still think you've lost everything that defines you?"

"Yes," Hunter admitted.

"All right, tell me," Peter inquired, "What defines you? Your job? A wife or lover? Are you defined by other's opinions?" Peter asked with emphasis. "All that labels the surface, but does it define a man? You know how I'm defined as a man? I'm dead," Peter replied, demonstrating his own aptitude for noting the obvious. Hunter admired his father's knack of reducing anything to its simplest core and wished he could apply that technique to his situation.

"My life turned out to be a big lie," he confessed. "I could point to things and say, 'that's me, that's who I am and what I do.' I could depend on some things. Now I find my entire identity was blindly walking a thin, fragile line. The things I embraced, rejected me, and the rejection hurts the most."

"The rejection hurts the most?" Peter questioned.

"Yes; and the loss..."

"A guy walks into a psychiatrist's office. 'Doc,' he says, 'I've suffered from rejection my whole life. In school, classmates and teachers rejected me. When I got older, co-workers and bosses rejected me. Worst of all, women rejected me my whole life. The important people I wanted to impress all rejected me.' So the doctor looks up from his notes, rubs his eyes and says, 'Yeah? Well, why don't you tell somebody who cares?'"

Hunter furrowed his brow and scowled. "You've gotten very annoying in your death," he said.

"Don't you get it? The only people you have to worry about impressing are the same people you don't have to worry about impressing. They don't care. They like you because they already like you. Just keep being you and don't worry about rejection, because you already know."

Hunter silently pondered his father's advice for fifteen seconds, but needed more clarity. "Because I already know...what?"

"What?" his father asked confused, assuming his point had been clear.

"What? What is it I already know?"

Peter sighed. "You are dangerously close to being rejected by me right now," he muttered. "Because you already know, you. You already know what's important to the people who are important to you, and they know what's important to you. They know your strengths and weaknesses. You shouldn't have to worry about opening up to those you love, and you shouldn't have to worry about exposing vulnerabilities to them either. If you still feel the need to impress somebody, ask yourself, 'Is it really important if I impress this person?' If it doesn't matter, congratulations, it doesn't matter. If you're trying to impress somebody who doesn't know you well, that's okay. That's how new relationships are formed. Just be aware of why you think it's important that they know," Peter finished with a vocal flourish. After a few seconds, he added, "Just don't be a jackass all the time."

"Where was this well of wisdom when I needed it twenty years ago?" Hunter asked annoyed. "I wish I could start over from scratch," he added.

"You can start from scratch," Peter stressed. "You say you have nothing; you've lost everything? If that's true, then I can't think of a better opportunity to start over."

"Yeah?" Hunter flippantly asked. "Where's the coin slot? The rewind button?"

"Think of yourself as a chain," Peter began. "Who you are is only as strong as the weakest link. Identify the weak link; maybe you have unresolved issues. It could be a bad temper or an addiction. Maybe you need culture. Maybe you should examine your spiritual life or social attitudes. You might have to reinvent yourself altogether; it could be anything. You find the link, take it out and work on it. Forge it so it's stronger and replace it. Then move on to the next. Eventually, all your links are stronger. So since there's always a weak link, you keep growing and improving. Yes, it could mean going backward or starting over, but sometimes that's better than living like a king. You'll know everything is yours, plus you get the benefit of doing everything for the first time again with the knowledge of previous mistakes. You get a clean slate, but with wisdom," he stressed. "That is the most enviable situation out there. So what if you don't get the country club or a wife to fill a house with expensive trinkets? Chances are, guys at the club would kill for that opportunity. And those trinkets that show 'you've made it'? One day you'd look around and notice they're tarnished, rusted, moth-eaten and didn't reflect the real you anyway. Your house becomes a shrine to avarice. Empty. Filled with accessories you can't use because you're too busy admiring them with blinded eyes."

Hunter quietly contemplated his father's latest lesson. It was simple and it was true. Still, what amazed him so profoundly, even more than his father's pan astral visitations, was the idea that Peter had become in death what he expected from a father; a wise sage dispensing advice, wisdom and truisms to teach and better his progeny.

There had always been lessons taught in the Damon home. The usual lessons passed from father to son to instill survival instincts and rules of civility. The axioms he'd learned these past few days were more profound than all that, and yet Hunter sensed they were so basic he should have known them all along. Like what Peter said about 'life being simpler once layers of confusion get peeled away.'

He fantasized about how different life might have been had his father given this insight while alive. Their home characterized the cornerstone of civility, integrity, respectability and grace. However, it lacked the more tender emotions. Shows of affection came easily and were genuine, but Hunter could not recall one time, the phrase, 'I love you' being uttered. Why do families withhold this most vital information from the exact loved ones who need it most? Certainly not out of hatred, jealousy or spite. Maybe the lack of emotional display comes from misdirected fear. The fallacy that exhibiting feelings or admitting vulnerability and devotion reveals a weak character — an Achilles heel of the heart left open to exploit. It made no logical sense, but something deep inside him convinced him there was credence in this theory. If not, then why was he having so much trouble expressing what he wanted to say?

Caught up in the moment, Hunter decided to fulfill a lifelong ambition.

"Dad, can I tell you something?" he asked.

"Sure, son," Peter replied.

"I love you dad," he said, his eyes staring straight at the road.

"I know you do boy. I know you do."

He expected an equally emotional reply after taking the risk of opening up, but his father had vanished again. Peter's response was reassuring and had delivered another lesson. Hunter smiled and shook his head.

"We do the best we can, with what we've got," he reminded himself, having no idea of the power of such a simple sentiment.

Chapter Twenty-Two

A few bucks means you're entitled, well it ain't that way with
me.
The privilege of excess comes with responsibility.
So the poor strangers you point at whose lives are tough
They're all your relatives if you go back far enough
Hey, I don't know your name, I don't know your life.
I don't know who's to blame, I don't know your strife.
I see your hungry heart when I look in your eyes
So you gotta know, buddy, I sympathize.
And I know a lousy dollar ain't gonna turn the tide
But at least one day, you'll have Jesus on your side

Louisiana was a fascinating state for about 100 miles. After 150 miles, it got depressing. To be fair to the good citizens of the Pelican state, Hunter's sour demeanor was caused less by the countryside's austerity and more because of overcast skies late that morning. He counted himself among those whose attitudes changed depending upon the weather conditions. Added to the dreary lack of color in the sunless sky was the ubiquitous humidity defining Louisiana more than Friday night crawfish boils. However, the gray sky wasn't the only ingredient in his melancholy. Since first asking himself how long his journey might last, his sole answer was a vague, 'it'll last as long as it has to last.' Hardly a comforting conclusion, considering the United States is a big country, and he'd only traveled through nine states...so far. Again, there was still cash to hold him for a while if he watched his spending, and of course he still had the 'generous' severance check from Paul Jones. How could he forget that? It was one more albatross pulling his neck down, and the idea of cashing it made him nauseous. Keeping the money would mean meekly backing away; denying his love for Hope — admitting it had been a fraud. The bastards of the world would have won.

Not long after reflecting how he'd traveled through nine states, he crossed into the tenth. Texas.

Like many northerners, Hunter had never been to Texas. Like most northerners, he envisioned a fabled land of swaggering giants wearing boots, hats, and six-shooters. Like all northerners, he would claim he hated Texas. He didn't know why, it just became a trendy target for northerners who love rooting for underdogs. If there's one thing Texas is not, it's an underdog. Texas represents opportunity. Texas represents resources and a spirit of individual achievement. And after examining the map, Texas represented pretty damn close to a thousand miles.

His introduction to the Lone Star State was Beaumont, a fairly sizable city he'd never heard of. He knew the major Texas cities: Dallas, Fort Worth, Houston, San Antonio and El Paso. Even the next tier of cities like Abilene, Lubbock and Waco, sneaked into popular folklore and news. Beaumont didn't show much of a skyline; mostly scores of industrial park-style buildings sprawled over nearly every acre. Still, if previously unknown Texas towns were this substantial, it's probably true that everything is bigger in Texas.

It didn't take long to understand that Beaumont's size was attributed as a glorified suburb of the mega-sprawling Houston. That wasn't a negative reflection of Beaumont as much as an observation about Houston. And the closer he got to Houston, the more he knew he was in Texas. The flat, ceaseless landscape exploded with oil derricks, a metaphor of its power and energy. The controlled rhythm of fulcrums was swiveling and gyrating, plunging their rods deep into the shuddering mounds, driving down, trying to release the pressure. Patiently waiting for the violent eruption of precious sweet liquid crude. "That about sums up Texas," he thought.

Like previous cities so far, Houston's skyline appeared all at once, like magic. One second he couldn't see it, the next second it appeared to bloom in full view. The central core of buildings sat clustered together, suggesting they'd be built within a few years during an economic boon. It had the cohesive appearance other skylines had, coming together as one enormous entity, but it lacked any amount of character. In size and numbers, the skyline was overwhelming; somehow though, it missed a defining element. Just steel and glass giants. Clearly the architects attempted to put artistic designs onto each building. Strangely, however, even the differences seemed similar.

With over two dozen skyscrapers, Houston's skyline was easily the largest he'd passed through. While Hunter was no architect, since hitting the road and noticing each city's first impressions, he learned it was easy to judge the citizens by their downtown. From an aesthetic viewpoint, Houston presented itself as an enormous, proud blue-collar town with little regard for anything interesting. Not that it looked ugly, quite the contrary. It was impressive — just not inspiring. These skyscrapers were simply too new and too unimaginative. In 70 years, if each building remained, aged, then became surrounded by new ideas, it might develop a little character. As it stood, this skyline was reminiscent of newly developed subdivision lots with a single sapling in each yard.

Houston was remarkably unremarkable. It lacked the elite feeling of New York City, the glamour of Los Angeles, the sensibility of Chicago, the style of San Francisco and the history of Philadelphia or Boston. It even failed to deliver the cowboy maverick business image of Dallas. Houston was just...there. In all its large, impressive mediocrity, this gargantuan skyline sprung up to be definitely and undeniably... there. An anonymous giant — an imposing figure with power and strength to shape, manipulate and change lives that the average Joe couldn't pick out of a lineup. And judging by appearances, zoning wasn't a priority in America's fourth largest city.

Driving past the oil refineries shed some light upon how this town grew so huge. Houston was, in large part, responsible for the growth of America during the 20th Century. Its refined black gold and gasoline encouraged people to travel cross-country to find their collective selves. Later, Houston guided America in another direction as the cream of the country's brightest engineering and aeronautic minds convened to undertake the space missions. Hunter's father often mentioned his days at the Space Center, but he rarely referred to the city. Houston was vital and important yet easily forgotten.

Constant oil references reminded him that since traveling close to 1500 miles so far, an oil change was not only a good idea before subjecting his car to the intense searing heat of the Southwest, but overdue. Exiting the highway onto a main artery on the western edge of downtown, it didn't take long to find a Lube-it-all®. Twenty minutes later another mundane task was taken care of and a little peace of mind ensured.

Pulling out of the service bay, he spotted a laundromat across the street. It seemed crazy to do laundry in an unfamiliar town, but nothing about the past five days had been sane. Besides, it needed to be done and there wasn't a familiar town within a thousand miles.

Hunter hadn't been to a laundromat in years, but it all came back. He staked out his territory, changed a few dollars into quarters, and bought detergent from the 'Laundromat Service Centre' (a vending machine selling a small choice of laundry supplies and a large selection of stale candy). The more things changed, the more Laundromats remained the same. The same TV tuned to the same trash shows; the same video games to help pass the tedium while liberating customers of more quarters. The same people slumped in the same plastic chairs, reading the same magazines. The alternative couples with outrageous hair, the college students, the middle-aged women guarding their laundry supplies and the random weird guy holding a philosophy book so everybody can see it. Even the same lint. No matter what gets washed, or where, lint is always the same shade of blue.

During the wash cycle, he amused himself with old entertainment magazines. When the wash cycle finished, his clothes smelled nicer. Mission accomplished; one more chore completed. Give his clothes about 45 minutes in the dryer, and he'd be back on the road.

Watching clothes tumble in the dryer held his attention for about ten seconds before he settled back with the special edition Envy!® celebrity gossip magazine. As he finished an unnecessary article about a recent unnecessary $1,000,000 Hollywood wedding, the 'ding' of the front door distracted him. Inside walked a very tall man dressed in clothes, which had not been fashionable in years, or clean in weeks. It wasn't the clothes that held his attention, though, as much as the homeless man's gigantic stature. As the bum scanned the Laundromat, targeting customers as an easy touch, Hunter couldn't help but stare, estimating the man towered at least 7'. Then the tall bum made eye contact and he'd been marked. That's the rule. Make eye contact with the homeless and become the mark.

"Hey man, can I ask you something? I'm sorry to bother you, but my car ran out of gas; could you spare a couple dollars?" the giant lied. On the sidewalk, any target could have responded with a standard 'sorry-I-don't-have-spare-change.' Unfortunately, this was a laundromat. Customers in laundromats have pockets filled with quarters. Not wanting to get caught in a lie as obvious as the bum's, Hunter grabbed several quarters from his pocket, as a fair price to maintain his honesty.

"Yeah, here you go," he replied dropping the change in the bum's oversized palm. However, as Hunter glanced way up into the man's face, he seemed familiar. He'd seen that face before and for a few seconds didn't know where. Upon processing the obvious fact that this guy stood seven feet tall, it dawned on him that behind the dirty hair and beard, this bum was former professional all-star basketball player Manuel Montrose.

"Hey wait-a-minute. Are you...?"

"No, I'm not," the man interrupted, as if he was tired of answering that question.

Hunter squinted, scrutinizing the man's face and hands. "Yes you are," he argued. "You're Manuel Montrose."

"So what if I am? You gonna give me another quarter, Mr. Big Spender?"

Manuel Montrose was the epitome of everything wrong and tragic with pro sports and greed. A one-time legend, he'd catapulted into the national spotlight as an All-American his junior and senior years at the University of Michigan. After his college eligibility ended, he went as the second overall pick in the draft to the Houston pro basketball team.

Manuel yielded immediate results, rocketing his team into the play-offs his first season, garnering 'Rookie of the Year' honors in the meantime. He averaged only seven points per game, but he dominated the boards with an astounding 18.5 rebounds per game. An extraordinary mastery of leaping from three feet inside the free throw line to grab rebounds earned him the nickname 'Flying Ebony' and guaranteed fans a performance of equal parts freak show-superhuman ability. Opposing teams dreaded playing Houston and the physical abuse at the flailing hands, reckless elbows, knees and dangerous feet of Manuel Montrose.

As is the case too many times, his fast fame, fortune and success had been way too much, way too easy and way too soon. After a stellar five seasons, posting potential Hall of Fame stats, Manuel Montrose got carried away with the press stories and lost his focus. He forgot he was simply a guy whose job was to grab the basketball when it didn't go in the hoop, and he started to believe he towered over not only the game, but also life itself. Omnipresent groupies and ravenous parasites led to outrageous parties, which led to destructive binges, which led to repeated brushes with the law and numerous rehab stints.

It wasn't long before the team owners came to their senses, realizing that Manuel's destructive personality was more a disruption to the team than his talent entitled him. But before they had a chance to unload him, his massive salary and his destructive ego, every other general manager in the league had labeled him a 'head-case.' Despite his incredible potential and abilities, no team dared to take a chance on Manuel Montrose. Bouncing around minor basketball leagues and European leagues for a couple years, his reckless escapades were just as frequent, only not as publicized, until one day, he became a 'whatever happened to' has-been. Now, Hunter knew what happened to Manuel Montrose; he'd been reduced to begging for quarters in a laundromat. Like Houston, Manuel had become an anonymous giant.

"I saw you play in college. I went to Minnesota. You kicked our ass every year."

Manuel's eyes lit up. A slight smile appeared under his

bushy, dirty mustache as he remembered years of glory like they were a lifetime ago. Hunter wanted to ask, 'what the hell happened', but spared Manuel the humiliation of reliving his downfall. Chances were he'd replayed his mistakes in his head every day since his contract was voided from the bottom-rung league. Regardless, Manuel beamed after coming face-to-face with someone who remembered his great skill in the days long before he fought off rats in the trash for a spoiled McWhatever[®].

"You saw me play in college?" Manuel asked.

"We were in school the same four years," Hunter replied.

As the novelty of meeting someone who remembered his celebrity status waned, his survival instincts returned. He stared at his mark, anticipating more money, until after much awkward silence, Hunter felt compelled to ask something, for no other reason than to break the long pause.

"So, did you like our arena?" he asked.

"I don't know. Yeah, it was all right, I guess." Manuel replied, searching his mind over ten years to recall one particular college arena.

Hunter searched his memory of experiences to find mutual ground, but the more he avoided asking, 'what the hell happened', the more pedestrian his comments became.

"They had the best hotdogs there."

Manuel didn't respond.

More uncomfortable moments passed as they stood there staring at each other with separate agendas. Hunter wanted to know what happened, and Manuel Montrose wanted more money. Finally, Manuel broke the deadlock.

"So, you gonna give me more money?" Manuel asked.

"What the hell happened?" Hunter demanded.

Manuel's reaction turned to annoyed indignation, masking his shame.

"Aw man, I ain't gotta explain nothin' to you. Who you think you are? If you ain't gonna give me money..." he said turning away.

"Wait a minute," Hunter interrupted. "Manuel...Manuel, tell you what. I've got almost an hour before my clothes dry. What do you say we get lunch?"

"Where we goin'?" Manuel questioned as if his decision depended upon the restaurant.

"Uh, I don't know," Hunter answered, taken aback, "wherever you want," he continued diplomatically. Manuel mulled the offer over then nodded.

"Okay," Manuel agreed. "There's a place four doors down. They treat me real good there."

Initially worried about leaving his clothes unattended in a run-down Houston laundromat dryer, the value of a story of buying lunch for a homeless ex-basketball superstar far exceeded some worn out casual clothes from the Old Banana Crew® store. Once outside, Manuel retreated behind some tall garbage cans in the alley beside the building where he retrieved a shopping cart filled with his belongings. Hunter looked at the cart's contents, making a mental manifest of the fallen star's kingdom. A pile of newspapers, two plastic buckets, a filthy pillow, assorted soda cans, a shoebox, some rags and a couple of shirts that might have been used as rags. Shocked that the sum of this once great man's empire had dwindled to a cumulative value less than a few dollars, he felt relieved there was no sign of liquor bottles, beer cans or drugs.

On their way to the restaurant, both men grew more conscious of their prominent polarity — a study of complete opposites. One average-sized, casually dressed, well-groomed white man strolling with his shoulders back, and one gargantuan, unkempt black man shuffling slowly, hunkered over as he struggled to push his empire in a stolen grocery cart over small stones on the sidewalk. As different as they seemed, they had more in common than each was aware of. Each man thought he'd lost everything important. With a lot of listening and a little luck, perhaps they could help each other.

Chapter Twenty-Three

Manuel's boast of being well treated at the Gallahadion Diner was misleading at best. The management tolerated him more than anything, and that was only because of his historic heroics as the city's premier sports star almost a decade earlier. When Manuel did scrounge up enough cash to indulge on the relative luxury of a sit-down meal, they relegated him far away from the rest of the clientele for fear his putrid stench might offend others. The hostess, showing surprise when he came in with a well-groomed stranger, quickly escorted them to his usual table near the kitchen and bathrooms. The table was surrounded by a half-dozen action photos of Manuel during his playing days and framed copies of yellowing newspapers praising his exploits.

The two studied the menu when an impatient waitress with blue hair came to take their orders. She kept an awkward distance from the duo, holding a napkin to her nose to avoid Manuel's rank odor.

"Hello Manny. Deluxe hamburger plate and water?" she asked, obviously annoyed with waiting on him.

"No, today I want the steak platter, with water," he replied, glancing to Hunter for permission.

"You got enough for that, Manny?" she asked as if he'd stiffed her before when he couldn't pay a tab.

"I'm picking up the check," Hunter chimed in. "I'll have the same, with an iced tea, please," he told the waitress.

Curious why Manuel just wanted water, Hunter asked him about it.

"I drink a lot of water," Manuel answered. "'Bout the only thing I drink to stay hydrated in this damn Houston heat," he continued, noticing Hunter's surprise. "You think I'm a drunk, don't you?" he smiled. "You think I'm gonna take your money and just go for gin and juice like some bum, don't you? Man, I ain't like them winos and crack heads. I don't touch that shit no more. I been straight almost two years. Two goddamn years. Cold turkey."

"Cold turkey? Must've been tough," Hunter sympathized.

"Shit yeah, it was tough. Spent three days in the hospital. Didn't have no choice," his voice wavered between pride and regret.

"Manuel, what really happened?" Hunter asked even though Manuel's exploits were well publicized.

"Hell, you know what happened. I partied, messed up and got kicked-out."

"But you're clean now, right? Why this?"

"A ban is a ban. Ain't nobody interested in me no more, anyway. The league sold some tickets, chewed me up, took what they could outta my ass, then spit me out," he stated morosely. "They already busy chewing up and sucking dry new kids," he chuckled with cynicism. "'Sides, I don't have skills I used to. The league ain't gonna touch me less I got something to offer. I ain't got that no more."

As Hunter unwrapped a packet of saltine crackers from a basket on the table and popped them in his mouth, Manuel grabbed a huge handful of the free crackers and stuffed them in his pockets.

"It's funny," Manuel continued with a tinge of resentment, "when I was drunk and high, the press followed me everywhere. We'd party at bars, dance at clubs. Hell, I paid their tabs. They watched my every move and printed their stories like my life was a damn circus report. Freak Show Central. They watched me slip down every rung, treated it like some joke. They counted on it; they prayed for it. People love them stories, and the journalists spoon fed 'em." Hunter looked away in shame, admitting to himself that he was one of those people.

"The lower I'd fall, less and less people cared. Can't say I blame anybody but myself, but when I got sober by myself, nobody cared. No press conference. No paparazzi dogging me then. That wasn't newsworthy. So, I live on the street," he expressed with shameful pride. "It's a long-ass fall from the penthouse to the street." Staring off over Hunter's shoulder in a melancholic daze, the steady timber of his voice turned desperate. "The worst part is, I remember what the penthouse looks like. I know how soft the towels are and how cool the sheets feel," he recalled as his eyes glazed over, as if pure concentration could magically transport him back. "Did you know, in hotels, the women got better looking the higher-up your room was," he reminisced as if the memories of his dalliances were as perfectly focused as when they happened. After a regretful pause, he rubbed his eyes, returned to reality and continued.

"People used to run up for my autograph all the time, like it meant something," he chuckled. "It was a trip, man. The more stuff I signed, the more they loved me. 'Here Manny, sign this ball because we love you.' 'Thanks Manny, you're my son's hero.' 'Manny, Houston needs you and appreciates everything you've done.' Now they don't even look me in the eye. They just see a tall bum. Sometimes, I wonder how many of them people who look away are the same people who waited by the locker room wanting a piece of my ass back then."

In a flash of inspiration, Hunter asked, "Manuel, what would you do if you had some money?"

"Shit man, I don't know. That depends."

"How?" he cryptically inquired.

"Well," Manuel reflected, "when I get five bucks or so, I get a meal. Ten bucks and I come here. After a good couple of days, if I have, say $50, I'd get a haircut and a room at the hotel for a night and take a shower." He smiled a distant smile. "I miss hot showers."

"What if you had $10,000?" Hunter asked with a straight face. Manuel, however, burst out laughing.

"Shiiiiit," he chuckled, "Man, ain't a lot of people shelling out more than a couple of bucks to a broke down homeless ex-ball player."

"Seriously though," Hunter pressed him.

"Okay," Manuel answered sincerely. He raised his chin and squinted his eyes, trying to visualize himself with that kind of money once again. After a few seconds, he answered. "With ten grand," he paused, "I'd get cleaned up, buy new clothes, hop on a bus and go to the casino."

"You would take a sure $10,000, go to the casino and risk

losing it all?"
Hunter asked stunned.

"Muthafucka, what do you think I got to lose? My cans? My dignity?" Manual chuckled again, "It ain't like we talking 'bout real money."

"Maybe," Hunter said under his breath.

"You wanna know something?" Manuel continued, "My peak year, I pulled in $10,000,000. Ten million dollars! I had no idea how much money that was. They didn't teach that at Ann Arbor," he paused with a smile. "Now, if I had one percent of that shit...one percent," he emphasized," I could rebuild my entire life. I have ideas and I know what money means now. But the farther you fall, the more you need to get out. Nobody, and I mean nobody, wants to take a risk on an old junkie, no matter who he was, if all he has is a few dollars and promises. Shit, I used up my chances, but you show up with $100,000, someone will notice you."

Hunter listened to his fallen companion's rationale. It sounded crazy, but made sense in a cynical-real-world way. To ease his mind, he had to ask the obvious question.

"You wouldn't blow it on booze and drugs?"

"Man, I don't expect you to believe me, and I don't care if you do or don't. You're just a nice guy buying me lunch and all. But it took me a long time to feel good again now that I'm clean."

Scrutinizing Manuel with the giddiness of a disciple listening to his mentor, this was unadulterated experience from someone who'd been high in an ivory tower and deep in the trenches. Up to that point, he thought enlightenment must have equaled personal achievement.

"You can't be happy with this life, though?" Hunter grilled.

Manuel looked at him not with contempt, but with confusion that someone could ask him that.

"What is wrong with you, man? I just got through telling you I don't have nothing except who I am, who I was and what I had. Now, I ain't got nothing, and no matter how tall I am it's a long way to the first rung. You wondering if I can be happy with my life? What do you think?" he lectured.

The food arrived in the nick of time to help the duo avoid

more awkward talk. Manuel's rank aroma nearly quelled Hunter's appetite, but thankfully, the tantalizing smell from the two sizzling steaks masked the stale stench. The conversation lagged as the men ate their lunches, until the check came. Manuel thanked his host and started to leave, making sure he wasn't going to have to pay. Convinced of Manuel's sincerity and need for a second chance, Hunter assured him he had no obligation and asked him to stay.

"I've got a proposition for you." Hunter quickly suggested. Intrigued, yet suspicious, Manuel slid back into his seat. Only minutes earlier he stole free crackers and admitted to nothing to lose.

"Uh huh?" he responded cynically.

"This is going to sound crazy, but I'd like to give you $10,000."

"Yeah, you're right, that sounds crazy. Thanks for lunch, but my cart is double parked," he joked.

"I'm serious. Listen, I have a check for $10,000 in my car, and I don't want it. Well, I want it, but...it's a complicated story, and I don't want to tell it anymore. Long story made short, this money would help you a lot more than I want it."

"Man, you ain't a fag are you? I don't do fag stuff."

"I don't want anything from you. I just don't like how I got this money," Hunter stated emphatically. He knew it sounded crazy, but he also knew it was something he had to do quickly before realizing exactly how crazy it was. The two men stared in disbelief at each other; one amazed that a stranger was offering $10,000 with no strings attached, the other befuddled why the first man wasn't jumping at the opportunity. Getting impatient, he pressed Manuel.

"Do you want it or not?" he demanded.

"Well, yeah. Okay. I mean, if you don't want it...sure I'll take it," Manuel replied confused, not entirely believing there was a $10,000 check, but willing to go along just in case.

After paying the tab, Hunter jogged to his car and retrieved the envelope. Manuel lagged behind and the two reconvened in the laundromat. Relieved to get it out of his car, Hunter pulled the check halfway out of the envelope, proving its existence. Manuel gaped at the check, hypnotized by the four zeros in a row, smiling as if seeing old friends he hadn't seen in awhile.

"Do you have a bank account?" Hunter asked.

"Sure," Manuel replied with sarcasm "at the same bank where I keep my good cans in my safety deposit box."

"If you carry $10,000 wrapped in a paper bag in a shopping cart, you're a marked man," he thought out loud.

"Ain't nobody gonna give me shit," Manuel interrupted, "I got street sense. I been out here a long time and ain't never been rolled. Some out of respect. Most because they're afraid of me. I busted some serious ass grabbing rebounds."

After several minutes of a one-sided argument while Hunter folded his clothes, he gave in and agreed to give Manuel cash. He didn't care; he just wanted the check gone before he changed his mind about giving it away.

"Okay," he said tentatively, "we'll do it your way. But I don't have a bank down here."

Manuel's eyes lit up, realizing he was one step closer to $10,000. Still, he remained calm and told his patron where they could cash the check.

While the neighborhood could not be described as 'glitzy', 'rough' would have been harsh. However, in many borderline neighborhoods, check-cashing stores are a standard fixture where people can cash checks for a convenience fee.

They walked two block to the check-cashing store and buzzed the security door to get in. The line wasn't too long, just long enough for them to feel uncomfortable since neither one had anything else to say to the other. Manuel mostly kept a protective eye on his cart. When their turn came, Hunter presented his check.

"Can you cash this check?" he asked holding it against the glass. Behind the bulletproof partition, the teller squinted to read the amount, reacting nonchalantly, as if they cash $10,000 checks every day.

"Sure," she replied in a heavy Mexican accent. "I've got to call it in to verify it and I need to see some ID. And there's a 5% charge."

The check was written on The Smarty-Jones Ad Agency account. Wondering if an amount so large might require confirmation from Paul Jones himself, Hunter fostered a sense of amusement from the horror he guessed Paul will suffer after learning his precious check, a check cut to buy his daughter's freedom, was endorsed at a checking cashing store in a seedy part of Houston. He only hoped he didn't have to talk to the bastard.

The teller made three calls, scribbling notes the entire time. The glass partition muted her conversation, but she nodded a lot, which they took as a good sign. Every second she spent on the phone forced Hunter to contemplate which was crazier; giving $10,000 away, or giving it to a man whose idea of safe-deposit box was a locker at the bus depot.

Finally, the teller hung up the phone and slid the check back through the small tray under the glass.

"Endorse it please," she requested.

"You can cash it?" he asked, genuinely shocked.

"Yeah. How do you want this? Big bills?" she asked getting out a key to open a special drawer. The men tried staying calm, but both men's eyes glazed over and their mouths hung open as she counted out ninety-five $100 bills, and passed them under the glass. Hunter grabbed the bills and, hypnotized by the money for a few seconds, considered keeping the cash. It was blood money, but it was ninety-five hundred dollars' worth of blood money. Reminding himself why he couldn't keep it, and remembering his promise, he closed his eyes, turned and handed the bills to Manuel, who shoved them into his deep pockets to comingle with the crackers. Hunter's integrity had nearly developed a price tag. Ninety minutes earlier, he almost didn't give this man $2. Now, he'd given him close to $10,000.

Upon exiting, Manuel Montrose made a gesture to prove he was a man of sincerity and not a run-of-the-mill homeless man. The value of the contents in his cart equaled nowhere near a fraction of the grant he'd been given, but displaying a show of good faith that hopefully his begging days were over, he grabbed his most personal prized possession as the only way to thank this stranger.

"Here, I want to give you this," he said, extending the dirty shoebox stained with black smudges and greasy fingerprints. Hunter objected at first, but Manuel demanded.

"What is it?" he asked.

Inside the stained, tattered box was a pristine pair of size 17 basketball shoes. Compared to sneakers with more recent innovations, they'd been outdated for years, but they had been well taken care of.

"These were my basketball shoes. I had a contract with a company that kept me in shoes and these are my last pair."

The sentiment was touching, but what he would do with a pair of sneakers at least five sizes too big perplexed him. Tempted to decline, Hunter peered into Manuel's eyes and saw a glimmer of pride, as if these shoes meant millions. To refuse this gift would have crushed his newly revived spirit. He graciously accepted the sneakers, completing their exchange. Shaking Manuel's dirty, oversized hand and wishing him luck, one albatross flew from his neck. That check was less of a severance from his job, but more of a severance from Hope.

He tucked the shoebox under his arm and turned to leave.

"Manny, you take care of yourself, okay?" he told him walking away.

"Hey, Mr. Ten Grand," Manuel shouted. "What's your name anyway?"

"Damon. Hunter Damon."

"Hunter Damon," Manuel repeated, committing it to memory. "We did kick Minnesota's ass every year, didn't we?" he added more as a statement of fact than a question.

"Yeah. You sure did, Manny," he replied with a wink and a grin as he got in his car.

Pulling away, he hadn't fully comprehended that he'd given away $10,000. Manuel Montrose hadn't fully comprehended that he was given $10,000 with no strings. Watching the back of the Mustang fade away, Manuel considered moving to Minnesota if people were giving out thousands of dollars.

At one time during his career, Manuel could have spent an easy $10,000 on dinner, drinks and prostitutes. That kind of money was walk-around pocket cash. Now, Manuel was not only grateful, he stood dumbfounded that a stranger just gave him that kind money. He never respected his basketball money. It was too much and he didn't think of the way he earned it as work. He didn't work for this money either, but he had greater respect for it, because this time the sacrifice had been his patron's. It bothered him not to have known the first thing about his benefactor, but as it turned out, the benefactor didn't know himself either.

Holy Spirit

Chapter Twenty-Four

*It's hard enough to get through life without the stumbling
blocks
Looking for success, but all you see are moving hands on
clocks.
(Tick-tock) What have you bought? (Tick-tock) What can you
save?
(Tick-tock) What have you got? (Tick-tock) What do you crave?
(Tick-tock) A little older. (Tick-tock) A lot less brave.
(Tick-tock) A little grayer. One tick-tock closer to the grave.
Validation. Vindication. Compensation. It's all fiction.*

His unscheduled stop in Houston, combined with bumper-to-bumper rush hour traffic, put Hunter far behind where he would have liked. Although there was no timetable or obligations to satisfy, his controlling mindset felt cheated if he hadn't gone close to 500 miles at the end of seven hours of driving. Rather than lose those miles, he decided to make them up with a couple extra hours on the road. Besides, there was still a good deal of daylight left and he was enjoying the unique illusion of a blue landscape from acres of bluebonnets along the highway.

Reflecting on Manuel's plight, it seemed unfathomable for a man to have the world at his fingertips one day then plummet to the depths of anonymous pariah the next. Of course that exact thing happened to him.

Shame washed over Hunter for comparing his trials to a homeless man's. Manuel's ordeal made his own story sound pathetic and his guilt instinct (as well as Big Mama Aristides) assured him life could be worse. Still, the best way to validate the guilt was to wallow in the misery of his losses.

His thoughts turned to Hope and her thick scarlet hair, and how he used to run his hand through it, sometimes hitting a tangle and tugging her head back. He worried that the tugging hurt her, but she assured him it felt nice. He remembered trivial things; how she needed six teaspoons of sugar in her coffee; how she panicked at the sight of any bug inside, or the way she leaned forward at her vanity to put on make-up. And her smile. Her smile was more than a simple facial manipulation expressing joy. It possessed powers to amplify a glowing ember of complacency into a roaring bonfire of rapture. Hope's smile held an angelic perfection that could charm the prince of darkness and convince him to change his ways.

Hope once confessed what she loved most about him was how good he made her feel about herself. A week earlier he was prepared to devote his life to her happiness as if his existence depended upon it. So what changed in her mind? One thing remained certain. He knew he still loved her because he wanted her to be happy wherever she was.

Although his love hadn't changed despite what she did to him, he couldn't deny lingering feelings of pain, confusion and resentment. For a year and a half, she played an essential role in his life as necessary as oxygen, and having no contact with her tortured him. It didn't seem right. The words they shared and the plans they made couldn't have just vanished, could they? How is it possible to tell someone you love them one day, then abandon them the next. It's impossible to plan a lifetime with someone and expect to let them go that easily. It's unrealistic to honestly love somebody, and then 24 hours later think terrible thoughts about them. Not honestly. If that was true, it was not only a reflection on Hope, but to a lesser extent, a tragic reflection on himself.

It bothered him not having any kind of memento to remember her by; a random piece of clothing, a silly prize from a carnival midway game, not even a photograph to stare at while he tried to remember intense passions they shared. All he had were memories and shame. Shame because after less than a week, he had to concentrate a little harder to see her face in his mind; a face so lovely, he wanted to wake up to it every day. Even the memory of her voice had become a far-off echo drowned out by constant wind whooshing into his car and the songs coming from the dash.

Style vs. substance, good vs. bad, peace vs. violence, happy vs.
sad
Black vs. white, night vs. day, flee vs. fight, leave vs. stay
Sedated vs. spastic, ground vs. sky, paper vs. plastic, live vs.
die
Light vs. dark, Heaven vs. Hell, formal vs. stark, buy vs. sell
Some are gonna win, but most are gonna lose.
But everybody plays, so you might as well choose
Left vs. right, right vs. wrong, read vs. write, short vs. long
Rowe vs. Wade, explode vs. fade, club vs. spade, diamond vs.
jade
Jade vs. pearl, cards vs. dice, boy vs. girl, virtue vs. vice
Lead vs. follow, light vs. heavy, spit vs. swallow, Ford vs.
Chevy
It's a game you can't win, a game made up of twos
But everybody's got to play, so you might as well choose
Loss vs. gain, love vs. hate, crazy vs. sane, gay vs. straight
Pain vs. pleasure, mountains vs. beach, work vs. leisure,
silence vs. speech
Stand vs. sit, quit vs. try, stick vs. split, truth vs. lie
Sound vs. sight, trapped vs. free, loose vs. tight, you vs. me
It's designed to confound, perplex, puzzle and confuse.
You don't wanna be left out, so you might as well choose.

Further into its wide-open spaces, Texas became a double-edged sword. The same solitude offering an opportunity to reflect and heal his mind lacked any distraction, making it almost impossible not to obsesses about her. Almost impossible anyway.

"That was a noble deed back there," Peter chimed-in not a moment too soon.

"What? The money?" Hunter replied. "There was no way I was going to keep that money just to ease their conscience," he replied.

"So if that check stood for everything bad to you, what do you think it meant to Manuel Montrose?"

"I don't know. Maybe somebody cares?" he answered.

"Maybe. Hopefully anyway," his father added.

Giving that much money to a bum seemed like a good idea at the time, but second-guessing the idea of subsidizing the mother of all binges quickly filled him with guilt. He imagined watching TV and hearing 'former basketball superstar Manuel Montrose was found dead of an overdose in a Houston back alley with his pockets filled with saltine crackers and $100 bills.' How ironic if people emerged from the woodwork to show love for Manuel Montrose after he was dead. What was done was done, and Hunter learned the hard way that he wasn't responsible for other's behavior. No, you give people the tools they need and have faith they'll do the right thing in their time. Still, Manuel's story rang familiar. The fact that a castle built up to the clouds rests on a fragile foundation, teetering precariously with the slightest breeze, proved terrifying.

Peter sensed his son's growing melancholy. "Okay, you've done this virtuous thing — this amazing act of charity bordering on insane. So what's bugging you?"

"You want to know?" Hunter answered after a reflective moment and a deep breath to collect his thoughts. He wanted to word his frustration in a way that would explain it to his father while simplifying it to himself at the same time. He was about to admit a fatal flaw too painful to think about.

"All right, I'll tell you. You know those success stories about people raised in horrible conditions? People on the wrong side of the tracks with nothing except hopes, dreams and a drive to succeed? They got nothing, but they succeed. They do it," he stressed, and then paused. Once he confessed, the door flung open. "I feel the exact opposite of those people. I had everything and I still couldn't make the pieces come together. I was given all the tools. Every single one. Now I look at me and I have nothing. God dammit that makes me feel guilty. I didn't fail out of complacency or laziness or arrogance; I don't know why. I don't know why I failed."

Peter saw the agony of confusion and frustration in his son's eyes. "Son, what you don't understand is," he paused for emphasis, "you're not using the right definition of success. You haven't failed if you haven't finished. It's a work in progress."

Hunter heard, but pretended not to have. It was easier to assign blame on uncontrollable mysterious forces than reduce his life to an extended experiment. His eyes stared ahead while his father continued.

"Son, sometimes things happen, and other times things don't happen. But somewhere in the middle, the murky gray void between chance and careful planning your destiny is cradled tenderly and gripped violently at the same time. Somewhere in the middle, between last night and tomorrow morning is the concrete reality you try to deny; the real life that contradicts and negates all the lies you've told yourself."

Peter's poetic words distilled eons of philosophies into one basic truth. 'Right now, things are, and you are.' As simple a sentiment as it was, Hunter struggled with his father's sage insight. Many times the undeniable truth, no matter how certain, is confusing. The truth often eliminates easy options, leaving only a small path that would be more convenient to ignore. Once that path is illuminated in plain sight, however, it's impossible to deny. And upon finding that path, only one question remains. Will we take it?'

Peter gave a moment to reflect then continued.

"At the end of the day, we take the bits, scraps and pieces of our lives, and wrap them up to show the world; the good and the bad, the beautiful and the homely, the sane and the surreal — in all their variations and degrees of possibilities. We can package them in a sturdy cardboard box decorated with colorful paper and tied with ribbons, or we can shove them into a plain brown grocery bag and bind them with nylon cord or burlap string. We show that package to the world as our own image, but nobody else can know what's in it. Even if someone peers into our package to see the elements of our psyche, all they see is the surface, like layers of sand covering a treasure chest. It's possible to get inside, but the emotional tools are too expensive, and more than likely, not strong enough to crack it."

Hunter stopped struggling and accepted that the truth is always there, although he wasn't sure what it meant. Wanting to leapfrog his soul searching in favor of the finish line, he asked the end-all-be-all question.

"What's the point of it all?" he asked.

"What's the point?" his father pondered. "The point..." said Peter with a dramatic pause, then chuckled as if he knew a secret, "...is don't worry about what the point is."

He'd expected a cosmic axiom, but got an ambiguous non-answer instead.

"Wait a minute," he protested. "Does that mean, 'there's a point, but I shouldn't try to figure it out?' Or does that mean 'the point itself is not to worry about it if there's a point in the first place?'"

Just like all the other times, his father vanished before he could finish getting out the last few syllables of his thoughts.

"God, that is so annoying," he muttered to himself.

Don't trust tired eyes deep in this grand illusion
And don't believe anything said amidst the confusion
Oh yeah, the best plan for you to start
To search for truth is to trust your heart.

Three hours later, most of the 'lost' miles had been made up. Hunter felt personal satisfaction for achieving his arbitrary progress, but also self-mocking regret for not getting a decent hotel room when he had the chance outside Houston. The muscles in his neck, back and shoulders permanently ached from days of constant driving, and his glazed, tired eyes had lost the ability to distinguish shapes, depth and color for the day, demanding their rest. As he struggled to keep them open, the distinctive flat Texas landscape blended and blurred, resembling the countless miles of background he'd passed for almost a week.

He pulled into a secluded rest area ten miles after the aptly named town of Flatonia, and sat alone in the remote parking lot where the brightest lights came from the soft colored glow of vending machines. Aside from the crickets, there was complete silence, and if not for an occasional truck driving past every few minutes, he could've believed he was the last man on earth. Settling in alone under the expansive Lone Star sky, he put in a CD. On the road a full five days, this had been the most tranquil he'd felt.

If the open road symbolized a blank page offering

possibilities, the stars represented permanent powers and a Divine plan put into motion long ago. This moment of solitude revealed an epiphany; a flash of awesome clarity when time seemingly lingers, allowing the mind ample freedom to comprehend a phenomenal gift.

The cruelest part of this trip was the isolation. Alone most of the time, it became impossible to share anything with anybody. Even worse, with no control of the situation, Hope seemed further away with a dwindling chance of finding her. The confusion, betrayal and abandonment hurt, but being alone was becoming agonizing. Strangely though, staring at thousands of stars calmed him. Growing more relaxed, he became aware of a heaviness in his hands, arms and shoulders, until the stress of his burning muscles flowed out of his limbs to complete his tranquility. A few minutes later, he felt thankful for being there alone.

Studying the stars inspired him. Every constellation had several stars, with each individual star enormous enough to be thought about separately. When considered independently, they offered a new perspective; a serene assurance that no matter how isolated one appears to be, no matter how many miles away, it's a vital piece of a larger, more magnificent picture. The individual prominence of each star confirmed that being alone can be cathartic.

There's a difference between being alone and being lonely. Being lonely is a tragic condition of the soul; a sad emptiness desperately needing to be filled by whatever is available to placate the pain for a awhile. Loneliness craves satiation from the outside, but too many times its gratification comes from filling itself in from the inside.

Pondering all life's wildest mysteries
And the answer is funny, but it's true
The only one who ever held the keys
Is the unexamined side of you.

Reclining in his convertible, well in the interior of the Lone Star State, he discovered firsthand how the song was true. The stars at night are indeed big and bright deep in the heart of Texas. Not only were the stars bigger and brighter, the moon loomed much closer that night with one of those red glows it gets, ironically, once in a blue moon. The moon crept westward until it hung just below — nearly touching — one particular star making it appear as if the ruddy moonlight radiated over to change its color. Staring up at the light painted pink star as it kissed the magenta luminescence of the moon, Hunter was reminded that it was the end of the day. Determined not to waste his father's advice, he wondered how he'd packaged his life, settled into the leather bucket seat and fell asleep.

Chapter Twenty-Five
<u>Friday</u>

A potent but peaceful combination of early morning sunlight and highway sounds woke Hunter up Friday morning. Sitting up and noticing rest area tourists walk past his car, it dawned on him how he'd become sort of a roadside freak show while he slept, drooling all over himself for all to see.

He shook his head, rubbed his swollen morning-eyes and ran his hand through greasy hair. The slick filthy texture of highway grime in his hair reminded him that, while driving a convertible is fun, there are drawbacks; like subjecting the hair and face to bugs that just pass over the windshield.

Self-conscious of his 'early-morning-just-woke-up' shuffle, he ambled inside the rest area building, used the facilities, washed his face, watered down his hair and invested .75 cents on an eight ounce cup of the weakest, yet somehow hottest coffee ever brewed. As the flesh on his fingertips seared, he wondered if perhaps vending machines used miniature uranium rods to heat their coffee before dispensing it into flimsy thin paper cups. Studying a map of Texas on a wall to chart his course for the day, his near blistered finger traced the line representing I-10 to the next large city in his path — San Antonio. Interestingly, I-10 connects with I-35 and heads straight down to Monterey, Mexico. That sounded intriguing, but after thinking about it, he figured Monterey is probably nicer to fly into than drive to. He stuck with I-10 West.

Spending the night in the rest area did provide a couple of advantages — catching up with the money spent on two exceptional hotel rooms, and getting on the road earlier. Driving in the early morning haze with the dew still hanging in the air boosted his ego, as if he got a head start on everybody else.

There's something at the end of this road, could be destiny.
Might be a new beginning or it might get the best of me
Oh yeah, you gave me so much. Your gave your heart, you gave
your touch
But there's something at the end of this road I gotta see.

If Texas offered anything, it had miles and miles of consistency. The highway scenery passed but hardly changed, as if his car ran on a treadmill in front of a painted curtain turning on a perpetual loop. Thankfully, as San Antonio approached, the landscape began showing signs of buildings, traffic and civilization. But more civilization meant more traffic. The time saved from his early start got nullified after all that civilized traffic slowed to a crawl on the eastern outskirts of San Antonio for road repairs.

The Texas Department of Transportation turned out to be as inefficient as the other 49 state DOTs. Orange diamond signs apathetically informed drivers of highway repairs and construction, while nothing offered any solutions or apology.

The road crew's responsibility consisted of gradually moving on-coming traffic into one lane. The three men wearing orange vests in the back of a truck took their time setting up a long stream of orange cones in a two-mile long line. Curiously, there were no lane improvements and nothing to warrant such a delay. Adding to his misery, the temperature in central Texas that morning topped 90 degrees when he found himself trapped behind a semi-tractor carrying a full load of cows. These unpleasant elements combined, simmering inside him for a half-hour, until he lost control with slight case of road rage. Stringing together several profanities and a few vulgarities, he cursed the other cars, he cursed the nonexistent road improvements, he cursed the orange cones, the road crew, and the entire Texas Transportation Department secretariat and finally, he cursed the cows and their awful bovine stench.

While blowing-off excessive steam and pent-up pressure, he took a perverse pleasure knowing the fate of the cows at the end of their trip. Chuckling to himself, he realized the redundancy of damning them, since they were already doomed.

What the cows couldn't have known was that their current situation was as good as it was going to get. For these bovines, a long, tedious, cramped, stifling-hot traffic jam granted a temporary stay of execution —— something rare in Texas.

With little to do but sit, sweat, wait and crawl five feet every two minutes, he regretted not finding a hotel room the night before; not for the soft bed, relative climate control or properly heated beverages, but just for the chance to wash Thursday's filth off. Studying to the Texas map, any hopeful prospects for a reputable hotel appeared bleak after San Antonio. There's a lot of west Texas before reaching civilization in El Paso.

Two hours of hot, crawl & stop, sweaty-olfactory hell later, he made it to the front of the traffic jam and found...nothing. There was nothing justifying stopping traffic. Not as much as a dead armadillo in the road. He'd already passed the last orange cone a half-hour earlier, then at some arbitrary point, cars started accelerating and the jam magically thinned-out. Taking advantage of the opportunity to punch down his gas pedal, the refreshing breeze cooled his sweat-drenched skin and, more importantly, cleansed the stench of doomed cattle from his nostrils. Cows only smell good when they're already dead and on a grill.

Like Houston, downtown San Antonio emerged all at once as a good-sized metropolis; and like Houston, San Antonio seemed to exist as an anonymous sleeping giant. An enormous town bustling under the national radar, he suspected, to avoid carpetbaggers who would invade their oasis in the plains should its secret get out. Unlike Houston, the handsome San Antonio skyline appeared compatible, charming and symbiotic. A diversity of buildings suggested imagination with varied industries. Older buildings offered romance and stability, while newer structures promised innovation of the future. It exuded character, history and an unpretentious honesty mirroring the prototypical image of a Texan.

As a testament to its size, the crowded traffic flowed briskly out of San Antonio continued for close to an hour, until like everything else in west Texas, the traffic became sparse. It might have been an ideal time for contemplative reflecting, but just as empty hands are the Devil's workshop, the scant landscape combined with the aural anesthesia of music provoked Hunter's nihilism.

The loneliness had intensified his pathos. For most of his journey, it was comforting to never be more than two or three hours from civilization. But Texas is another matter. In some parts of the country, it's easy to drive three hours and travel through three states. In Texas, it's easy to drive three days and still be in Texas. Trying not to complain, he reminded himself of the night before and how peaceful being alone could be.

> *Every once in a while life will wear you out*
> *And it'll make you wonder what the hell it's all about*
> *Wherever Fate's gonna take me, I suppose it's gotta have a*
> *plan*
> *But it's a mystery to me, because I'm just a man.*

These few days on the road taught Hunter that he'd led a pretty sheltered life in Minnesota, but since jumping on the road, he lived the American experience one-mile marker at a time. Gaining a better understanding of the human condition from interacting with strangers at gas stations, hotels and restaurants came from improvising, and all he had to do was follow his heart and the asphalt under his tires. And much like reading tea leaves at the bottom of a cup, the past several days could be interpreted by the remnants of bugs on his windshield.

A few hours later, he reached Ozona, Texas. On the map, Ozona was a small dot beside a notation indicating a memorial to beloved Alamo defender, Davy Crocket. In real life, Ozona couldn't have been much more. If Texans loved Davy Crocket so much, Hunter wondered why they erected his memorial in such a secluded location where nobody would see it.

Several more miles down the highway, Hunter had somehow become fourth to last in a convoy of at least a dozen vehicles. So used to not paying attention in the isolation—zoning out — he hadn't noticed the gradual increase of cars merging onto the highway from the previous three or four exits. Apparently, the Davy Crocket Memorial drew more traffic than he gave it credit for. The isolation of this stretch of road created a kindred bond with these other drivers, like a chain reliance for survival. At the same time, he fostered a growing resentment for them, since these Johnny-Come-Latelys likely lacked the fortitude to traverse all of Texas starting with Beaumont.

Another annoyance stemmed from three mammoth sport utility vehicles blocking his immediate view down the road. This 'blind-follow-the-leader' parade continued at a brisk clip, with each driver maintaining a consistent, comfortable and communal 75 mph rate. Nobody tried to pass and nobody slowed down. He flirted with the idea of accelerating to the front, but didn't want to break the convoy's unspoken protocol, especially if the other drivers conspired to speed-up to thwart his selfish attempt. So for a long 30 miles, this modern day cavalcade proceeded in perfect lock step like happy sheep at the beginning of a migration.

Suddenly their symmetrical ranks were broken as the SUV in front of him swerved abruptly hard to the left, following its predecessor's lead, to avoid debris in the middle of road. With his view blocked, Hunter didn't have the same advantage or time to react to the debris. He'd barely had a chance to see the truck in front of him swerve when he felt, then heard, the debris pass under the front end of his car, jolted the car and thumping loudly as it smacked against the bottom. In his rear view mirror, he saw the trash as it spit out the back, sliding closer to the shoulder, safely away from the drivers behind him. Although it felt as if he'd run over a rhinoceros, a glance in the side mirror confirmed it to be a cardboard appliance box with stud reinforcements. Checking for a "Massive Undercarriage Damage" indicator light on the dashboard, no bells, whistles or alarms sounded, and everything seemed fine. Kudos to the American automobile industry. What's more, he'd fallen on a grenade for the troops behind him, confirming his image as the only real disciplined grizzled veteran of the long pack.

Less than ten miles down the road however, his status changed to martyr. The Mustang abruptly pulled hard to the right as he heard the dreaded "thwack thwackity-thwack-

thwackity" grow louder like an approaching freight train. Surrendering his position from the caravan's formation and easing onto the shoulder, the three cars behind him slowed down as they passed, then sped up to stay with the pack. So much for that kindred brotherhood. Traitorous bastards.

His pride wasn't the only thing deflated as his tire rim rested in a deep groove it carved into the soft asphalt. Standing there, scowling at the shredded rubber and steel belts, he spied the top of a large nail worn flush with what little tread remained.

"That tire won't fix itself," Peter said by the side of the road.

"I thought you forgot about me," Hunter said smirking.

"Impossible," Peter reassured him.

"I'm beginning to think I should have just stayed in Minneapolis and gotten drunk for a month."

"And miss this adventure? This is the best thing you could've done."

Failing to see his father's suggested silver lining, Hunter walked to the trunk, popped it open, lifted the false bottom and stared down at the abomination every driver dreads — the pathetic, miniature spare tire tucked away in its tiny wheel-well like it was the stale five hour old coconut doughnut nobody wants. The baby tire sat there mocking him, daring him to put it on. If given the chance, he'd rather buy a brand new car than put this demi-tire on his car, but he didn't have that choice. He grabbed the lug-nut wrench and jack, knelt on the ground and started cranking. Peter took advantage of this downtime to teach once more.

"Son, you're looking at it the wrong way."

"Really? Please enlighten me wise and sage apparitional patriarch," he said, straining against a lug nut.

"Hunter, this isn't a road trip, it's an odyssey. The difference is; an odyssey is not confined or defined by lines on a map or subject to laws and boundaries of the corporeal world. It's a spiritual journey. You've become more concerned about where you've been, what you've done and where you'll end up, when you should be thinking about what you want or what you'll find. You can drive until all the wheels fall off and not find satisfaction until you realize that," Peter continued. Hunter listened, but focused his concentration on changing the tire. As Peter went on, his insightful message drew his son in.

"I admire you, though" he continued. "Everybody needs to make a spiritual odyssey, but not many do. Nobody can seem to find time to examine themselves. I'm not talking about church or museums or books or staring at the ocean from a condo — although all those help. But here you are, thrown into a situation where you were compelled to begin this odyssey. Ironically, it was this unfortunate situation that allowed you the time to commit total concentration to it. It really is an awesome gift. It may not seem like a good thing now, but in the long run...down the road you'll look back and know. You learn, you grow and you know yourself a little better."

Almost finished with the tire, Hunter paid more attention to his father's words.

"Before you can find those things, before you can start an odyssey, you have to find your road," Peter continued. "And that is the hardest, most important part of the trip; the customized route to your ultimate destination. The path to salvation. True, there's only one path, but the brilliant thing is, that one path is different for everybody. It's the one path that you know is best. And true, the path to peace is narrow, but what does narrow mean? One man's narrow is much wider than another's. Some won't need much room to begin with, while others deserve more leeway because they got a bad deal somewhere. It's arrogant to assume there's a single road for everybody at the same time. There's one path, but it's different," Peter reiterated.

The 'path' metaphor seemed elementary, but Hunter had never considered comparing the size and length of his path to others, or the notion that, good or bad, people get the path they deserve.

"Everybody has a road to follow, and many do take an easy route," Peter continued. "Maybe it's convenience. Maybe they have three kids or work 18 hours a day and don't have time for an odyssey. Some will stray, get lost and wander aimlessly, while others stay on their path their whole lives. Some journeys last a lot longer, and a few people may find a shortcut. But you know what? Things tend to equal out and all that matters in the end is that we get there. Now many folks are so proud of how well they've stayed within the lines, they'll shake a jealous vindictive finger at others who they judge are taking an easy route. That's plain presumptuous. You can't begrudge somebody because of their path. You can't know where their odyssey might lead. They may go a thousand miles out of their way and find profound answers along a brand new smooth, straight path. The other guy? He'll get there. He may get there before you if you help him. Don't judge him; just be mindful of your road. Don't be jealous of him. Carry him if he needs it. Don't worry about the extra load because maybe you were carried or will need to be carried one day. Help people. Be happy for their success. Where you end up and how you get there — that's all you need to worry about."

Peter's tone changed. What started as a confident voice from a wise teacher subtly softened to something inspirational. Hunter stood with his back to his father, inspected the epic pastoral vastness while reflecting.

"Coincidentally, your own spiritual odyssey is like this trip. There are signs, limits and boundaries. There are long stretches where you wonder, 'when will this be over?' Other times you'll have to stop and fix things. But most important, you're in the driver's seat. I can join you, come along for the ride, give direction, but I can't take you there. I will tell you that no matter how it works out, you'll know yourself better."

For the first time that week, Hunter developed a faraway gaze in his eyes as if the indisputable truth in his father's words could be discovered by scanning the horizon. He understood it was an odyssey, but only days removed from the pain of his big loss, instead of looking beyond it, he continued analyzing it, trying to figure out how the fuzzy edges of constantly mutating pieces fit together. Peter noticed that spark in his son's eyes, but opted against pushing for too much too soon. One virtue traveling in tandem with wisdom is patience. Hunter had traveled a long way on this path so far, but it was still unknown how much of either of those virtues he had secured.

Chapter Twenty-Six

Of the numerous innovations and celebrated ideas in the history of the automotive industry, the miniature spare tire falls way down the list. Many car enthusiasts insist the only product keeping the idiot wheel from the bottom slot is the 1974 AMC Pacer/Gremlin – a car created for teenage boys who wanted to repel teenage girls.

As if the puny spare wasn't aggravating enough, Hunter resigned to keep his speed under 40 mph until a replacement tire could be bought. If Texas seemed big, flat and boring at 75 mph, being forced to drive 40 mph magnified it. Driving that slowly was so humiliating, he avoided eye contact with drivers passing him, maintaining a never deviating forward gaze, like a defiant woman who knows she's slow but doesn't care.

The first available exit lead him to Bakersfield, a small town evidently stuck in 1972. A quarter-mile down a flat dusty stretch of road, he found Hooper Donau and Sons Tire and Parts Auto Service Station, an anachronistic oasis in the middle of Texas. Throughout the years, Donau's had remained a true 'Service Station' from days of old when there was reverence for the word 'service'. The bow ties and snappy white uniforms were long replaced by jeans and blue shirts with names patches, but employees retained that old time level of friendliness and helpfulness. While one attendant squeegeed not only the windshield, but all the glass, a second attendant checked tire pressures and the oil level. After days of gassing up at plastic hybrid convenience stores with contrived names like Pump & Run®, Snack & Go®, Petro-Mart®, SpeedEZ-Way® and Fuel Town®, a gas station with mechanics on staff and air-filters, wiper blades and oil cans displayed beside the pumps seemed romantic.

Pulling his Mustang beside the building next to a large window front gave him a clear view of the waiting area. Donau's couldn't boast a large selection of snacks, trendy sport juices, beef jerky or sundries. They had a soda machine with a photo of a longhaired teenager with muttonchops enjoying a refreshing Coke, while an emaciated, stringy-haired companion happily sipped her Tab through a straw in the can. Next to the soda machine was a vending machine selling candy that hadn't been popular since about that same time period.

Barely out of his car, a sprinting attentive attendant met Hunter. Noticing the name on the shirt patch read 'Hoop Jr.', he figured this must be the oldest of Hooper Donau's sons.

"Howdy sir, you need some help there?" the friendly attendant inquired, wiping his dirty hands with an oily rag.

"Yeah..." Hunter answered. "Hoop, I need a tire."

Hoop glanced at his out of state customer quizzically, searching for familiarity in a stranger who knew his name, until he remembered the patch on his shirt. He smiled, then turned his focus to the doughnut wheel. "I say you do," he responded with charming hayseed sarcasm. "Let's see what you need."

Hoop Jr. squatted to examine one of the remaining good tires. He ran his fingertips around its sidewall, reading raised numbers as if he'd discovered the Rosetta Stone, then stood up and wiped his fingers on his blue jeans, dirtying-up his pants and spreading black carbon grime more evenly over his hands.

"Well sir, I've got good news and bad news," Hoop Jr. warned.

Hunter's mind raced with the negative possibilities.

"We can get you the tire, we just don't have it in stock right now," he told him." We sold our last set of four, the kind you need, just yesterday. You know you're 'spose to buy tires in fours don't you?" Hoop informed for future reference.

"Of all those tires up there," Hunter asked, pointing at two-dozen tires inside the service bay, "you don't have one I need?"

"Y'see sir, what you have here is a sports car requiring a high performance tire handling speeds well above 100 miles per hour."

"But I'm not going to drive 100 miles per hour," Hunter replied in frustration.

"Don't matter, the tire still needs to fit the rim," Hoop said pointing at the tire. "See them numbers on the side? That means tires on this car got to handle, what they call, a V-

Rating," Hoop informed. "Now, you could try Mitch Barton's gas station cross town, but frankly, they don't carry much selection. Besides sir, Barton's closes up at 4:30. By the time you got there, they'd be gone. 'Course, you could try driving on that doughnut to Odessa. But you see here?" he added pointing at the tiny tire, "'Do not exceed 35 mph on this doughnut,' which I'm guessin' you already ignored, seein' you were on the highway and all. Nah, you might as well enjoy Bakersfield's hospitality and let us do the job right," Hoop's voice conveyed smugness countering his customer's spiteful sarcasm.

It's not that Hunter had to be anywhere that frustrated him as much as he hated the idea of time lost he could have used for finding a decent hotel somewhere to get cleaned up. Visibly annoyed, he understood it wasn't Hoop's fault, and to his credit, Hoop sympathized with his customer's frustration and tried making him feel welcome in town.

"You just gotta face the fact that you ain't going nowhere tonight. Tell you what sir, when we close, I'll have Azra drive you to the Old Rosebud Motel in town. When we get the tire in from Odessa tomorrow, we'll get it fixed fast and get ya on your way. Now, that's the best I can offer, unless you want to sleep in your car tonight. But I reckon you won't want to be here after we let the dog out."

Left without a choice Hunter agreed.

For the next half hour, he watched mechanics work on his car from the waiting area, like a fascinated foreigner exposed to a new culture, until at 5 o'clock, a dirty, grizzled mechanic stuck his head in.

"You the guy Hoop says I gotta take to the Old Rosebud?"

"Yeah, I think that's the plan," Hunter confirmed.

"Well c'mon," the mechanic replied, "I'm in a rush."

Hunter followed Azra to a jacked-up, modified pick-up truck. A custom paint job along the passenger side showed an optical illusion of a huge Gila monster clawing his way out of the panel. On the tailgate, Azra had a fairly realistic rendering of DaVinci's 'Last Supper.' The truck's brand name fit nicely into the mural, giving the accidental illusion that the Christ party of 13 enjoyed that Thursday night dinner at the

'Chevrolet' restaurant. On the truck's hood Azra airbrushed the nickname of his beloved truck —'The Dust Commander.' It was the tires, no doubt, that gave him command over all dust, dirt or rocks. They were at least four feet in diameter and set the truck up so high, Hunter had to stand on his toes to reach the door and hop up to get his foot on the chrome sideboard for leverage into the cab. Once inside, Azra started his truck, showing off a few modifications to the engine and exhaust system. The truck's seats vibrated slightly, and the motor's loud rumble reverberated in his stomach.

"You don't mind if I make a quick stop at my girlfriend's," Azra snarled.

"I've got time," Hunter agreed compliantly.

"Heh heh...I hope you do," the driver growled sarcastically.

The dusty road out of Bakersfield was long, straight and full of potholes. Azra's arrogance in the superiority of his truck meant not swerving around a pothole and in fact, often adjusting his steering to hit them. More disturbing was the great joy he seemed to feel after running over two deer carcasses lying in the road. After ten miles, Hunter realized this would not be a quick errand. His polite gratitude for the lift turned annoyed, especially after seeing a road sign.

Leaving Pecos Co.
Entering Upton Co.

About ten miles later they passed through Lawrin, a town no different from Bakersfield, then drove another mile or two to a crossroads in the middle of nowhere with five small homes in a row. Azra pulled into the gravel drive of the middle home and cut his engine. The stillness of the silence was dramatic after almost 30 minutes of rumbling.

"Wait out here. This shouldn't take long," Azra said with a menacing chuckle.

Strutting casually to the door, Azra was met by a woman wearing a bikini. Not long after they went inside, a girl — maybe seven years old came out. Initially upset about being kicked out of the house, she skipped to a rusty swing set in the yard and hopped on. With several kicks, the persistent young girl tried to get started, but soon quit out of frustration. Spotting Hunter in the truck, she cocked her head to the side and stared at him with curiosity. Hunter climbed out and met the girl at the swing.

"You ain't from town, are you?" she asked innocently.

"No, I'm not," he replied. "Your mother's friend is giving me a ride."

"You best wait out here with me," she assured him. "They like they privacy."

"Oh, I see," he responded, realizing he was in for a long wait.

"What's your name, mister?" she asked.

"My name's Hunter. What's yours?"

"Stephanie. But most folks call me Stevie."

"Stevie, it looks like you're having trouble getting started. You need a push?" he offered.

Without uttering a sound, Stevie grinned and nodded her head. Something in the girl's grin pushed all the right buttons. One healthy shove sufficed, then he got out of the way. For several minutes, the young girl seemed giddy, concentrating on maintaining the proper rhythm with her kicking legs, until her face grew serious. She stopped kicking, and instead dragged her bare feet in the dirt as brakes.

"Sir, you think there's a Heaven?" she asked, out of the blue.

Taken aback that a child would ask a stranger such a profound question, he remembered his father's answer. "Sorry, that's one's against the rules," he snickered, making an inside joke to himself. Stevie stared at him confused.
"Why do you ask?" he questioned her.

"My daddy got killed, and when I asked Mama if he's in Heaven, she told me she don't much care where my daddy was, since she never knew where he was when he was alive, most times. Mama says th' only good thing she ever got from daddy was me."

Hunter looked away and bit his lower lip out of sympathy for the girl. She couldn't know the many levels of tragedy she conveyed with her naive answer, and sadly, she had no idea how it would scar her for life. Consumed with pity and compassion, his first instinct was to pick her up and hold her. But as a stranger, the last thing he needed was to get arrested in another small town for an innocent misunderstanding. Hunter lowered himself on one knee down in the dirt and got eye to eye with her as she sat on her swing. Now it was his turn to be in teaching mode.

"Let me tell you about Heaven," he offered. "Have you ever wanted to go somewhere special, but your mother said you could only go if you were good?"

Stevie grinned enthusiastically, nodding her head.

"And maybe you were bad, but she took you anyway because she loved you?"

Stevie nodded again, but her dour and penitent expression gave Hunter the uneasy feeling that the girl's mother not only kept her threats, the resulting punishment was perverse and severe.

"Well," he continued softly, "Heaven is like that place, only better because you get to stay there," he explained, then paused. "So, say you get to go to Heaven? It's good for you because it's fun; everybody likes you and there's lots to do. But because you're there, you left people behind, right? Now, don't you think they'd miss you and feel sad because they couldn't see you anymore? But you know what? Hopefully, they'd be grateful because you're at that special place where you're happy all the time."

"I know there's a Heaven and I'll see my daddy someday," Stevie declared. Then she added, "I don't even 'member my daddy. I was only a baby when he gone off, but I know I love him anyhow."

Although she couldn't have known it, Hunter was grateful for the girl. She confirmed that some bonds formed remain forever.

Young Stephanie quizzed her new friend and teacher about the world outside of Lawrin, Texas. She hung onto each of his descriptions and insights, fascinated with a miraculous world that offered her a new hope far away.

An hour and a half later, Azra finally emerged then strutted past Hunter and the girl without so much as a glance. Motioning and whistling that he was ready to leave, he jumped in his truck and cranked its engine. Hunter saw his ride was in a hurry, but couldn't leave the poor girl with the same insensitivity she'd been getting her whole life. He got down on one knee and Stevie took the initiative by wrapping her thin, scarred arms around her new friend's neck as if begging him not to leave. When she did loosen her grip, Hunter held her at arm's length by her tiny shoulders and looked her in the eye.

"You're a good girl Stephanie, okay?" he expressed with a sincerity that he prayed would endure her whole lifetime and ease inevitable pains and fears bound to evolve. Again, she cocked her head, confused, as if she'd never heard that combination of words before. Hunter winked at her and she grinned. Her smile manipulated everything good within him. Her mother sternly bellowed her name from inside the house, ruining their moment and giving Hunter an uneasy feeling of foreshadowing. Stephanie left him kneeling in the dirt, wishing for one more smile. It took every ounce of his energy to let her go.

Back in Azra's truck, neither man spoke for several miles, until Hunter broke the silence.

"Your girlfriend's daughter is something," he said.

"Stevie? Yeah, she's something all right," Azra echoed in his ominous tone and disturbing chuckle.

"Are you and your girlfriend gonna get married any time soon?"

"Marry her? Ain't no way in hell I'm gonna marry her," he declared emphatically.

"Why not?" Hunter challenged him.

"For one, I don't think my wife would take to that idea too much."

Hunter's heart sank. Not another word was uttered all the way back into town to the hotel.

The Old Rosebud Motel turned out to be located only a mile from Donau's Service Station. The fact that Azra drove over 15 miles out of his way and made him wait nearly two hours revealed more about him than his callous demeanor and bitter attitude. Hunter couldn't wait to get out of the truck, but as unpleasant as spending time with Azra was, the Old Rosebud was not much better.

Checking into a hotel had become a simple series of affirmative or negative grunts while filling out forms. His new checking-in know-how paid off well since the front desk clerk had the attitude and vocabulary of a badger. His room at the Old Rosebud was, in one sense, a new experience. Like everything else in Bakersfield, the room key was a holdover from ancient days when hotels had metal keys on big plastic fobs. He opened the door and surveyed his Friday night accommodations.

"I am in Hell," he said aloud.

The floral wallpaper, peeling-off in each corner, had nicotine stains in some parts, water stains in others and faded sun damage on two-thirds of the wall opposite a sliding glass door which opened to a swimming pool outside that had been filled-in with dirt. The towels were small and threadbare, and the carpet probably hadn't been cleaned since its burnt orange color was fashionable. The bed's sunken mattress had a look of thousands of 'noon affairs with the secretary' and the over-efficient jet engine air conditioner he'd grown accustomed to had been replaced by a rattling rusty inefficient non-oscillating fan — particularly ineffective in west Texas. Perhaps most telling of all, the 13" television had a black & white picture. To add further insult, the archaic TV and its accompanying obsolete bulky remote were bolted down 30 years earlier to prevent what would become an irrational theft. In short, the owners of this lodging suite assumed guests were either not interested in watching television or their hospitality options were limited in Bakersfield, TX. In either case they'd be thankful to find a room.

Each room had a door that opened up into the adjoining room. The Old Rosebud was built with thick, substantial walls, however, the thin door allowed Hunter to hear that the couple next door was not at all interested in watching their 13" black and white TV. From what he could hear, her name was 'Baby-Baby' and his name was 'Gawd', because that's what they kept calling each other at the top of their lungs.

The bathroom, no larger than a small walk-in closet, had a shower stall with not much more room than a phone booth. To make matters — not to mention bathing — worse, the showerhead sprayed little more pressure than a constant trickle from a garden hose. As pathetic as this experience was, the opportunity to finally wash off two days of sticky Texas filth thrilled him.

Ironically, just being in the Old Rosebud made him feel dirty as soon as he stepped out of the shower booth. The tiny lightweight towel wrapped around his waist reached only as far as the top of his thighs, giving him the appearance of a slave in a gladiator movie. With as much modesty as he could muster, he sat at the foot of the bed reflecting how his life had transformed from exactly one week earlier, when he and Hope enjoyed their rehearsal dinner. What was supposed to begin as a carefully planned-out journey with the woman he adored had turned into an emotional tempest with no clear course of action and even less idea of an outcome. Hunter stared into a mirror over the desk until the eyes of his mirror image blurred. He searched deep into his irises, praying for the gift of even a glimpse into his soul, wondering if there existed a glimmer of untapped truth it kept secret from his rational mind. Focused on his reflection's eyes with unyielding concentration, the rest of his face morphed into bizarre, grotesque shapes, then turned smooth and white like the surface of the moon. Frustrated that he couldn't find any new revealing clues, he grasped another cruel life axiom. The human condition only allows people to feel truly comfortable when answers are readily available. Unfortunately, Hunter didn't have any more answers than that first night back in Eau Claire.

He scooted to the top of the bed, leaned his head against the headboard and propped the thin, stained pillow behind his back, just as the 'Baby-Baby & Gawd Show' resumed. After several seconds struggling frantically with the fastened down remote, he clicked the archaic TV on and set the volume just loud enough to drown out his neighbor's ecstatic screeching. Reaching over to turn the clock so its display faced him, it was relatively early by most people's standards for a Friday. Never mind that this Friday had been a long one, starting out over 13 hours earlier when he woke up as the unexpected drooling main attraction to gawking travelers in a rest area. He closed his eyes and tried convincing himself that he wasn't going to fall asleep; he was only resting his eyes for a minute. Then his subconscious asked, 'who are you trying to kid?' Predictably, like a hundred times before, he'd fall asleep with the light on and the television playing reruns in the background.

Of all the events of that day, his last thought before dozing off was, 'damn idiot-wheel spare tire.'

Chapter Twenty-Seven
<u>Saturday</u>

Hunter rarely remembered his dreams, but for the second time that week, a vivid dream remained clear upon waking.

He's standing near the edge of a rocky cliff like those off the coast of Maine. A hundred and fifty yards to his right he sees a lighthouse, painted gold with a wide white spiral stripe. Twenty yards behind him, his boyhood home stands dilapidated, having fallen into a state of depressing disrepair. Chipped paint and sheets of warped pressboard covering the windows portray a sad shell of the home he remembers, but it's still recognizable. In a small, blooming dogwood tree beside it, two mockingbirds chirp mating calls, jumping from branch to branch teasing each other in avian foreplay. Although the birds are less than 20 yards away, their song sounds distant, as if being carried to him by a dying echo.

The ocean's tide rolls in with a soft, steady rhythm, its waves encounter surround, smother and envelope the rocks near the shore, instead of the usual powerful display of violent crashing. A half-mile out, he sees a three-masted schooner drifting dangerously close towards a massive jagged rock jutting up from the sea. Looking to the lighthouse for help, he discovers a lone man with shoulder-long white hair and a full-length black leather coat has joined him. The stranger, standing in silhouette ten yards away, remains still in a solemn pose, contemplating the ship, oblivious to anything else, while his black coat and white hair whip and flutter in the slight wind. Hunter tries walking to the mysterious figure, but the loose, unstable rocks underfoot make it impossible. Horrified, he's forced to watch helplessly as the ship smashes bow first into the rock, crumpling upon itself as if it were built of paper. In shock, he gapes at the mysterious figure only to realize it's his father. No longer bald, Peter's long, flowing white hair lends an air of a philosophical sage. Peter glances at Hunter and murmurs, "Well. There you are."

Hunter woke up and heard voices in his room again. He sat up in bed and saw that the television had been on all night. What kind of shows could induce and influence such a bizarre, vivid dream? Old reruns? Infomercials featuring the 'King of Inventions?' Get-rich-quick schemes presented by men who got rich by selling get-rich-quick schemes? The farm report?

It didn't matter. Hunter had always found television reassuring, since it could be on, even when he wasn't. He remembered reading a bizarre newspaper story years earlier about an Eastern European man who died in his apartment watching television. The story reported that since this man had no family or friends, nobody knew he was dead for ten years. So for a decade, or as long as it took the Eastern European Socialist Power Company to turn off his electricity, this man decomposed in his favorite easy chair, rotting in front of the warm glow of television, while fine state-run Socialist propaganda programming (presumably free of commercials and infomercials) went on and on.

Jumping in the shower for the second time in ten hours, he again cursed the low water pressure. Getting clean didn't make much difference since his bags were in his car and he'd been wearing the same clothes he put on Thursday morning in New Orleans.

Checking out that morning, a new Slacker front desk clerk, immersed in a quasi-pornographic Japanese comic book, showed complete apathy to Hunter's situation — not even asking about his night or suggesting that he 'come back real soon.' Clearly, education and personal skills were not a high priority in the hiring process of this establishment.

Unlike the three economy hotels he'd stayed in, the Old Rosebud had no peppy motivational posters or corporate plaques on the wall. There was no free newspaper, basket of bagels or complementary coffee. There was, however, off to the far side of the counter, a cardboard bakery box with a telltale trail of powdered sugar leading from box to the clerk. Sadly, when he peered inside, all that was left was one lonely stale coconut doughnut.

As he paid the $59.95 bill, he held his breath trying to avoid the piercing stench of stale pine-ammonia disinfectant mixed with various cheap colognes that had been lingering in that same spot for twenty years. Unfortunately, the morning Slacker's snail pace made it next to impossible to hold it long enough. Exiting this Bates Motel knock-off, he drew a deep breath, replenishing his lungs, and fantasized about a taxi waiting out front to drive him back to the service station. His reality re-entered earth's atmosphere upon discovering he was the only man on the 'strip.'

Walking up to Donau and Sons Service Station close to 11 a.m., he saw his Mustang parked in the exact spot from the evening before. Reaching in and grabbing his overnight bag, he was greeted by Hoop, Jr.

"What's the word on getting that tire?" Hunter inquired.

"To be honest sir, we didn't get a chance to call Odessa yesterday, "Hoop Jr. confessed." There's a chance they sent it with the regular shipment,"

"And if they didn't?" he asked with premonitory trepidation, suspecting the worst.

"Well sir, you may have to stay here until Monday, seeing we're closed on Sunday."

"Monday?" Hunter asked incredulously.

"Yep, Monday," the rube repeated, bobbing his head and smiling.

"So, what time does your shipment come in from Odessa?" he asked annoyed.

"Tim Tamez gets here 'round 1 o'clock," Hoop answered.

Accepting that his stay in Bakersfield had been extended by at least a couple of hours, Hunter's determination to change into clean clothes hadn't wavered. He grabbed the rest room key (soldered to a Cadillac hubcap to thwart the cabal of thieves who steal gas station bathroom keys), and changed. His mood improved substantially.

Waiting once again in the reception area, he passed the time paging through out-of-date periodicals. One sports magazine cover hyped an upcoming Super Bowl as 'perhaps the closest, most defense oriented Super Bowl of all time!' In truth, that game was played three and a half months earlier and was a blowout by the middle of the second quarter.

Donau's had at least three dozen tires on a shelf on the back wall inside the garage bay, and Hunter scanned them all several times over the next 30 minutes in the off-hand chance they'd overlooked the one he needed. Finally convinced the tire wasn't going to magically materialize, he turned his attention to the cashier engrossed in her supermarket tabloid. His curiosity roused after noticing a few of her exposed tattoos, he wasted a few more minutes examining her art, discovering generic tattoos popular with generic small town girls – rainbows, unicorns, dolphins and such. When her ink-work stopped holding his attention, he counted how many times she popped her chewing gum, stopping at 27 because it grated on his nerves and forced him outside.

Thanks to missing dinner the night before, his hunger offered a prime excuse for a diversion. He poked his head inside and asked the 'Bakersfield Charm Queen' where he could grab lunch.

"Kingman's Cafe is down yonder," she answered sweeping her finger three directions in the air, never looking up from tabloid tales of Pygmy-kangaroo babies and JFK's randy ghost, while popping her gum not once, but twice.

"Down yonder?" he asked, needing more specific directions.

"Go to the corner, cross the street, go past the liquor store and the drug store. Take a right at the grocery, go three blocks," she explained, popping her gum another seven times, including a double-shot at the end.

In spite of her directions, he found Kingman's Cafe; but it was more of a bar serving bar food during lunch hours than a restaurant. It was dark and rustic, decorated in anything Texas: Texas flags, old Texas license plates, Texas football memorabilia, armadillos, cowboy hats, western movie posters, jack-rabbits and photos of historic politicians who hailed from the Lone Star State. In the middle of the room stood a well-worn pool table, and against the wall, a shuffleboard table and a vintage pinball machine.

Taking a seat at the bar, he caught a glimpse of himself in the long mirror behind four rows of liquor bottles. Above the mirror hung several neon beer lights and a sign proclaiming 'Kingman's Cafe. The Burgoo King!' At the end of the bar, a middle-aged man with a three-day stubble and a sports coat enjoyed a liquid brunch and read a newspaper.

The waitress-barmaid placed a glass of water in front of Hunter and asked if he knew what he wanted. He scanned their limited menu, written in chalk on a blackboard:

Fried chickin / Fried pork chop
Chickin fingers / Bufalo Wings
Country fried steak / Fried oysters
French Fries / Onion Rings
Hamburger/ Cheeseburger
Chile / Burgoo!

"What's burgoo?" he asked, pointing to the sign.
"Where you from?" she questioned.
"Minnesota."
"You won't like it," she assured him.
"What's in it?" he asked.
"Venison, rabbit..."
"You're right," he interrupted taking her word for it. "I don't suppose you have any whitefish back there?" he asked knowing the answer even before crossing into Texas.
"We've got fried catfish," she countered.
"I'll just have a hamburger, fries and a Coke, please."
She scribbled down his order and disappeared into the kitchen.
"Hey. Hey you," the unshaven man at the end of the bar slurred as he folded his newspaper. "Where'd you say you were from?"
"Me? Minnesota," Hunter replied,
"Minny-soootaaaahhh," the man exaggerated as he sat up straight. "I was in Minnesota once. Too goddamn cold if you ask me. Went ice fishing in one of them damn outhouse lookin' shacks with this guy I sold a car to. This was back, must of been...15 years ago when I was running my daddy's car lot in Johnstown. This fella comes in, says he needs a car right away for whatever some-such reason. Talking this and that. What the

hell do I care? I was pushing tin for crissake. But I'm a salesman, I'm 'spose to get friendly with customers, make 'em feel special. So this guy gets all Midwest buddy-buddy, right? Tells me he's a sporting goods distributor on a trip with his wife when he suddenly realizes he has to rush back to...Minny-soootaaaahh right away. Why? I dunno and I didn't care. Anyway, this guy needs a car fast, but since he was a salesman too, he gets all competitive like he wants me to know he's not being suckered by my pitch, right? So, he tells me he'll buy the leather package if I go to Minnesota to Lake Damm-It's-Friggin'-Cold-Up-Here, and go ice fishing. Clyde Van Dusenberg. You know him?" the man asked.

"No," Hunter answered, trying to ignore him.

"Weird sonuvabitch," he continued. "About 6'5, blonde hair, must have been the whitest man I ever met. This guy was so white, he was damn near transparent. Thought he might've one of them Albanians."

"You mean albinos?" Hunter corrected.

"Yeah, albino, whatever. But guess what? 'Ol Clyde wasn't no albino, he was just Norwegian," he cackled to emphasize his point. "So, I tell him whatever just to sell him the damn car, and you know what? Not five months later, out of the blue, this weird, white sonuvabitch calls me. Now, I'm a man of my word, so the next thing I know, it's 20 degrees below zero and I'm sitting on a goddamn pickle bucket in a wood shack on the middle of a frozen lake sippin' some kind of funny cider-schnapps concoction, and I got a fishin' pole stickin' in the damn ice! Ice! Craziest thing I ever saw; fishin' in ice. They don't cast out and reel in. They just sit on buckets in tiny wood shacks in below freezing weather drinking nasty Minnesota moonshine and talking 'bout hockey. All day long he's spouting off promotional ideas, how we can be partners. Buy a car, get a fishing rod. Buy a sports car and get bucket seats or whatever. To be honest I couldn't hear half of what he said, 'cause my damn teeth were chattering and I got drunk from that homemade hooch. He just wouldn't stop talking. It was blah-blah-blah-cold-'nuff-fer-ya...blah-blah-blah-goin'-to-see-Gophers-play-hockey...blah-blah-blah-sales-promotion-ehh? Don't you hate people who just keep talking, when it's obvious that you don't wanna listen? Sheesh, that fella was one weird hombre. Knew how to catch fish, though. Knew cars pretty good too."

The man only stopped talking long enough to finish off his drink.

"The important thing is, I sold that weird sonuvabitch a car at full price. And Jenny, I'll have another one of these," he said raising his empty glass in a mock toast. "So whut're ycu doing down here in the great state of Texas?"

"Just passing through. Got a flat tire and I'm waiting for a spare."

"A spare?" he asked suspiciously. "Where?"

"At Donau's."

"At goddamn Hoop Donau's place? That goddamn sonuvabitch will cheat you and ruin your goddamn life before he's done with you. You mark my words," the man warned, like a Gypsy in a werewolf movie.

The waitress placed a fresh Bloody Mary in front of the man and chastised him. "Settle down Mr. Mayor. Don't bother the customers." She stepped down to the end of the bar to apologize.

"I'm sorry 'bout that," she offered. "The mayor usually keeps to himself."

"That's your mayor?" Hunter asked astonished.

"Yeah," she verified timidly.

"He's drunk at 11:30 in the morning?"

"Hey, screw you my Minny-soootaaahhhh friend," the mayor interjected. "It's a Saturday. Weekdays I wait until three," he snickered to himself, proud of his restraint during work hours.

The waitress rolled her eyes and leaned in closer so the mayor couldn't hear. "Y'see, he got caught having sex with a...well that don't matter. But to avoid a big scandal, the town figured to let him finish out his term instead of having a bunch of national publicity and such. There was enough damage done. The election's just a few months away," she rationalized as she left.

With the waitress gone, a calmer, placated mayor recognized his opportunity to restart his conversation.

Stumbling over, he plopped down two stools over from Hunter.

"As I wuz sayin' 'bout Minny-sootaahh, the weather is cold, but I'm sure the people are nice. Nicer than they are here, I bet," he shouted toward the kitchen. "Lemmee tell you 'bout people," he started, with a nasty sneer.

As the mayor's bitter babble went on, his story sounded more like an unabridged autobiography. Hunter was reminded of a classic joke, where a man recounts several amazing deeds he'd accomplished, and how his town's residents marveled so much in said achievements, they bestowed upon him honorary titles matching his feats: John the Barn Builder, John the War Hero, John the Lawyer, John the Senator, etc. The punch line is, "...but you fuck *one* sheep..."

Vaguely admitting to an indiscretion in a moment of weakness, no more information was disclosed the waitress didn't already reveal. He reasoned that in a town with very little intellectual or mental stimulation, there was little else to do but concentrate on carnal stimulation and that most of Bakersfield condoned a 'free love' attitude; no doubt a symptom of being stuck in 1972. In the mayor's defense, Hunter agreed that he's seen nothing in the way of entertainment. However, as soon as the mayor mentioned his trysts took place at the Old Rosebud Motel, Hunter's mind drifted far away from the one-sided conversation and the motel he remembered he was trying to forget. As the mayor prattled on and on, his drunken homespun banter showed qualities of both a salesman and a politician; self-celebratory and extremely long winded.

"...so the point of the story is," he declared with a dramatic flourish several minutes later.

"Oh thank God," Hunter thought to himself.

"...you can't reduce a man's whole life to his most recent shortcoming or unfortunate incident!" the mayor exclaimed with executive proclamation as he slammed down his Bloody Mary.

Had Hunter been paying attention, he could've been one step closer to going home. Unfortunately, the mayor had cast his pearls before whine.

The waitress finally brought out his food, and other than an occasional hiccup and grumble from the mayor, Hunter ate in silence.

On the walk back to Donau's, he glanced at his watch, wondering how much longer his wait might be. It was noon. One week earlier to the minute, he was finishing up mundane errands, counting the hours until getting married. Stranded in a two stoplight 'free love' town where the most interesting things worth mentioning were a drunken mayor and a skuzzy motel, he admitted with a slight smile, "Funny how things can turn."

Chapter Twenty-Eight

Back at Hooper Donau and Son's Service Station, Hunter's pensive mood suddenly turned optimistic after spotting an oversized pick-up truck with a shipment of tires and car parts being unloaded. With the giddiness of a child on Christmas morning, he ran to Hooper, Jr. wondering when his car might be ready.

"I'm 'fraid I got some bad news. Tim ain't got that tire here."

Within seconds, blood pooled in Hunter's brain. His fists and teeth clenched, his eyes fluttered in disbelief and he lost control.

"Wwwait-wwwait-wait," he stuttered, trying to maintain his composure. "Are you saying, that in this entire region of west Texas, I can't buy the tire I need?" he exaggerated in an attempt to berate Hoop.

Unfazed by his customer's belittling tone, Hoop tilted his head and shrugged his shoulders. "I can't speak for the entire region. They got themselves a Sears in Fort Stockton, but I'm tellin' you our distributor ain't got what you need today."

"So I'm stuck here in...in...Where the hell am I again?"

"Bakersfield, sir."

"...Bakersfield? Until Monday?"

"Not unless you want to drive on that tiny spare wheel all the way to Fort Stockton. By the way, how was your night last night?" Hoop asked sincerely.

Pointing his finger with an accusatory annoyance, he ignored the question. "Your mayor warned me this would happen."

"You see the mayor down at Kingman's?" Hoop asked innocently, unaware that he'd just been insulted. "I hope he wasn't already too far gone," he added, checking his watch.

Feeling trapped in some perverse 'Abbot & Costello Meet the Twilight Zone' parody, Hunter spun around in frustration and kicked at a rock in front of him. The rock skidded across the parking lot and in an unsettling omen, ricocheted off the rim of his own flat tire.

"Why couldn't this have happened in Nashville or New Orleans, where hotel rooms are comforting and beds are used for sleeping," he thought out loud. As soon as Hunter resigned to spend another two nights in the austere accommodations of the Old Rosebud, Hoop Jr. sensed his despair and a moment of inspiration, realized a third option he hadn't thought about.

"You know, if'n you're dead set not to spend any more time here, it dawned on me, we may have them tires we took off the other fella's car 'round back. We can go check if'n ya want," Hoop Jr. offered as he picked up two trash bags filled with discarded oil and air filter boxes.

Hunter's attitude changed back. His head sprung up with new life and his eyebrows rose with the prospect of this problem disappearing. "Now," Hoop continued, "I cain't make no promises 'bout any of them tires, and I cain't give you no warranty; but if we find one, I reckon we can git it on yer rim so you can git on your way. That is, if you're dead set on not waitin'."

"I'm pretty dead set, Hoop," he responded excitedly.

"C'mon then. Jes help me carry back some of this garbage if'n you will," Hoop requested.

Back behind the garage at the garbage dump/used parts storage, they found the four tires arranged alongside rusted water-pumps, engine manifolds and faded faux-leather car seats Hoop Donau, Sr. kept, 'just in case.'

"Yep, there them tires," Hoop pointed apprehensively. "Y'see, they sure ain't much."

The two men scrutinized the tires, fingering what little treads were left, trying by process of elimination to determine which tire promised the best prospect of lasting a little longer. Hoop, Jr. patted the tire he favored. It was bald to the point of its steel belts showing through, but they weren't as badly frayed as the others.

"I figure this one's prob'ly your best bet."

"If that's your professional opinion..." Hunter conceded rhetorically.

"My professional opinion is fer you to wait til we have the proper tire in stock," Hoop reiterated sarcastically, "otherwise, let's just git this tire on yer car, if that's what ya want."

Using an antiquated, yet incredibly efficient jack, Donau's tire-jockey raised the Mustang's flat tire two feet off the ground with three quick pumps on the long lever. Furthermore, it took him less than two minutes to switch tires using a pneumatic wrench. Had Hoop remembered the discarded tires earlier, Hunter's whole Bakersfield detour could have been drastically minimized. As they settled up, Hoop included a couple of addendums.

"Now, you realize, this is probably very illegal," he stated clearly. "You didn't get this tire here, and I can't give you a receipt, understand?" he stressed, covering his bases. Hunter didn't care. Nearly ecstatic, he would've agreed that the earth is flat if it meant getting out of Bakersfield. In hindsight, he felt ashamed for believing the mayor and prejudging the Donaus as crooks, especially after Hoop only charged $10 to change the tire.

Merging back onto I-10, Hunter celebrated his reclaimed freedom by gunning the engine and testing the tire. At 65 mph, all systems worked close to normal. At 75 mph, the steering wheel shimmied a bit. It wasn't until the speedometer read 90 mph that the car's handling suffered noticeably, compared to its usual performance. Satisfied the envelope had been pushed to acceptable limits, he felt relieved. Even if that tire had been bound to the wheel with electrical tape, twine and safety pins, it beat spending another 48 hours with the Slacker Twins back at the Old Rosebud.

A comforting wave of relief engulfed him momentarily, and he gratefully embraced the open road – an understatement in west Texas. The low, flat horizon teased him with the illusion of being able to see as far as two days into the future. "Too bad," he mused. "I'd like to know how it all works out; if it works out in less than two days. Or if it works out at all."

Surrounded by the wicked is a test of sanity
So you shout your alibis from moral high ground.

Samuel Miller

To make sure it's honest and not just your vanity.
Wait for the echo and listen to the sound.

With close to six hours of daylight driving left, he estimated escaping Texas by sundown. His spirits lifted from his perceived victory, he knew it wasn't that a good thing had happened as much as he'd just avoided more of a bad thing. Regardless, his gratitude gave him new perspective as he watched the scenery zip past. The epic west Texas surroundings could've easily been the birthplace of monotony, yet they offered an enigmatic quality, a unique Spartan beauty unavailable up North.

He theorized that every northerner should drive through Texas one time to fully appreciate it, or if not to appreciate it, at least respect it. He quickly scoffed at the improbability of his novel notion, since most northerners would rather immolate themselves than deal with the Southwest — and frankly, immolation wouldn't be half as hot. Besides, Texans like as little interaction with northerners as possible.

Deep in thought, focusing on an optimistic future beyond the constantly shifting horizon, Hunter stopped paying attention to exit signs and absent-mindedly forgot about getting a new tire.

I was told when very young, that from the moment of birth
I'm entitled to my Father's world, both his grief and his mirth
It's a heart sewn on a sleeve, but it's not hard to believe
When it's taught through the agony, it's best to grieve

During the next three or so hours, the elements of the west Texas landscape grew easier to count. Turf decreased dramatically as the amount of sagebrush drifting along the ground increased. The grassy plains he'd grown used to all week had turned to scorched ground, dead brown grass and small scrubby bushes as he passed through dusty towns like Saragossa, Plateau, Allamore, Sierra Blanca, Riva Ridge and

Esperanza; towns that were few and far between and just a half-dozen deaths away from official ghost-town status.

This peaceful serenity subsided and succumbed, however, replaced by a lingering sense of loneliness; the lack of cars in sight intensifying that alienation. The loneliness, the desperation, his frustrated feeling of failure all magnified his withdrawal into solitude. In a moment of honest reflection, Hunter discovered another basic axiom.

Isolation from people may be the worst condition a soul can endure. Isolation eliminates the vital stimulus humans crave, imprisons the mind, and forces a monotonous repetition of thoughts. Isolation results in no contact, no exchanging, no sharing or growing. If a soul can't share emotions, those emotions become wasted. If those emotions are wasted, then there's no point to even having them in the first place. If Peter was right about souls being defined by emotions, then ultimately a soul with no emotions possesses no measuring stick to define existence. He doesn't exist. He's a lost soul.

If $A = B$, $B = C$, and $C = D$, then $A = D$. Isolation = Lost Soul.

People spend their lives proudly defining themselves. Fulfilling instinctive urges to impress others, validating their importance, convincing others of their productivity. Without understanding it, people's lives revolve around themselves. A four dimensional canvas created to express the most complete image of themselves. It's such a universal obsession; it's simply called 'an identity – who we are.'

Isolation means taking solitude too far. Often, for different reasons, spending too much time alone comes at a price – the loss of humanity around us. What use are emotions if there's nobody to share them with? How satisfying is good news with nobody else to revel in it? How much comfort can a man get after devastating news without a sympathetic shoulder to lean on? There will always be periods when a man needs to satisfy a wanderlust in favor of the silence in his imagination, but it means nothing if he doesn't rejoin the pack to share himself and his lessons.

Alienation manifests in many toxic forms. Perhaps the worst is when people turn their backs and ignore those who want to share with them.

"It's so simple," he exclaimed to himself. "Life is about sharing. Life is about other people."

With his latest emotional discovery, a random thought about Hope popped in his head, and for the first time in a week, he knew he could never marry her. Even if he found her, forgave her and they reconciled, there would always be a scintilla of residual doubt scraping away at the paper-thin protective layer of trust. Not always, but too many times, scorned lovers beg to be taken back. Running to someone who only hurts you is the exact opposite of turning your back on someone who wants to help, but it's just as poisonous.

> *Trouble begins when your mind's become ground zero*
> *And the battleground tactics have all been tried*
> *Don't be fooled by a boastful anti-hero*
> *'Cause all the best saviors have already died.*

"Good Lord, you're still in Texas?" Peter suddenly asked, popping-in the passenger seat.

"Hey, there you are," Hunter answered surprised, shaken from his contemplation. "Where've you been all day? Where were you last night? I could have used the company."

Peter sighed with disappointment that his son had not grasped the concept that he's always there. Deciding to let it go, instead he asked a simple question.

"So how are you hanging in there?"

"Ahhh, you know," Hunter replied with a timid nervousness.

"No, I don't know," his father answered.

Pondering isolation and loss forced him to dwell upon his depression. By putting so much stock into an illusory life that rejected him, he assumed his identity had collapsed. Was there any meaning? What could he look for?

"It's like, life rolls by and you rarely notice anything wrong day-to-day. There's stability. Bills are paid, there's gas in the car and condiments in the fridge. It's an ordinary day under control. Then one ordinary day turns into another, then an ordinary week and an ordinary month. Eventually, 15 ordinary years pass and you've done nothing. Nothing's happened and there's no progress to show for it. You look in the mirror but it's the same face as always. The changes are too gradual to notice. Then one day you look around and you're lost. But how can you get lost if you weren't heading any particular direction. Can you be lost if you have no destination? What do you look for?"

Peter paused, dramatically, organizing the right words.

"Son, think about this. What makes up those things people search for? Broken down to its simplest elements, in history, there are two continuous threads connecting all philosophers. From intellectuals dead for thousands of years to regular guys drinking beers with buddies; the search for truth and beauty. Everything important is the search for truth or beauty. Now, they're not the same. Truth is not always beautiful and often, beauty is a lie. Thankfully, the degrees of variations in the eye of the beholder keep things interesting. Even if the majority declares someone or something is true or beautiful, there's always a dissenting view. And without unanimous consent or proof, nothing can be absolute. So where can you find truth and beauty? On the inside? On the outside? Both? It's a matter of perspective. You can search for one, while the other is under your nose. Or you can accidentally stumble across one when it's least expected. Peel the distracting layers away from anything and at its essence you'll always reveal some level of truth or beauty. They remain the last pure things on earth, but they cross into every area. They're the two things that make life worth living. The continuing, sincere, committed search for truth and beauty."

Peter had somehow managed to reduce an immense abstract to its simplest basic core. Without looking over, Hunter knew his dad had already vanished.

Determined to test his new learned insight, he applied this philosophy to the passing Texas landscape. If he could strip an already desiccated west Texas scenery down to its barest essentials, and still find truth or beauty, somehow the rest would be easy. Before he could scrutinize the landscape, however, the monotony started breaking up as El Paso neared. In his excitement over the prospect of not being quite so isolated in the vastness of nowhere, he felt relieved. The signs of civilization reappeared and he forgot about the insightful gift, losing the fire to discover and losing his lesson.

El Paso was not only bigger than expected, it was simply big. Not as colossal as Houston and perhaps three-fourths the size of San Antonio, still, El Paso loomed as a major Texas metropolis nonetheless. As he got closer, his attention was grabbed and held by the beginning foothills of the Rocky Mountains. He stared in awe, inspired by snowcaps dramatically jutting up from the land like a primitive skyline. He imagined hiking the steep hills, climbing challenging passages and conquering well-trodden serpentine paths, until reaching the apex and being closer to the Heavens.

"Now that's beauty," he said aloud.

Figuring the view couldn't get any more dramatic, he caught his best glimpse yet of the Rio Grande and Mexico. After traversing the plain flat vastness, signs of beauty unfolded before him: a major city, the foothills of the Rocky Mountains, the Rio Grande and Mexico. Finally, a scrap of redemption for the perseverance.

Mesmerized by the foothills, these were the humble beginnings of a major natural wonder stretching thousands of miles. He remained awestruck until remembering that, being from Minneapolis, he'd crossed over the near-genesis of the Mississippi River every day and never thought twice about it.

It was no different he realized. Like any significant landmark, the Rockies had been roughly the same size and shape for millions of years, waiting for each new set of eyes to discover them all over again. They could be seen exactly where they had always been and their awesome beauty and impressive majesty had not changed. It was Hunter who had to change to witness their grandeur.

And that was truth.

Chapter Twenty-Nine

Most men, their lives revolve around their honey
And a few go pretty far, because they're really smart
I've know many whose lives are run by money
And some who dedicate their existence to making art
Several live for travel to see the world's attractions
Others are fortunate to do well with careers
I've never had the benefit of those distractions
'Cause I've been running on faith for all my years

On the other side of El Paso, the panorama returned to the parched Southwest surroundings he'd grown accustomed to. The only proof of escaping the immense boundaries of Texas was another sign.

Welcome To New Mexico
"The Land of Enchantment"

The setting sun baked the harsh landscape to a dry brown-red tinge, suggesting everyday life resembled an 1880's sepia tone daguerreotype. A thick, encompassing curtain of swirling dust, stirred by a desert zephyr, filtered the sunlight, dividing it and allowing only a few rays to penetrate to the ground. Road signs partially obscured by dust kicked-up by cars 'just traveling through' protected the region's sacred anonymity for area residents. For most folks, southern New Mexico does not typify an ideal locale for settling down and setting up shop. Rather it remains a mysterious, exotic place only imagined about in passing.

The blinding sunset gave him a good excuse for calling it a day and checking into the first available lodge. Not long after passing Las Cruces, he found a motel with a diner next door. The Gato Del Sol Motel was a somewhat fake looking adobe structure on I-10 between Las Cruces and Deming, which is to say, in the middle of nowhere. Like many things in this region, its catchy Spanish name perpetuated a mysterious image, so tourists from ordinary places like Buffalo, Omaha and Spokane got the impression of visiting a strange land where 'hardly anyone spoke English.' The most promising clue the Gato Del Sol Motel might have been a notch above the previous night's accommodations came in an elaborate antique flashing neon cactus in front. The glowing turquoise cactus, cutting-edge decor decades earlier, stood as a kitschy monument to those glory days of the Route 66 mystique. That nostalgic image shattered after spotting a plastic pennant posted beside it:

Free HBO in all rooms!

The 21st Century was bound to happen sooner or later, even 20 miles outside Deming, New Mexico.

By now, his check-in experience had bloomed into a precise expert synchronization. The front desk manager's semi-professional disposition alleviated his fear of this motel being as bad as the Old Rosebud, but the ultimate proof was in the bedding. Anybody can wear a tie, smile and sell garbage.

Scanning his room left him reassured, yet also a bit disappointed. The hotel's cement block facade promised at least a little authenticity. Once inside, the rooms were as common as they come. What he first assumed was a sturdy, sentimental relic ended up as a contrived marketing idea; a cynical letdown likely concocted by a travel industry magnate who saw a chance to cash in on an image of a neglected hotel he'd stumbled upon.

Checking his watch, it read 9 o'clock — an awkward time given his situation. Not particularly hungry and not quite on the threshold of drowsiness, he wondered how to occupy himself for a couple hours until exhaustion kicked in. Turning on the television, surfing through the available free channels, there was nothing mildly interesting. Even HBO, the big promotional draw, proved disappointing, showing a documentary on the making of 'Typhoon II,' a disaster movie sequel about a luxury Pacific resort that was rebuilt two years after being obliterated in the original blockbuster. Yes, the 21st Century did indeed arrive 20 miles outside Deming, New Mexico, but apparently it didn't make it any more entertaining. As soon as he felt relieved that 'at least it's not 8 o'clock,' he glanced at the cheap clock radio on the bedside table. It was 8 o'clock. He had passed into Mountain Time.

Strangely, though gaining an hour, he felt cheated, as if the passage of the previous 60 minutes had been lost. Ignoring the uncommon luxury of reliving time, he reasoned it would've been more convenient had the hour already passed. So in addition to everything else lost, (his fiancée, his job, his brother, complete control over his life, and quite possibly his mind), in some warped way, he lost one hour. And not just any 60 minutes. Exactly one week ago to that hour, this whole episode began. He would have given everything to go back in time to change that hour, and now he had to relive that same Saturday 8 p.m. hour one week later. He chucked the television remote on the bed with exaggerated disgust and headed back out the door for an evening walk.

Twilight in New Mexico glowed unlike any time of day in any part of the country he'd seen so far. Intense reds, brilliant oranges and earthy browns converged in a unique way, making it difficult to judge where the horizon began, while distant shimmering desert mirages suggested the illusion of Native American ghosts standing sentry over their beloved land. One glimpse of the bleeding sunset made his annoyed feelings about the lost hour fade. Spotting a bench beside the sidewalk, he sat down to watch the rest of the show.

It was the precise cusp between day and night when the sun could have belonged to the evening and the moon might have held dominion over the late afternoon. But like every other dusk, the night stars popped out as the day star abandoned its reign, dimming in the west.

"I've seen a lot of things in this world, but not many like this," Peter remarked.

Glancing at his father he asked, "Remember the other day when you said we all have a purpose?"

"I said you're here to do one thing but you're not supposed to know what it is," Peter corrected.

"So there's a Divine plan or something?" Hunter inquired.

Seeing where his son was heading, Peter paused and drew a deep breath.

"You know, people are so arrogant, everybody thinks their destiny should be grand. A general who wins a decisive battle. A chemist who cures a fatal disease. An author who writes an inspirational best seller. People obsess that life should have dramatic meaning. Celebrities, important men who deserve respect. If their name isn't on the lips of strangers, life is a dismal failure," he mockingly emphasized. "What people don't understand is the most meaningful acts they perform are so simple. The small simple acts are much more indicative about their true nature than any grand gesture. One simple deed leads to another and so on. Millions of modest dominoes falling in a never-ending chain-reaction, providing insight and helping others along the way. Together they add up, exponentially creating a beautiful mosaic of potential," Peter expressed, adding a sweeping motion toward the sunset.

"Even if you are a great man of achievements, they probably don't have much to do with the reason you're here. Yes, it's noble to help others, but man's accomplishments are not part of His master plan," Peter asserted pointing at Heaven. "He's not too easily impressed."

"Also, sometimes people finish their task and die immediately. Other times, they get the job done early and live another 80 years. Fair or unfair, who cares? It's the big picture that matters. Every man is a single dab of paint in a masterpiece. Individually, each one is unique and vibrant, but it only makes sense when viewed as a whole."

Listening to his father explain the fairness of inequality, an impatient Hunter showed a nervous anxiety, clenching his fists over and over as if time had become a vital issue. His own soul may have alerted him to imminent calamity. Peter saw the stress but resisted a confrontation, deciding instead on dipping into his knowledge of the cosmos for his next point.

"You see that star?" he paused, pointing at the sky. "That star is 10,000 light years from earth. The light you're seeing from that star was emitted 10,000 years ago, and it's taken that long to reach Earth. Now, what if something happened sometime during those 10,000 years and that star burned out? That could be a dead, dark star right now and you wouldn't know because the light, the power, the energy it gave off millenniums ago still exists on its way here and beyond. It's the same thing with your soul. When a body gives out, the soul and the power and energy it gave off, still exists. Just understand this; your life belongs to you, but not as much as your soul belongs to God. You're in control of your life, but God's in charge of your soul. Give up control, boy. Just trust Him. "

Wanting to believe his father, giving up control was too massive a leap of faith. His mind fought it, racing with flimsy excuses to counter his father's advice — and before Hunter could come up with a rationale challenge, Peter disappeared, just as the last trace of daylight vanished. The New Mexico sky had completed its metamorphosis to a dark, serene vastness.

Instead of returning to his room right away, he stayed on the bench another half-hour debating the pros and cons of 'just letting go.' As if there wasn't enough turmoil jockeying for position in his mind, this internal struggle added one more facet to the billowing angst. If his life had floundered up to then, how well could it go by surrendering all control? On the other hand, maybe he faltered because a fixation for control stifled his options. More interestingly, how does one go about 'just letting go'?

Back in his room, the darkness had grown relaxing, surrounding him with isolating calmness. The only breach of light was a consistent glow of turquoise smoothly blinking around the edges of his drawn curtains. Slipping under the latest set of rough, unfamiliar sheets, Hunter came to one conclusion.

He was tired and needed the comfort of a home.

Chapter Thirty
<u>Sunday</u>

Sleeping-in until after 11 o'clock on Sunday morning wasn't something he planned, but his three days in Texas had exhausted him. Besides, he hadn't slept in such a nice room or decent bed since New Orleans — which wasn't a positive reflection on the Gato Del Sol Motel as much as an indictment of the previous two night's arrangements. As a pleasant result, he woke up refreshed and recharged. Nearly twelve hours of sleep can do that.

A lingering awareness weighed heavy in his heart, however. Thinking less about being jilted and fired, the memory of the previous night's talk with his father left him engulfed in confused desperation. Something hidden had to be done. Something was left unfinished and the frustration of his inability to define it left him feeling empty.

An emptiness much easier to pinpoint was hunger. After dressing and checking-out of the Gato Del Sol Motel, he tossed his bags in the car and walked next door to Lil E. Tee's Place, a diner that at one time was presumably part of the motel since they shared similar over-the-top Southwest architecture. Judging by the condition of the upkeep, the motel and diner had separated several years earlier.

Lil E. Tee's Place had 12 cheap chrome-trimmed Formica tables with two chairs at each, six stools at the counter and four variably ripped Naugahyde booths along two opposite walls. The linoleum black and white floor tiles were mildly scuffed, and by happenstance the ceiling almost mirrored the floor since many of the floor's black tiles were directly under dark holes where fiberglass ceiling tiles were missing. On the walls were a few unrelated posters hung in random places to take up space, including a Georgia O'Keefe print, a badly stained poster of a past New Mexico State University football team and a colorful cartoon of sheep grazing at the edge of a cliff. The main focus, however, were large posters showcasing beautifully prepared and garnished meals available from the menu. He doubted if the real Waffle Plate Special or Fruit Bowl Medley being served bore any resemblance to the professionally produced photos, but they all looked appetizing and made choosing difficult.

The only other patron in Lil E. Tee's Place that morning was an elderly Native American sitting in a booth. Hunter greeted the old man with a polite nod as he passed by, but the old Indian, perhaps harboring decades of resentment toward the White Man, ignored him and his greeting.

Taking a stool, Hunter grabbed a creased, wrinkled menu and glanced over the choices, scanning the walls for each item's poster hoping to sway his decision. At the end of the counter, set back near the corner, a television tuned to CNN drowned out the sizzling sounds of the grill.

The diner's sole employee sat hunched over the counter, concentrating on a crossword puzzle in a folded newspaper. Perhaps in a ploy to lend his restaurant a measure of elegance, the cook wore a heavy starched white jacket embroidered with black block letters — 'Elwood Taylor'. If Elwood Taylor was the proprietor of Lil E. Tee's, there was nothing 'lil' about him. A rough, whiskery hulk, Elwood wore a long mullet and had ears that curved forward. Most prominent, however, was Elwood's lazy eye. Hunter was uncomfortable with lazy eyes, never knowing which eye to look into. He wondered if people with lazy eyes knew about it, or when they looked in the mirror, did the lazy eye skew their sight to the point that it appeared normal? Like most, he never mentioned it, in case they didn't realize they had one. Seeing that Chef Elwood was figuring a crossword puzzle, that brought up a whole other question; because of his lazy eye, could Elwood be scribbling his answers in the wrong squares?

Before he had a chance to order, Elwood took a few seconds to scrutinized his customer's face, asking, "Hey, you look familiar. You a famous celebrity?"

Amused by the obvious irony, Hunter answered, "If I was famous, you wouldn't have to ask, would you?"

Confused at first, Elwood got the joke.

"I guess yer right," Elwood chuckled, "I jes thought I seen your face before. What'll you have?"

"Coffee, orange juice, English muffin, hash browns and bacon, please."

"Have that in a minute," Elwood replied, turning back to his grill to work his breakfast magic. With everything sizzling on the grill, Elwood returned his attention to the crossword puzzle, struggling with a clue.

"This is the damnedest thing," he remarked. "Nineteen across – 'Biblical garden', starts with 'G', but it ain't 'Garden of Eden' cause there's only ten spaces."

"Gethsemane," Hunter returned.

"G-g-gedsenin...?" Elwood tried repeating.

"Gethsemane. G-e-t-h-s-e-m-a-n-e," he offered.

"a...n...e! Hey, that fits. Thanks. I got another one here. Twenty-two down, six letters. 'Harvey's friend, Mr. Dowd."

"Elwood," he answered.

"Yeah?" Elwood asked expecting something else.

"El-wood," he deliberately repeated, a little louder and slower.

The chef stared his patron in the eyes as best he could arching his eyebrows in anticipation of a question or comment to follow his name. 'Gethsemane' was tough, but if a man named Elwood had never heard about Elwood P. Dowd and his companion, Harvey the Invisible 6' Rabbit, he didn't deserve the answer and probably shouldn't be doing crossword puzzles. Instead of explaining, Hunter just pointed out that his breakfast was close to burning. The chef acted quickly, managing to salvage everything.

As Elwood placed his plates in front of him, Hunter turned his attention to the television news.

"We'll have an update on Saturday's tragic plane crash in France that claimed 157 passengers at the top of the hour. Now here are the top sports stories."

Elwood heard the word 'sports' and spun around pointing at the television.

"Hey, you gotta hear this," he exclaimed. "They been showing it every half-hour with the sports headlines."

"For Headline Sports, I'm Corben Alison. Here's a feel-good story from the 'where are they now' file. In a bizarre turn of events, former basketball superstar and homeless MIA Manuel Montrose won an astonishing $325,000 at a Louisiana casino on Saturday."

For the umpteenth time that week, Hunter's jaw dropped like he had a mouth full of molten lead. On the screen was Manuel at a casino. True to his word, he'd gotten cleaned up with a shave, a haircut and new clothes — not at all resembling the man scrounging quarters days earlier. Instead he recaptured the glorious Manuel Montrose of old. The reporter continued.

"According to the one-time hoops phenom who disappeared after several self-destructive binges, the initial seed money came in the form of an extraordinary $10,000 handout that he parlayed into his incredible winnings. All Montrose said he knew of his mysterious benefactor is that he's a man from Minneapolis named Hunter Damon."

If the story alone wasn't nauseating enough to Hunter, CNN put a photo on the screen of Hope and him posing while raking leaves in his front yard. Taken the previous fall by Mrs. Buchanan, the elderly widow next door, he remembered the exact moment the photo was taken. For months she'd promised to give it to him, instead, she must have handed it over to the news crew when they knocked on her door, after realizing he wasn't home.

He didn't know what stupefied him more — seeing a painful reminder of his ex-fiancée on national TV, or learning a homeless bum made over a quarter million dollars from his altruism.

"...Montrose positively identified Hunter Damon from this photograph, and went on to explain that he had never met Mr. Damon before their chance meeting and didn't know where he went after they parted ways. Manuel Montrose said he is eternally grateful to Mr. Damon and thankful for a second chance at life. Efforts to reach Mr. Damon in Minneapolis were unsuccessful."

Elwood, watching the story with great amusement, began commenting on the absurdity of a total stranger giving away $10,000.

"Don't that just beat all?" Elwood chuckled. "I wish a sucker handing out ten grand would come in here. Can you believe some jackass would...?" Elwood began.

As he turned to address his customer with his astute observation, Elwood, even with his lazy eye, recognized the face on TV as the same face at his counter. After a double, then a triple take, he stared at Hunter dumbfounded. Now an official demi-celebrity, Hunter smiled, nodded and answered, "Yeah, I guess that jackass would be me."

Contrary to Hunter's taunting attitude, Elwood decided to test the potential for opportunity knocking on his greasy spoon's squeaky screen door.

"You know, as long as you're handing out money," the cook hinted.

Rather than answer rudely, he ignored Elwood.

Embarrassed by his faux pas, a humbled Elwood hoped he hadn't alienated his philanthropic customer too badly and wondered if he could still profit if he played his cards right. "Your girlfriend in the photo is real pretty," he blurted out, trying to curry favor.

Hunter sat stunned, tilting his head a touch to the left, staring directly into Elwood's lazy eye. Elwood searched for an inkling of reaction to his roundabout request, until a few seconds of Hunter's offended face answered his question with little doubt.

"Can't blame a guy for asking," Elwood muttered under his breath, turning back to his grill.

The diner's atmosphere remained polite, but every sound, carried an awkward tension fed by Hunter's sudden fatalistic mood. It had taken a full week to reach the near nadir of his mentality; that vile place where the only silver lining is 'at least there's nowhere to go but up.' After hearing of Manuel's good fortune, that standard further plummeted.

Peter and Lee Damon had run their household with a strong Christian-Judeo ethic. Good things happen to good people. Bad people get their comeuppance. That's justice. While Manuel didn't necessarily fall into the bad category, he certainly squandered a lot of talent and money on self-destruction and vice. What bothered Hunter was how the severance check stood for everything evil that happened to him. A buy out for their conscience at his expense, the check represented a cancer that deliberately ate the noble pieces of his soul, leaving the bitter, sour parts like fear, rejection, betrayal and anger to fester and infect his psyche. He didn't want the check, so he gave it away with good intentions hoping it might help someone who needed a chance; but this ironic twist of karma bordered on cruel. He was the one who needed Divine Intervention after being abandoned and emotionally drained. He was the one being punished for doing nothing wrong. He was the one who went above and beyond to make an extraordinary gesture. Yet it was Manuel who'd won the chance to reclaim the foundation of his castle. In short, Hunter fell victim to the time-honored, well-worn plea uttered by shortsighted people.

'That's not fair.'

His appetite understandably shot, all he could do for five minutes was push at his food and scratch his plate with a fork. Finally, he grabbed his wallet from his back pocket and pulled out the smaller denominations of bills. Counting out $10 for the check, he tossed it on the counter, shoved the remaining cash in his pocket and headed to the door, crushing his wallet in his hand.

He'd already reached the door by the time the other customer got up to follow him. The elderly Indian shuffled as fast as he could to catch him, but Hunter saw him and ignored the old man who'd snubbed him minutes earlier.

"Wait up," the Indian yelled. Hunter stopped, put his wallet down on his car's trunk and leaned on his stiffened arms. Glancing skyward he addressed Heaven.

"This just keeps getting better, doesn't it?" he asked God. In a moment of defeat, he hunched his shoulders and hung his head down.

"Please, I am old. Don't make me run," the Indian pleaded as his gait slowed. "I want to talk to you," he tried again.

Hunter leaned up and, assuming the old man wanted a hand out, spun around in a frustrated pose with his hands in his pockets.

"What?" he asked, exasperated.

"You are the man on the news who gave away $10,000?"

the Indian asked.

"Yes, that was my picture on TV," he growled. "I'm sorry, I don't have any money to give you," he continued, patronizing the old man. "It was a onetime thing."

The old man seemed confused, then broke into a huge smile. "I do not want your money. I have lived here all my life, and have been turning down the White Man's money the whole time. I don't plan to start taking it now."

Ashamed at his presumption, Hunter walked closer to the Indian elder.

"I'm sorry. Then what do you want?" he asked.

"If you are the man who gave a homeless stranger $10,000, then I would like to shake your hand," the old man responded as he extending a bony, leathered arm. Confused, Hunter took the stranger's frail hand and shook it gingerly

"You know," the old man continued, "as long as I can remember, the White Man has taken and taken and taken, but he rarely gives back. When the White Man does give, he makes sure he still has much more in his home. He does not have the faith to give his all. You look comfortable, but do not look rich; and yet you gave so much."

Hunter's humility kicked-in. Instead of being hit up for money, he was being praised.

"Well Mr. ..." he started.

"My name is Ben Brushwolf," the elderly Indian filled in. "Like I said, the White Man takes. This is the first time I can remember that he has given, yet I sense in you an anger of this great deed you have done. Why?"

Not even tempted to tell his story again, Hunter gave a succinct answer.

"I didn't want that money, but I don't think it's fair that someone should benefit so much from my heartache."

The old man bellowed on the verge of a coughing fit, then answered. "Now, you know how we have felt all these many years." Hunter couldn't help but smile along with the old Indian, then Ben continued. "Why should that matter to you? You did what you wanted to do with the money, he did what he wanted to do with the money. Had you not seen it on television, you would not have known about it, but the result would have been the same. Do not worry about your neighbor's prosperity; just know the condition of your own home. But what we do to help others comes back to help us. You will receive a valuable reward for your kindness and patience. It may not be money, but it will be of great value. You will see."

"Karma?" Hunter confirmed to himself.

"Call it what you will, the Great Creator does not make differences between people and their beliefs. God is an elephant."

He understood what Ben said to that point, but the 'elephant' comment confused him.

"What?" he asked.

"God is an elephant," Ben repeated. "It is an old White Man's story we tell to teach our children about the Great Creator. You see, there were six blind men who came across an elephant. None of them had ever seen one, so they did not know what it was. The first man grabbed the elephant's tail and said, 'An elephant is like a strong rope.' The second man had his arms around one of the feet. 'No,' he said, 'an elephant is like the trunk of a great tree.' The third man felt along the beast's side. 'No,' he said, 'an elephant is a rough wall.' The fourth felt the tusk and claimed, 'An elephant is more like a sharp spear.' The fifth man was touching the ear and said, 'An elephant is like a fan.' Finally the sixth blind man felt the elephant's squirming trunk and told the others, 'You are all wrong. An elephant is like a big snake.' So even though none of them had ever seen an elephant and didn't know what one looked like, they all had faith. Each blind man was partially right, but they were all wrong."

"The Alpha and the Omega," Hunter said to himself remembering his father's lesson while showing the wise elder he understood.

"Exactly," Ben responded, proud of his new student.

The old man's face beamed. Hunter looked into Ben's sincere eyes and saw his own sincerity reflected back. Ben then grabbed Hunter's cheeks, and turned his face left then right, inspecting it with careful scrutiny. The elder didn't say anything, rather he let out a couple grunts signifying his approval. He patted his student on the shoulder, nodded, turned and started walking back to the diner. Halfway there, Ben turned around.

"You are a good soul. I saw that in your eyes. You will see," he said with a chuckle of confidence.

"How?" Hunter asked cynically.

Ben grinned and raised his right hand as if offering the classic Indian greeting. "How...indeed," he replied with a wink. "You will see," the old man reiterated continuing back inside the diner.

To anyone else, the past week would have been an eventful, bizarre learning experience. Even the nonevents promised enormous potential for securing answers. Unfortunately, obsessing about his losses blurred his rational, skewing his priorities. Instead of reflecting upon the Indian's sage words, he couldn't focus past his face plastered on TV (with his ex-fiancée) as the guy who gave thousands of dollars to a burned-out bum, who then won a quarter-million dollars with a few rolls of the dice.

Sitting in his idling car, he tried to put a positive spin on Manny's windfall, fantasizing about Paul Jones' reaction after learning his buy-out check went to a vagrant. Paul Jones, captain of industry, proponent of capitalism and a lifelong advocate of honest wages for hard work, had indirectly helped 'a derelict with little or no social redeeming value' make the quick dollars. Hunter's grin was short lived as it changed to a sour sneer after remembering a time he overheard Paul bragging about a beach condo he'd bought with tremendous dividends he'd 'earned' from a stock broker's tip.

An unrelenting feeling gnawed at Hunter. Where was his incredible luck? Why had the powers-that-be overlooked him? Had he been forsaken in his hours of need?

Fed up, he put his Mustang in gear and jammed down the accelerator – kicking up small stones and leaving the gravel equivalent to peel-out marks.

I had so many grand dreams in my younger years
Ended up with silent screams that magnify my fears
There is no denying it, life took another route

Spend the nighttime's crying, when I really want to shout.
Staring in the mirror, I'm confused by who is in it.
I don't know how I got here, — but I remember every minute.
Scenarios inside my mind didn't happen as I planned
And facing the future blind is like walking on hot sand
Easy to blame the vice, but I know just what I've lost.
Had to pay a higher price, I didn't know the cost.
My world is a slowing sphere and I have no way to spin it.
I don't know how I got here, — but I remember every minute.

This latest implausible episode dominated his musings until its shock faded. In a disturbing pattern, his obsessions began creeping back into consciousness, and for an hour his mind reviewed chaotic scenarios, jumping back and forth, but allowing little effort and no time for figuring solutions.

The barrenness of the Southwest landscape had become a paradox. Its bleak isolation kept him aware of the emptiness of his existence, but at the same time, the lack of development and progress along this untouched vista introduced what a pristine world resembled during primordial eras — reminding him of the beautiful, pure part inside his soul that remained unsullied.

The primeval panorama inspired a last gasp attempt at spirituality. Squinting his eyes, he gazed again to Heaven.

"Is this what You want me to do?" he began with reverence "Am I on the right path?" he asked, recalling Peter's analogy. Despite a respectful tone, he hoped that since his request for Divine reassurance had been satisfied so quickly in Mississippi, perhaps 'Help Hunter Damon' took top priority on the Almighty's list of 'Things to do today.' Guilt-ridden by that grandiose presumption, he continued with a touch of self-abasement.

"I mean, I know You're busy with the sick and the poor and the dying and...everybody else much more deserving. Also, I'm sure it's hard enough, running a successful Universe, without some guy tugging at Your robe every five minutes. I don't mean to sound greedy...but I could use another sign down here — maybe something less abstract, a little more direct this time?"

His understatement and brash request was intended as an ironic show of humility to the Good Lord. With the casual nature of his prayers, combined with his less-than-conventional notions, he was already in way too deep if Almighty God, in fact, did not have a sense of humor.

"Hello?" he appealed almost comically. "Are You up there? Where are You?"

Like his reaction when the crucifix didn't transubstantiate and divulge Divine advice, Hunter felt alone and abandoned. However, less than two miles down the road, he received his second literal sign in a week.

Entering Lordsburg, NM
Pop. 6000

"You are good. I'll give You that," he smiled, shaking his head with amazement and appreciation. Both this latest sign and the Mississippi hotel marquee could have been disregarded as 'vague coincidences,' but he had been seeking calming reassurances that God heard him and followed his travels with omnipresent attention and endless patience. Hunter craved a more concrete suggestion. A specific mandate with no room for interpretation; a cut and dried message — like an old highway Burma-Shave ad:

Got a dollar to invest?
Don't know where to stick it?
Hunter, God *strongly* suggests
You buy a lottery ticket!

Falling deeper in contemplation, he reviewed concepts he'd faced on the road so far. Loss, love, fear, evil, truth & beauty, irony, karma, eternity...God, and even a few more. Each concept — far too colossal for a single man to grasp in a week, if at all. Combined — a formidable strain driving an already anxious mind to unexplored depths of panic and confusion.

Aware of how overpowering his introspections had escalated, he'd become stuck in the middle of mental and emotional anarchy. His compulsion for control had taken over, and like a slip-knotted rope binding his arms and neck, the more he resisted, the more damage it caused.

Lacking distractions or a reason to pay attention, it wasn't until he'd driven close to 40 miles to Thunder Gulch, Arizona before he realized he'd crossed into that state. Spotting a sign for a state highway approaching and needing to control anything about this odyssey, he figured 1400 miles was long enough on I-10, and turned onto Highway 191 just for something new.

Refusing the luxury of considering consequences, the value of a change of venue outweighed familiarity. He knew every action had opposite and equal reactions. What he didn't know was, his wallet, money and identity lay among the dust and gravel in the parking lot of Lil E. Tee's Place.

Chapter Thirty-One

Ever since I had to leave my Father, I've only wanted to go
back
He said, "Learn these lessons, or don't bother, it is these
things that you lack."
You may never hear my voice, but you know that I know all.
To claim my name, you have no choice -character comes from
the fall."
Now then living through those years, nothing about my life was
light.
And I cried so many tears, but stood straight for the good fight.
So imagine one day to my surprise, I got a call on the
telephone
Son, you've done well, it's time to rise, and I need you to come
home."
I'm going home.

Hunter believed each day of the week has a separate personality (although Tuesday and Wednesday seem similar). Each day fosters unique energies weaving through the air, manifested from the aura of millions of people performing daily routines. It was possible, he theorized, to be locked in solitude for an unknown number of days, walk outside and guess the day purely by perception.

This day was different. The surreal quiet of the Arizona desert around Highway 191 stifled his instinct. It lacked that usual Sunday silence of restful calm comprised of serenity, leisure and potential. Instead, the stark desert atmosphere conveyed an ominous warning, a distorted tension that mirrored and mocked his subconscious.

The isolation began smothering him like a thin plastic tarp wrapped around the contour of his spirit, cinched taut by a dozen strings of self-doubt, worry and uncertainty. It allowed light and air in for survival, yet just enough to inspect and rehash the same top of mind subjects causing his anguish and torture.

"Reminds you of old western movies, doesn't it?" Peter asked.

Shaken from his daze, Hunter looked over at his father. "It is Arizona. It's dry, it's hot, it's dusty," he replied proving his continued grasp of the obvious.

"No, it's a metaphor. C'mon, think out of the box for a moment," Peter pleaded. "The lone cowboy on his mustang; the rugged individual living by his own rules, defining his own morality, but still doing the right thing. It's quite inspiring."

"I'm glad you're amused," Hunter responded.

Seeing his son slipping into melancholy again, Peter grabbed his opportunity. "Alright, what's up now?" he asked.

Hunter sighed a long exasperated breath. "I thought after some time and distance, I'd get Hope, my job, everything, out of my mind. I know she's gone. I accept that. But every time I think about her, I wonder what the hell I'm doing out here. The emotions get stronger, like I should've fought harder."

He'd wanted to clear his head and find answers deep within himself but felt nowhere closer to truth than when he began, which frustrating him more. His reflections had been brought to a stymieing standstill by a dense fog of denial swirling in his mind, until Peter put truth into motion with wisdom that could only come from an insightful sage, able to break down a situation to basic facts.

"Hope?" Peter responded stunned. "This trip isn't about Hope. This trip hasn't been about Hope as soon as you renounced all possibilities by heading east in Eau Claire, when you committed yourself to this odyssey in the first place."

"What are you talking about?" Hunter asked in a shaky tone, a nervousness revealing that a small defiant part was beginning to understand.

"You're not doing this because of your losses," Peter continued. "It started out like that, but now it's become testing your mettle, reevaluating priorities, finding anything genuine you can trust in the back of your mind."

The first few pebbles of Hunter's wall jarred loose and

trickled down, but his resistance still tried pinning his defeats on uncontrollable forces.

"I've been out here a week," he lamented, "and I haven't learned a thing."

"My boy, you have no idea how much you've learned and how far you've come," Peter hinted mysteriously. "If only you open up a little more, the skies will unfold."

Hunter shuddered as if shaking off his father's advice, yet he knew it contained a swelling element of truth. His subconscious started the week with a faint tapping, but had begun pounding louder with each passing road sign while the rational mind scrambled to ignore it. No matter how secure his muddled thoughts bound him, the idea of abandoning control terrified him. His agonizing thoughts were not only the last things he could control, they were all he had left — and each one became a tiny dose of poison killing him slowly. Being emotionally naked to the world, showing friends and strangers the dark crevices of his psyche was like standing naked in public. He would rather die than expose who he was or who he thought he was to the world.

"Son, you know what the hardest thing to do is? Watch someone you love self-destruct before your very eyes. You've been driving for God only knows how many miles, and you don't know what you're looking for. What do you want?" Peter asked.

The dark brittle mortar cementing his protective wall began cracking, cascading away like heavy black dust. Larger stones loosened and fell into the void where the sound of symbolic stones smacking the wall on the way down, rang with a vibrato that grew louder and louder in his mind.

"What do you want?" Peter repeated more firmly.

"I don't know," Hunter shouted back in frustration.

"You don't know? Think, goddamn it. This is too important not to know."

Hunter calmed down and answered with confused vagueness.

"A reason," he said to placate his father.

"A reason? A reason for what?" his father pushed.

"A reason...for being," he half-heartedly confessed.

"A reason for being?" Peter repeated in a mocking tone, letting his son know he wasn't letting him off the hook with such a vague, universal answer. The decaying bastion fortifying Hunter's emotional wall prepared for one last clash. How much would it take to cause a man ruled by quiet restraint and utter control to lose it all and break down? It was forcing Hunter to face the demons he'd been barely dodging for days. Since the demons showed no sign of letting up, Peter's last best chance was misdirection: when a barking dog runs at you — run straight at the dog and bark even louder. Although Peter still had his trump card, he swung one last calculated blow to his son's wall. It could have pushed the pendulum in either direction, but at this critical crossroads, it was the final piece of advice to give his son.

"It's ironic," Peter said as if he had firsthand knowledge, "downright cruel if you think about it. You can never get a complete sense of what it's like to be human until after you die."

Hunter turned visibly agitated by his father's guru-like answers. Those bits of laser sharp wisdom seemed much too easy to be answers in a complicated life. His grip tightened on the steering wheel as he fought moistness forming in his eyes, but as he learned days earlier, it was impossible to lie to himself. They weren't tears of fear, weakness, hatred, or sadness. These tears were the final refuge of a confused, frustrated man. They were the last strips of cloth of a rejected castaway, lost and forgotten in an apathetic world that didn't care that he'd become emotionally exposed, abandoned and betrayed.

"You know dad, maybe you're right," he answered. "Death does have its advantages."

In an impulsive fit of rage, he stomped down on the accelerator and squinted his eyes, searching ahead with a fierce maniacal determination. The engine's hum swelled from a low, consistent purr to a higher pitched roar booming like chaos in his ears.

"What are you doing Hunter?" Peter asked, concerned but not afraid.

"Something I should have done before now."

It was only a matter of time before an ultimatum clicked in

Hunter's mind. Unable to keep them at bay any longer, the isolation, the loneliness, the pain and rejection all converged into one crossroads.

"Son, son...you don't have to do this," Peter assured him with a calm voice.

"No," he panicked. "Maybe I do need to do this. Maybe this is one thing I can control. What do you say I join you over there on the other side and find out?"

Hunter Damon's spiritual odyssey had lasted seven days and 3000 miles, but his dizzying descent into madness was a much quicker trip. His once impenetrable wall quickly decayed, becoming as fragile as the stem of the last leaf on a tree in Autumn.

Peter had no choice but to play his trump card.

"Son, listen to me carefully. You're ready to tell yourself," he hinted in a loud whisper. "It's been you this whole time. I'm not here. I'm just a manifestation in your mind. I'm how you remember me. And the things I've taught you? They're all truths and ideas already deep inside you. What you admire about me is in you and always has been. Your soul has memory. You've known that truth the whole time. You're the one telling yourself these things, not me. You know what I'm saying is true, and a small part of you has known all along. In fact, you know I'm not even here. Son, I don't exist, except in your..."

Hunter looked over and saw he was, indeed, alone. It had been him all along. The stories, the insight, the advice, the jokes, even the 'Other Side' rules were revealed as his own speculations. Unable to cope with his painful reality, fantasy took command, and yet through it all he managed to find truth.

Stunned, his mind shut down and his mouth hung open as he gawked blankly at the empty passenger seat, trying in vain to contain the flood of varied emotions. His foot, however, stayed smashed down on the accelerator in frustration. The Mustang cruised faster and faster and still faster, its cylinders pounding furiously, generating massive horsepower as if the car dreamed of this unbridled opportunity to stretch its 'legs.' But before Hunter could comprehend this latest epiphany, before he could appreciate the value of the gift he'd given himself and before he could slow down — disaster struck.

The bald replaced tire blew out.

The next several seconds were out of his control. Imprisoned in a 2500 pound machine and hurtling at over 100 mph with no way to stop until friction and force took over, time slowed down as distance stretched out, distorting all perceptions. Hunter strained and struggled with the steering wheel, instinctively fighting to regain control, but the car kept skidding on a thin layer of silt covering the road. The convertible swerved hard and fishtailed unpredictably, and each desperate jerk of the wheel only induced more radical over corrections. Then the unthinkable happened. The Mustang veered sideways, tipped over and started to whirl away in a rapid succession of violent flips, rolls and somersaults. Fear ruled and he lost his bearings as the horizon spun wildly. The ground and sky flip-flopped and the landscape streamed into blurred shades of red-brown and brown-red. He was thrown left and right and back and forth with no restraint, until at some point momentum spat him out, tossing him over the door onto the hard, dry, dusty shoulder where his body rolled several more feet. The car continued flipping, and each time its metal scraped against pavement, the screech sounded like Satan's laugh.

Eventually, all things put into motion come to a state of rest.

After the catastrophic chaos, the scene reverted to the eerie, harsh calm prevalent in the desert. The stifling, oppressive heat was bearable only because of a mild wind. Except now the desert boasted an extra reminder of its unforgiving harshness. The scraped, dented, twisted corpse of the Mustang laid upside down, its windshield nothing more than glass shards strewn across the highway. Its underside faced the sky while smoke and steam escaped upwards in a steady gray plume as if its soul ascended to Heaven.

Twenty seconds after receiving the greatest revelation of his life, Hunter Damon lay contorted and motionless on his back at the foot of a giant Saguaro a few yards from the road. His scraped, bloody arms stretched up and out, mimicking the cactus' limbs. And for the amount of pain he'd endured over the previous week, somehow, he finally looked peaceful.

Chapter Thirty-Two

As if given a mandate from God Himself, Hunter fluttered and opened his eyes. When he raised his hand to shield his eyes from the blinding sun, a wide stream of blood dribbled down his near-skinless forearm. Within moments of regaining his bearings, sharp pains screamed from every inch of his body. After a few more moments of enduring surging ceaseless pain, he groaned at the graveness of his situation with an assumed doom.

And that's when he realized the most ironic reality of all.

"I'm alive."

'To be or not to be' has always been the question. Spurred by tremendous anguish and not wanting any further injustice or calamity, Hunter thought he'd made his decision. But when Fate intervened, proposing to oblige, it was kind enough to extend an escape clause asking: 'Are you really sure you want to do this?' His instinctive fight to regain control of the careening car brought to light the severity of that choice and his instinctive gratitude for being alive unveiled his true answer. Upon recognizing his subconscious choice, that he didn't really want to die, his soul reverberated with profound elation.

With great effort and agony, Hunter sat up in the cactus patch, feeling stabbing pangs from broken ribs that pierced his breathing. Reacting in agony, he grabbed his torso with scraped crimson arms and shredded bloody palms, only to feel shooting sharpness from a broken left wrist. As he bit his lower lip while rocking back and forth, trying to subdue the pain, dozens of cactus needles pierced his lower back and thighs like tiny fiery nails. Finally, a steady trickle of blood oozed over his brow then down his face from a gash below his hairline. Although the suffering was excruciating, Hunter relished it. The pain let him know he was still alive.

He'd spent the week searching for a reason for being and he found it.

Being, is its own reason for being. It was that simple. The only alternative to being is not being. While nonexistence permanently removes pain and anguish unique to the material world, it also eliminates the incredible wonders, profound feelings and potential awakenings only available to the living. Those appreciations that make people fear death and cling to life at its most mundane and hopeless times. Those small pieces of truth and beauty that reveal themselves every day to inspire. Besides, nonexistence in the corporeal world would come one day, soon enough.

Loss seemed trivial. Loss is a necessary part of existing. Thankfully, so are discovery, renewal and novelty. It's all a matter of perspective. Hunter had lost everything he thought was important, and in the process gained back more than he ever imagined. He'd secured a small piece of Divine truth, and with that piece came peace; the good with the bad, the ordinary with the bizarre. Everything he needed already existed within him, and no matter what happened for the rest of his life, Hunter Damon would be thankful simply to be alive. By giving up and losing control, he regained control. He was his own man, and he now understood what was important.

The trials and tribulations also seemed petty compared to the only thing he possessed with any genuine worth. The broken hearts, the gross violations and the cruel injustices paled when compared to his next breath. And if every breath taken into his lungs was free, that meant the things he thought were lost had a combined value of less than nothing. It became clear that 'being,' with its range of tremendous emotions, is reward enough. Laughing is no better or worse than crying, and pain, as much as it hurts, is as crucial to life as pleasure. Truly, giving and taking equal out in the end.

What began as self-imposed exile from the world ended as serendipitous self-discovery. Rising above cruel betrayals and callous abandonment by lovers, friends and even family, Hunter's reality was no longer a series of cynical circumstances tossed upon his shoulders; the perverted values and insincerity of a hypocritical culture could never be his yardstick for standards anymore. Instead, his new reality emerged — born of his rational principles then tempered by the fire of this emotions. He knew he was right, and what's more, he'd discovered truths found outside the rat's maze. Despite its intentions, the world be damned.

Unaware of how long he'd been unconscious, he lifted his arm in grueling agony to check his watch. All that remained was a scuffed blood-soaked leather band and the back casing. Glancing at the sun's position in the sky, he estimated 6 o'clock and watched two buzzards circle above, biding their time as if waiting for a table. He stood up with a lot of effort and limped to his car to examine the wreckage. By then, the smoke and steam had stopped rising and his overturned car stood as a metaphorical and literal sign that his odyssey had ended. Staring at the underside of the mangled Mustang, he chuckled. Everything accumulated during that week lay strewn across both sides of the road. Compact discs, his overnight bags, plastic bottles, paper sacks, Styrofoam cups and one very elegant envelope with his name printed on it. His whole awful week was on public display as a testament for anybody traveling that section of Highway 191.

Among the debris he spotted a side view mirror sheared-off cleanly. Feeling the warm wet bloody trickle past his temple and down his cheeks, he picked it up to examine the gash on his forehead. All that was left of the shattered mirror was a long, thin shard of glass. Unable to fit his whole face in the thin shard's reflection, Hunter held mirror up with deliberate maneuvering so its image showed the damage he couldn't see. The gash didn't gush with blood, rather it just seeped-out in a steady trickle, but what there was smeared most of his face and had begun to congeal.

Stranded in the middle of nowhere on an Arizona highway, he wasn't sad, angry or worried. In fact, he felt freer than he had in his whole life. After all, what was there to be afraid of? What was the worst that could happen? That he might collapse and die in the desert? Hunter knew every second he lived after the crash was bonus time. His former life had ended and he appreciated the potential for a new one.

Unsure of his exact location, he scanned up and down the road for a car or a telltale plume of dust. All alone for miles, he spotted one last sign about

50 yards down the road. He limped closer.

Phoenix - 82 miles

Only beginning to appreciate the extraordinary gift he'd given himself, he remembered.

"Faith Byrdsong," he uttered in amazement, realizing the final piece of this miraculous puzzle unveiled his destiny. It hurt his ribs, but Hunter cackled as powerful as he did that first night.

Amid the shattered glass, scattered CDs and tattered bags and cups, he spotted the shoebox Manuel Montrose gave him. He took the sneakers out, struggled to put them on with his one good arm then stared at them on his feet. In the box the sneakers were pristine and white. On his feet, however, smeared bloodstains running from the laces to the toe of each shoe served a sanguine reminder of the suffering he had to endure to reclaim his life. And even though the sneakers were at least six sizes too big, they were far and away more comfortable for what he had to do. In hindsight, $10,000 was a bargain for Manuel's shoes considering the comfort they would provide for the miles he might have to walk. A car had to drive-by sooner or later, but until then he decided to end the last leg of his journey, by beginning a new journey on his last leg.

Still reveling in his revelation Hunter began the trek to Phoenix in intense pain, but alternating between fits of laughter and groans of agony as his broken ribs rattled after each guffaw. He laughed so hard it hurt, but the pain reminded him he was alive and that made him happy — which made him laugh even harder. As he hobbled down the middle of the white line of the dusty road, he remembered something his 'father' told him days before.

"If you're not moving forward, you're just standing still."

Epilogue

'And they lived happily ever after' has become an overly simple cliché; an often heard, yet rarely pondered six-word phrase compressing the gamut of emotions, hard work and intangibles into another package to show to the world. It might be trite to casual observers on the fringes, but for any couple fortunate enough to secure it, 'happily ever after' is a blessed Godsend no matter the degree of unseen effort behind closed doors.

Unlike other packages, it's what's on the inside that matters. People at peace put little credence into appearances. They don't care about what others say or think. They only answer to themselves, those they love and with whom they share.

Hunter made it to the next town, got a ride to Scottsdale two days later and found Faith Byrdsong, MD. She bandaged his wounds, physical and otherwise, they fell in love, got married and enjoyed a honeymoon in Venice (after a quick stop in New Orleans). Her practice prospered, and he opened his own ad agency with friends he met after moving to Phoenix. As a karmic bonus, he lured three major clients away from Paul Jones and became the agency representing Manuel Montrose's successful bold venture: Rebound© — a line of comfortable, affordable sneakers, allowing more people a chance to walk in his shoes.

But Hunter never reduced the results of his serendipitous odyssey to a mere cliché. Soon after finding Faith, he understood it was Providence which guided him out of the shadow of pain, suffering and emotional death, onto the open road and into the arms of the woman he will love for the rest of his long, happy, productive life — and yes, even into death when their souls will be united again.

The irony was not lost on him that he had to lose Hope to find his Faith.

And although he had to endure pain and loss to find out

things about himself he never thought were possible, the point was...don't worry about what the point was. More importantly, he wasn't afraid anymore. Not because he thought he was invincible. Quite the contrary. If anybody respected the precious fragility of life, it was Hunter Damon. His physical, mental, emotional and spiritual pieces had all been tested to the brink, and after the dust had settled, literally, those frail parts were torn down with a fury. Each piece, however, was rebuilt stronger than ever, and his faith never again as much as quivered.

The point of this epilogue though, is not about reviewing one man's epic adventure, as much as it's a showcase of destiny, fate and the hand of God. There is a plan, but some people have to work a little harder and a little longer to find peace. Hunter began his odyssey unaware that he was searching for truth and beauty. And while he found out that chaos is the complete lack of either, he learned that love is the ultimate blending of both.

Life offers no stock answers, which is fine because it's not a test. It's a journey to be taken alone, even when surrounded by family and friends. Hunter began his journey by asking common questions, and Providence led him to the open road where he found answers not found in most books. It turned out the only books he needed were a Road Atlas and a Bible.

If there was anything to be learned, it was that strong people who never doubt their faith are rewarded with the knowledge that pain, anguish, torture and suffering are simply precursors to the promise of prosperity ahead. His odyssey wasn't about forcing mismatched pieces together to create a picture that was never intended. Rather, he had to appreciate and accept the accidental design of random sections and their individual inspired intricacies. Truth and beauty were always inside of him, just waiting to be tapped.

He often thought about one of the last things his 'father' told him. 'You never get a true sense of what it's like to be human until after you're dead', and it's true. Hunter came as close as possible to verifying that without dying, but in reality he was dying long before he hit the road. He'd become complacently comfortable, stuck in the pleasantly poisonous routine plaguing people with both eyes hyper focused on the American Dream. Wallowing in a cultural mire of apathy, mediocrity and empty gratification, by the time he made it to the Arizona desert he typified an empty shell of the man he could have been.

Ironically, heartache and humiliation granted him the opportunity to win his battered soul back. With his cognizant mind busy running and jumping from one denial to another, his subconscious orchestrated and executed a brilliantly planned spectacular bid to secure a last chance at redemption through sacrifice. From then on, his reflection in the mirror was extraordinary every day. His smile amplified his serenity and made his goodwill contagious.

His life had been affirmed.

The journey home is a constant. It can be a daily trip or a once-in-a-lifetime pilgrimage. It's often a literal trek over relative distances, conquering challenges and misfortunes to reach a home — a familiar habitat, a simple dwelling containing comfortable memories and cherished people; a haven to relax in the refuge of a favorite chair, protected from the world and at ease. The truth is, however, home is not always where the hearth is; it's where the soul is. That's when the journey home becomes an allegory.

When a soul is lost or misplaced, the search and restoration carries vital consequences. Because without a soul, the grandeur of life and the splendor of love are impossible. The irony is, if existence can be reduced to the search for truth and beauty, then if we're lucky, we'll see our soul was always very close the entire time.

To the optimist, it's easy to be a cynic. To the cynic, it's foolish to be an optimist. Hunter realized it's easy to be foolish and it's foolish to be easy. Rededicating his life to being alive and having fun, he couldn't deny that he'd been shown the difficult road to righteousness and he took it. Many paths cross, many run parallel and many end much too abruptly. But after all is said and done, we find our own truths, make our own way, create our own being, and make a beautiful imprint on the spiritual force surrounding and enveloping everything. One life touches more than it can ever know.

Sometimes things happen, and other times things don't happen. But somewhere in the middle, the murky gray void between chance and careful planning is where your fate, your destiny is. Cradled tenderly and grasped violently at the same time. Somewhere in the middle, between vague memories and dreams not yet imagined, is the enduring reality you try to deny. The proof that contradicts and negates all the lies you want to embrace.

Hunter Damon thought he'd lost everything, but in the end he got the whole country and all the trimmings in life accompanying success. The difference was, the accouterments didn't define him anymore. They were no longer the carrot at the end of a stick to keep him going. Rather, they became the garnish complementing the main nourishment in his life. After searching and hunting elusive shadows, Hunter understood life. Hunter understood love. But most important, Hunter understood how to love life.

And yes, they lived happily ever after.

Acknowledgements

Okay, where to start? I don't think anybody knows this, but this book represents a potential fulfillment of a promise I made to my Dad on his deathbed. I've been carrying that around for quite some time, so I'm keeping my fingers crossed that this book 'does well'.

To the several or so people over the years who read my manuscript as a Microsoft Word document while it languished on my computer, ignored and rejected by scores of literary agents and publishers. These were the friends who reassured me that I *might* have something good. Thank you for buying this copy, even though you already read it for free. Todd Mitchell and Robin Hilton come to mind.

My appreciation to Starbucks Coffee Frankfort-Lexington Rd. in St. Matthews for countless hours of keeping me fueled-up for revision after revision. Also, thank you to Lynn Tincher for her astute editing skills and Kerri Klawiter for awesome cover art.

A big thanks to all the great friends who kept me laughing and (mostly) legal during the tough economic times: Donald & Ann Kohler, Tom O'Brien, Adam Kohn, Charisa Calabrese, Cols. Kevin & Reneé Finnegan.

I owe a debt of gratitude to all my friends on social media who have expressed their approval and excitement for this novel.

To my Mother, Lydia Miller and my 3 brothers Hayes, Andy & Jim, I thank you for all the support you've given over all these many years.

Finally, a big THANK YOU to Tony Acree and the good folks at Hydra Publications. Without your interest and backing, this novel (and future novels, depending on the success of this one) would've never seen the outside of my computer.

About the Author

Samuel Miller was born, raised and currently resides in Louisville, KY.

Follow him on Twitter @samuelmiller64, or email him at <u>samuelmiller64@gmail.com</u>.